A Degree of Murder

DCI Garrick - book 9

M.G. Cole

A DEGREE OF MURDER
A DCI Garrick mystery - Book 9

Copyright © 2025 by Max Cole (M.G.Cole)

All rights reserved. No part of this publication may be reproduced, distributed, or transmitted in any form or by any means, including photocopying, recording, or other electronic or mechanical methods, without the prior written permission of the publisher, except in the case of brief quotations embodied in critical reviews and certain other non-commercial uses permitted by copyright law.

Cover art: Shutterstock

A DEGREE OF MURDER

Chapter One

Ice cold air puckered the exposed flesh into a sea of goose pimples. It took on the image of a rash as blood rushed to warm skin in an unwinnable battle against the numbing cold; the zero point that all creation, all matter, all life, inevitably succumbs to.

And for some, it is already too late.

Bare heels slid across the icy floor with almost no friction. Physics made it easier to drag a naked hundred-and-twelve-kilo body under such conditions. The noise of naked skin across ice made a pleasing sound, like gently brushing soft silk. The thud of fat and bone dropping onto the hard surface was more jarring, especially to the soothing ASMR the assailant was used to. Even the metallic swish of the blade being unsheathed from its scabbard gave a relaxing, almost sensual sound.

Gripping the long handle with his insulated gloves, the killer slid the thick door closed. The door's wheels made a gentle rumble over the guiding rail before it sealed shut with a soft thump that blocked the noise of the world beyond. For several precious seconds, there was a silence so deep that the blood pounding in the killer's ears became a soothing rhythm.

Then the fans whirled to life, waking from their economy mode now the door was open, pumping in air to maintain the -20C environment. The blast of sharp air tasted metallic and was intense the killer blinked rapidly, before angling their cap's peak to shield their eyes from the airflow.

Then came a groan from the body on the floor.

The killer mused. The human body was an incredible machine. Fragile, yet at times almost impossible to destroy. Clinging to life with the faintest whisper of the soul. Something that the killer found incredibly fascinating, and studied at every available opportunity. Such as this one. But why should others be privy to such secrets? What had they done to deserve such a gift? Nothing, as far as the killer was concerned.

The body issued another low whimper, barely audible above the thrumming of the fans. Its right leg trembled on the icy floor, slowly stretching in an involuntary motion. A last, futile, scramble for survival. A fighting spirit was a good sign. It was something to be admired as the killer waited for the victim's core temperature to drop to twenty-one degrees, which killed most people, but keep the flesh soft and malleable. Easy enough to shape.

A satchel on the floor was unzipped. The cold metal snagged a few times as it had become prone to do when longer it was left in the cold. Inside, the instruments were laid on top of one another in an orderly fashion, separated by a layer of soft black felt. Each had been methodically cleaned and sharpened between each use; an ethos that taking pride in one's work always ensured success, but for now their favourite blade was selected.

The body writhed again, issuing a louder moan. This one was a fighter. After double checking the locker door was firmly closed, they drew in a lungful of frigid air, held the breath, then slowly exhaled. In an act of mindfulness, the killer felt their shoulder muscles relieve their tension, and the blade felt lighter, almost an extension of one's hand.

Slipping a foot under the figure's pelvis, it took all the assailant's strength to flip the body over. A sheen of ice glinted from the exposed smooth abdomen which gently moved with each shallow breath. The tip of the knife teased the flesh. At this temperature, they would feel no sensation. That was about to change and, with the gentlest of pressure, the steel sank into the skin in an almost artistic gesture.

Then the screaming began. And it would not stop for a long time.

Chapter Two

The screaming was incessant. A sound designed to attract attention and shred the listener's nerves until they did something - anything - to intervene.

DCI David Garrick was on his feet in an instant. His blood was pumping, despite the hazy fog swirling through his mind that disoriented him as he reached the doorway. He was acting in instinct and tried to recall *exactly* where he was as he rushed towards the closed door ahead - and shouldered it open with such force the wood almost splintered.

His blurry eyes struggled to adjust to the soft light coming from a nightlight in the plug socket. The impact of the door as it slammed against the wall aggravated the screams to a piercing level. Then a startled woman's hissing voice jolted the last of his sleep away.

"David! What the hell are you doing?"

The accusation in the words chilled Garrick to the marrow. He realised he had been caught in the sluggish middle-ground between dream and reality. Chasing some sleazebag through a rain lashed field had somehow merged with barging in on Wendy and his three-month-old daughter.

Wendy gently rocked Amy Elizabeth Garrick and encouraged her to continue breastfeeding. After a few moments of spluttering from both David and the baby, the ruse worked, and Amy fell silent as she clamped onto the nipple. David sheepishly swung the bedroom door back and forth to check he hadn't jolted it off its hinges. Even without looking, he could feel Wendy's glare.

"You really need to do something to stop flying off the handle like that" she muttered.

Since David Garrick had clawed his way to consciousness after a car crash in the line of duty, the world had moved on. He had been in a coma for five weeks following a brain contusion as he was tossed around the back of the Audi. He had been abducted as a human shield during a sting that had gone wrong. In a high-speed pursuit across Hampstead Heath, innocent civilian lives had been at stake. His vehicle had been rammed off the road by Garrick's colleague, DC Fanta Liu. No doubt she had saved lives by terminating the chase. But it had almost killed Garrick. Seconds before impact, his kidnapper had been attempting to choke him to death with a seatbelt.

That had saved his life.

Although not belted in, it had restrained his head enough to stop his skull being mashed to pulp. He'd broken his left arm, which was just out of a sling, and two ribs. The contusion was his lucky escape. But that had meant he'd missed the birth of his daughter, and had been on medical leave for a further two months which had placed him in the direct line of fire for a newborn's sonic weapon.

Since Amy arrived, sleep had transformed into a luxury

commodity. David constantly felt on edge, and Wendy had become irritable twenty-four-seven. At least in his eyes. Garrick wasn't in any position to tell if she was suffering some sort of post-maternal depression, or if he was. When Amy was not screaming, he felt himself overwhelmed with amazement at the being he and Wendy had brought to life. The sense of love and protection that surged through him stole his breath. But on nights like these, he often fantasised about walking out of the house. At least he recognised they were not the healthiest of thoughts. Wendy had been nagging him to discuss it with his therapist and ask for medication.

That bumped against the progress he'd been making over the last few months, despite the crash. Following an operation to remove a growth pressing his brain, Garrick had been under strict instruction from his doctor to avoid any strenuous activities that could result in injury. Dr Rajasekar had meant contact sports, but that hadn't stopped Garrick from hanging from clifftops, getting into fights, and crashing cars. Rajasekar was at a loss as to how he was still alive, but she assured him he won't be for much longer if he kept this lifestyle up.

Ordinarily, Garrick would have laughed the comment off, but now when he looked into the face of his daughter, his own mortality had come into sharp relief. Almost overnight, he had started to focus on his health. Eating sensibly, stopping drinking, and even jogging - despite the pain it caused - had become the norm. He'd begged Rajasekar to wean him off his medication, and his new therapist, whom he pointedly kept at arm's length, had only seen him for half the scheduled sessions. He should be in peak condition - ignoring the recent coma, broken arm and freshly mended ribs. But fragmented sleep was now his new enemy.

Feeling too wired to fall back asleep, David made two cups of tea, a builder's mug for her, and a green matcha for him. By the time he returned upstairs, Amy was fast asleep in her cot and Wendy had returned to bed and was gently snoring. Fighting a growing sense of uselessness, David returned downstairs and sat in front of the television. His hand hovered over the remote control, but he decided it best not to create any noise. Just in case. He thumbed through the printouts of the houses he and Wendy had been browsing on Right Move, in the hope of finding somewhere with more space and - ideally - soundproof rooms. After selling his own home, he had moved into this cramped terrace and promised they'd find somewhere better once Amy was born. Now they had reached that milestone, David found his heart wasn't in house-hunting, it was focused on living. After watching his sister die in front of him, his own mortality was something that now accompanied him every night when he stared into the shadows.

"Morning, guv." When Garrick didn't respond, DC Harry Lord repeated a little louder. "Guv! Morning!"

Garrick's head jerked up from slouching over his keyboard, betraying the fact he had nodded off for less than a minute. He desperately tried to cover this in the only way the guilty do - by overacting.

"Harry. I didn't hear you. I was engrossed in this," he indicated his screen.

Harry gave it a brief glance. "Your lock screen? Fascinating." Garrick noticed his terminal had reverted to the password prompt due to inactivity. "Another Amy night?"

An irrepressible yawn escaped Garrick's lips before he could answer. He nodded instead. Harry patted him on the shoulder.

"Good job for you the criminals of Kent have gone quiet. Don't say they don't do anything for you. Cuppa?"

"It'll be my sixth. They don't do anything."

"It's that herbal crap you drink. You should hit the hard stuff. Coffee."

Garrick pulled a face as he logged on to the system and checked his messages. "I've been trying it. Tastes horrid but keeps me awake, I suppose."

The Serious Crime Unit had been unusually quiet while he had been on leave, which gave his team time to address the dreaded paperwork that never ended until cases wound up with a prosecution, and that could be a year or more after the arrest. Yet, due to a slew of high-profiles incidents, the team had desperately needed the time. Because of his sick leave and the baby, he'd managed to avoid the dreaded paperwork, and his detective sergeant, Chib Okon had also escaped midway when she finally took her honeymoon to the Maldives.

Now the team were all reunited, although the lack of cases appeared to have put everybody on edge. They were not used to being confined within the office. Garrick's fatigue made him feel both sluggish and irritable, and there was a terse atmosphere between him and Fanta. She was living with the guilt of almost killing him. No amount of praise from anybody else, including an official commendation for saving lives at Hampstead Heath, had salved that wound. Garrick had even tried to cajole Fanta by reminding her he had almost killed her when they'd broken into a house that had been booby-trapped with explosives. He assured her they were equal now. All that had achieved was to fuel her desire to seek a promotion. It was an unspoken threat that indicated she would leave the team.

Garrick was torn by the prospect. She was a young detective constable, but her track record had catapulted her to lofty heights. She'd become an instrumental part of the team and losing her would be like losing a limb. On top of that he felt a slight betrayal that she would *want* to leave, but his level-headed side knew she was meant for bigger things.

When Harry returned with the drinks, he placed Garrick's down with an overly loud clunk onto the desk to wake his boss up from another micro-sleep. Garrick snorted in surprise, but took Harry's chuckling with good nature.

"See the job's really keeping you on your toes then."

Garrick took the drink and sipped deeply. Maybe it was psychological, but the caffeine already seemed to wake him up.

Harry sat on the end of the desk. "How's the old memory?"

"Memory's as sharp as ever, mate. Just a few more clunks on the old noggin, and they're going to knock out all the stuff I'd desperately want to forget."

I just wondered if that was making you, you know, lose your sleep a little bit."

Garrick's head bobbed non-committally.

"I don't know. Maybe it's made me more sensitive to Wendy's moods. Sometimes I get the feeling that she's permanently pissed off with me."

"She's a new mum; that's a big transition." He caught Garrick's look. "Come on, you only got whacked around the head. She delivered a bowling ball out of her..." he nodded towards his lap. "I mean, that's eye-watering just to think about it."

Garrick drank deeply as he considered. "You know, part of me has considered quitting. And the other part of me has realised I really need this job, just to keep my family afloat. And God help us if we actually buy a house."

"That wouldn't be the end of the road. You have transferable skills."

"Like what?"

"There must be something," Harry said vaguely. "When I was thinking of leaving, you told me not to be an arsehole."

"I was saying anything to make you stay. Are you going to say the same thing to me?"

Harry shook his head. "Nah, you've always been an arsehole."

"Yeah, but now I worry about being a dead one, especially with Amy relying on me." He took a deep breath. "And that's when my mind starts venturing into dark places, and I wonder if Wendy thinks she'd be better off with somebody whose job's a little less of a rollercoaster."

"You know it's not supposed to be. I mean, chasing perps across the tops of trains and running into burning buildings ain't exactly a prerequisite of the job. That's more of a human..."

"Condition?" said Garrick with a smile.

"I was going to say faulty personality."

They both laughed, but it was laced with grim, dark humour.

"I think it just boils down to one basic thing. Are you happy?"

Garrick almost spat out his drink. "Blimey, when did you

become a philosopher? Am I happy? Now I know how you interpreted the last few minutes of conversation."

"That's not what I meant. Are you happy with the job? Are you taking risks for the right reasons. You know, you've got somebody like Fanta who's desperate to fill your shoes."

He caught Garrick's look. "But let's face it, you'll probably be retired by then anyway."

"Oh, cheers, mate. That's another thing to think about. Retirement. Being old, redundant, useless."

"You're only three of those things. People retire early all the time. I sometimes think it's my best shot, hopping out of here." Harry's brow deepened. "The more I started thinking about getting out, the more I started thinking how much I'd miss this place. Hanging around here, busting bad guys, winning bets against all you losers. It's nice to have that extended family. You know what I mean?"

Garrick did, but he was loath to admit it. He quietly continued sipping his tea and enjoyed the trickle of energy that was washing away his fatigue. Lack of sleep, he thought to himself, combined with heavy paperwork equalled feelings of uselessness and desperation. At least he hoped that was the cause. A gentle ping from his email got his attention.

"Ooh," he said, placing the cup down and going for the mouse. "Something of interest might've finally happened." He opened the message and quickly read through. "We have a body."

"Thanks, I work out," Harry deadpanned.

"Chib's not in. You want to come with me?"

In past, Harry would have leapt at the chance to come with him and see a little bit of front-line action, even if that action was taping off the crime scene. But since he had an accident while trying to apprehend a subject, he'd been left with a permanent limp, and after being part of the operation that had seen Fanta ram her boss off the road, Harry had shown no desire for fieldwork.

Garrick read into his hesitation. "Find out where Sean and Fanta are and get one of them to join me."

He stood up and drained the rest of his matcha tea.

"At least I know one of them is going to be pleased to get out of the office."

Chapter Three

Whitstable fish market was one of the oldest in Kent. Over a century it had cultivated the finest Dover sole, oysters, whelks and other seafood from the British shores, none of which the average Brit would entertain eating so it was mostly exported just a few miles across the Channel to the continent. For all these years it stood as a bastion of British industry. Despite fishing being one of the smallest in the UK economy, worth less even than leather tanning, it was still politically powerful enough to make the public turn away from Europe after Brexit. The steeply sloped black rooftops and black walls lent a Scandinavian vibe to the quayside, which came alive in the wee hours of the morning as wholesale customers dashed in to claim the finest catches, before leaving it as a ghost town as the rest of the world woke up.

The other firm stamp of authority the market imposed on the town was the intense smell that had Fanta gagging the moment she opened the door of her car as they pulled into the gated storage facility that stood between the market and Whitstable Castle.

Garrick almost had to bite his tongue to stop himself from smiling. "What's the matter, Fanta? Don't like the scent of fish and chips?"

"Chips I can handle," she muttered. "But fish shouldn't smell like that."

Garrick frowned. "Fish smells of fish. It's one of those inescapable truths that we'll take to our grave."

"Trust me, guv, if the chippy smelt like that, we'd all be eating snails and croissants after the pub."

Garrick gently shook his head, and looked through his phone to refresh his memory of the report. The security guard at the gate had waved them through when Garrick had flashed his identity card, but he now made no move to greet them. A few milling workers in stained white aprons were hosing down the floor, outside a long aisle of large black wooden units that faced one another, all housed under an elevated metal roof that kept the weather at bay. Garrick and Fanta approached the unit with a police car parked outside. Garrick rapped on the glass, jarring the young, weak-looking officer sat inside, his head bowed to his phone. He stuffed his phone into his pocket and got out of the air-conditioned car. He looked green as he put on his hat, his eyes watering, as if attempting to waft away the lingering stench with his eyelashes.

"Morning, sir. Ma'am," he said, nodding at Fanta.

Fanta pulled a face and mouthed the words *'ma'am'*. "How old do I look?" she whispered to Garrick.

Garrick ignored her. "What do we have here?"

The constable sucked in a breath to speak but then immediately regretted it as he drew a lungful of fishy air.

He indicated the hut, which they could now see was a large wooden shed some twenty-five-feet square. The weather-beaten wood was cladding a large freezer locker. They became aware of refrigerating fans from the units all around them, creating a deep, bass-laden concerto. Garrick imagined the wood had absorbed centuries of the heady scent and nothing short of an inferno would rid it of the smell. A quick count told there were thirty units on the site.

"A body found inside unit sixteen by a worker this morning." The constable didn't seem to know what else to say, then added. "I've been keeping everybody out."

Garrick extended his hand. "Lead the way."

They followed him to a large sliding door that was firmly closed and opened by a lever-handle that was hung vertically. A chain hung from the wall, appearing to be the only way to lock the unit.

"Are these all owned by the same people?"

The officer gave a slight shrug. "I'm not too sure who owns them. I know individual fishermen rent them."

"I see you've been using your time to make enquiries," said Fanta, provoking a shy smile from the constable, whose detective powers clearly didn't extend to sarcasm.

At least he had the presence of mind to wear gloves as he put his body weight into sliding the door open. It gently rumbled on well-maintained castors, and the blast of cold air was a brief, gentle relief that blew the smell, and Garrick's breath, away.

The copper pulled his all-weather jacket tighter as Garrick threw him a warning glance. "They're kept at minus-twenty around the clock." He nodded inside. "After you."

Fanta entered. Despite wearing a light rain jacket, she

didn't react to the cold. Garrick shuffled in after her, keeping his head bowed.

"Don't tell me you're not freezing you knackers off," Garrick said in a low voice.

"That's the advantage of having no knackers to freeze off." She pointed. "There it is."

Garrick's eyes had started watering the moment he'd stepped inside the locker. He wondered if the tears would freeze to his cheeks in the short time he planned to be in the locker. He blinked to get a better look. A naked calf and bare foot were poking from underneath a stack of fallen crates. The plastic boxes had split open, throwing dozens of frozen fish across the floor.

The young cop clearly didn't want to get any closer. "The guy who found it said he was removing stock for the market, when the stack fell over and he saw that. He legged it out and call us."

Fanta frowned as she knelt next to the limb. Her gaze moved from the calf to the crates.

"I suppose the body was stashed behind the boxes," mused Garrick. "And its weight made the boxes..." With one hand he mimed the stack falling. It was preferable than sucking in cold air.

"I don't think that's what happened," Fanta said thoughtfully. She was already fishing in her jacket pocket for a pair of blue latex gloves. "Can't you see what's wrong with this picture?" she gestured to the toppled crates as she pulled the gloves onto her increasingly numb fingers.

"Are you suggesting the deceased was killed by the weight of frozen herring?" Garrick said with more than a hint of sarcasm.

"They're mackerel."

"Oh, a fish expert now, are we?"

"You mean an ichthyologist?" Fanta said smugly. "No." She tapped a white strip written with a black marker pen. "It says so here."

"You're going to nail that detective sergeant interview."

"I've got to do the NPPE exam first. I missed the last window in March. The next one is coming up soon. She gestured to the fallen crates. "This doesn't look right." She took her phone out and took several pictures of the scene from multiple angles. Pocketing the phone, she then lifted two of the crates away.

"Oh..." Garrick blinked in surprise. It was now obvious what Fanta had been driving at. He was annoyed that he hadn't spotted it.

There was no body. The limb had been perfectly severed above the knee. It was now obvious there was no room under the stack for a corpse.

Fanta knelt again to get a better look at the limb. She'd never been comfortable around corpses; it was a desensitisation that Garrick had built up after a long career, but at least she was making a concerted effort to override her natural repulsion. Garrick's knees clicked as he joined her. The cold from the floor shot through to his kneecap and made him shiver.

"It looks like a skilled job," he noted as Fanta took more pictures.

White frost coated the limb which had frozen solid throughout, making the cross-section cut look like a cartoon representation of a steak, with the ringed sections of white fibula and tibia clearly visible. Fine hairs covered the limb, indicating it was a man's.

"The cut looks almost surgical. That takes a lot of time."

Garrick glanced at the pale grey floor. A fine layer of ice coated the surface, fragile enough that their soles had melted distinct footprints. His head jerked sharply up to the open door. "Close that now!"

The copper hesitated for a moment, then reached across and drew the door almost to a close before stopping.

"I don't wanna be locked in here," he mumbled nervously. "Especially with that."

"It's just a leg, son. All it can do is boot you up the arse if you don't stop the warm air from melting evidence in here. Besides, the door opens from the inside."

The policeman used his bodyweight to drag the door closed with a soft thud they all could feel as the air pressure changed.

Garrick stood and circled around the crates as Fanta took more pictures. "When was this discovered?"

"Call came in at 6:36. I didn't get here until about an hour later. I was dealing with a DUI in Dover," he added as an apology.

"Nothing's wrong with doing your job correctly." Garrick felt embarrassed for snapping at the officer moments ago. Lack of sleep and anxiety was his problem to deal with, not one to take out on others. "Talk us through what you saw."

"It was a young guy who found it. He's hanging around because I said you'd want to talk to him." He waited for Garrick to nod approvingly, before continuing. "By the time I arrived he'd closed the unit. I think a few of the fishermen had popped in to take a look, but they didn't move anything."

"I'm sure there's some sort of health and safety violation stopping surf and turf being stored together." When Garrick didn't receive even a grim chuckle from the younger officers,

A Degree of Murder

he looked up to see they were frowning at him. He shook his head. "Never mind. Carry on."

"I walked in. Saw the leg and immediately called it in. I didn't see the point in hanging around in here. But outside was no better, as the stink has made me want to throw up all morning."

"Anything strike you as out of place when you came in?"

"Apart from that." He nodded to the leg. "I thought it was some kinky dogging session that had got out of hand. I asked around, but nobody saw anything odd beforehand."

"What about cameras?" said Fanta who was now inches away from the limb as she examined it. The hesitation from the officer indicated he hadn't thought to ask. "Let's talk to the guy who found this." She stood up, before noticing Garrick was staring at her with a half-smile. "That's, um, if you think it's right, guv."

"Carry on, DC Liu."

They all welcomed the suddenly balmy air as they stepped from the locker, even though it had been a chilly eight-degrees according to Garrick's dashboard when they arrived. The officer led them to a small portacabin that was used as a staffroom. Inside, a thin young man was hunched at a table, drinking a coffee as he pored over his Instagram feed as if digitally hypnotised. A small electric heater was on, two bars glowing cherry red, but despite that the man still wore his thermal jacket over a stained apron that had once been white, and dark jeans. He only looked up when he heard his name from the constable.

"This is Simon Evans. He found the, um, body."

"Thanks. You can leave us. Make sure nobody enters the locker until forensics arrive."

The copper nodded, and hastily retreated to his air-conditioned car. Garrick and Fanta drew up vacant seats from another table so they could join Evans. He nervously turned his phone screen off and nodded at them.

"I hear you had a heck of a morning," Garrick said warmly.

"It's always an early start, but I'm used to it now. And the money isn't so bad."

"I meant what you found."

Evans chuckled nervously. "Oh, that. Yeah. Bummer."

The detectives waited for him to continue, but it was clear that was the extent of his emotional trauma.

Fanta made notes on her mobile. "Didn't it freak you out?"

"Well, I wasn't expecting it, so I guess I jumped. I ran out and told Trev."

"Trev?"

"My boss. Trev McDonald. He's the skipper who runs *Trev's SeeFood*. He's the one who called the fuzz... I mean, you."

"Walk us through what happened."

Evans shrugged with teenage indifference. "I'd been here since three. Trev has his boat, the *Sea Mutt*. I meet them on the quay and help them bring the catch here so it can be stored. It's divvied up, most take to the market." He jerked his thumb in the direction of Whitstable Fish Market. "We try to get the fresh stuff out first as that sells quickly when the market opens. But lately there's a lot left over so that that to go into freeze for the next day."

"You mean that mackerel was yesterday's leftovers?" Evans nodded. "So, you were in the locker yesterday?"

"Yeah. Trev rented three of them, but most of this year we've only used two. I put that stack up yesterday and swear there was no body in there then. It was empty even after Trev asked me to move stock out of the other locker. I think he's managed to cancel the lease, catches are low. Sales are low."

"Are the doors locked?"

"There's a padlock on the outside when nobody's here. There are about twenty companies use this place, and I wouldn't trust 'em not to nick a bit of stock."

Garrick leaned back in his seat and laced his fingers across his chest. Fanta had leapt in with the questions and he was quite happy to let her continue.

"Was it locked when you came in?"

Evans nodded. "Trev has the master key and there's one hanging in the security office at the gate. I went in about three or four times. It was when I was reaching for the top crate... It was a bit out of reach. I tugged at it and the whole lot fell. That's when I see somebody is wedged under there."

"Did you close the door?"

Evans nodded emphatically. "Trev goes nuts if you don't."

"And what about rats?"

That got a surprised reaction from both Garrick and Evans.

"Rats?"

"Lots of food around. Do they often get into the lockers?"

"Never. There are rat traps everywhere, but I don't think I've seen one on site. There are two cats that hang around after a bit of fish. And the lockers are sealed so rats aren't getting in."

Garrick didn't have much to add as the questions wound down. They took Simon Evans' details and let him go. He was clearly over the worst and eager to continue the rest of his day away from the fish market.

"I remember back in my day finding a corpse was a big deal," Garrick said as they walked to the gatehouse.

"Typical Gen-Z," snorted Fanta.

"I thought that's what you are?"

She shot him a look. "I'm not *that* type. Did you smell it?"

Garrick was about to nod, but realised he didn't know what she was referring to. The scent of fish smell had overridden his senses. He shook his head.

"He stunk of pot."

Ignoring petty misdemeanours was always a balance when investigating serious crime. Even the most innocent person instinctively clammed up when talking to the police, so a small fine or wrap on the knuckles was a surefire way to stop a witness from being cooperative.

After checking the status of the locker keys with the gate guard, they requested video footage, they headed back to their vehicles. Trev McDonald had already left the site, but Garrick called him, and he agreed to come into the station at the end of the day to answer questions. Garrick opened his car door and paused as Fanta was about to get into her vehicle.

"Why did you bring up that question about rats?"

"Oh, because of the marks."

"You're being cryptic, Liu. My brain is half asleep at the best of times. What marks?"

"On the leg. Didn't you see? They looked like bite marks." She looked around. "I'm not entirely sure this place is hygienic."

Chapter Four

"I don't think in all my years here, they've ever got this thing working right." DCI David Garrick thumped the air conditioning panel in the small interview room. He paused for a second to listen if there was a change in the unit's tone - but it just kept churning out overly warm air. "Sorry about this."

Trev McDonald gave a dismissive gesture and smiled at the suited solicitor next to him. Garrick returned to his seat next to DC Fanta Liu and looked at his notes, which were mostly printouts of the pictures Fanta had taken in the storage depot, as well as her notes from Simon Evans' statement.

"Thank you for coming along, Mr McDonald," he said pleasantly, although the truth was that if he hadn't, they'd be having the interview someplace else. It wasn't optional. "And, although I have no issue with you bringing your solicitor along, this is only to clarify facts surrounding what was discovered this morning."

"A slur on my company is just as bad as a personal attack on me." McDonald's Scottish accent was pronounced and his speech bordered on being almost impenetrable.

"I hope it doesn't come to that."

Garrick studied the man who defied his expectations of a fishing vessel captain. McDonald was in his forties, trim, with a stylish beard and long but equally fashionable hair. He wore a loose-fitting Ralph Lauren sweatshirt and chinos, and looked every bit as if he'd be comfortable in a trendy Soho members' club. Garrick had returned home to exchange his clothes from the fishy specimens he'd worn at the depot. McDonald smelled of expensive cologne.

"You own Trev's SeeFood?"

"Aye."

"'See' with an 'e' not an 'a'?"

McDonald rolled his eyes. "I'm dyslexic, but I knew what I was doing. See and in 'I *see* some delicious food'. It's a pun that I now waste most of my time trying to explain to people."

Garrick stopped himself from asking an annoying follow up question. "You rent three storage lockers at the market."

"Two now. It was three, but they charge an arm and a leg for each unit and the market has been very soft recently."

"Another pun!" Garrick said with a smile, which disappeared when he realised McDonald wasn't fully aware of *what* had been found. He heard a soft groan of embarrassment from Fanta and forced himself to concentrate. "So just two now."

"That's right. As of this morning. I asked Si to empty the third yesterday. Not that there was much in there."

"Why is business slow at the moment?" Fanta asked before Garrick could think of another gag.

"It's difficult to export over to Europe now. I've had loads spoil in the time it's taken for the paperwork to go through. The irony is, Brits don't eat the sort of fish we catch on our own shores."

Fanta frowned. "I thought that's what Brexit was about. Protecting you guys?"

McDonald gave a low harrumph. "Let's not go there. I know I have me solicitor here, but he's tired of hearing me bang on. Do you know where the fishing business ranks in the UK? Between *seventy* and *one hundred*." The bitterness in his voice increased. "*Vets* rank above us. Driving schools are just below us. We contribute about nought-point-one per cent to the GDP, but we get the blame for leaving the EU. It killed our industry and took just about everybody else with it!" He slammed his palms on the desk to vent his frustration. He took a deep breath to calm himself. "Sorry, but it drives me mad. Me own business is only about a third of the size it once was. Nobody cares now."

Garrick was about to add *"That ship has sailed,"* but thought better of it. Instead, he formed a more serious question. "I suppose that means there is a lot more competition between companies?"

McDonald's eyebrows shot up in agreement. "That's putting it mildly."

"Would any of them be interested in seeing you out of business? Hypothetically?"

McDonald frozen. His gaze darted towards his solicitor. "That hadn't occurred to me. Hypothetically, I wouldn't be against kicking me rivals in the bollocks. Purely legally, of course."

Garrick nodded. "Understandable." He tilted his head to

Fanta. She selected a photo of the leg poking from under the stack of crates.

"This is what we found this morning."

McDonald gave it a cursory look. "I saw it. When SI came running in to tell me, I had to take a gander before I called it in. Who is it?"

Fanta licked her lips before continuing. "We are ascertaining that now. There is no body. This is a *severed* leg."

"A severed leg? So, maybe not murder?"

Fanta started several sentences, but each came out as a spluttering response, before the words formed. "Well, I don't think his leg fell off and he hopped away. The assumption is there is more of him. That's why the market is closed until forensics can sweep the area."

McDonald's eyes went wide. "What about the next catch? Me lads are out there now!"

Fanta looked at Garrick for backup. He leaned forwards. "That is the depot's responsibility to inform you about their contingency plans." McDonald pulled his mobile from his pocket. "You can't make any calls during the interview."

McDonald looked sidelong at his solicitor who nodded in agreement. With a sigh, he lay the phone on the table.

"You may have guessed me time is now somewhat limited. What do you want to know?"

"Do you have any thoughts regarding the victim's identity?"

"No." He stared challengingly at Fanta. All pretence of being pleasantly cooperative had dissolved. "And before you ask, I don't know who might have it in for me. Not specifically, but I also wouldn't put anything past that shower of sharks."

"We are interviewing them," Garrick said calmly, keen to

defuse McDonald's temper. He had set Chib, Sean, and Harry to speak with the other tenants. The owner of the depot had so far been avoiding calls, but he supposed they had firefighting to do with their unhappy customers. "What about your own employees?"

"I've been working with them for years. When you're out on the water you've got no choice but to trust the man next to you."

"And Simon Evans? How well do you know him?" Fanta asked.

"He's been with us for a couple of months. Was a bit of a slacker when he started. I didn't think he'd last a week, but he wised up and got used to the graft."

"But you don't trust him enough to have a key to the locker."

McDonald laughed. "Why would I? There are two. Mine and the one on-site. No need for any others."

Garrick shifted in his seat to draw attention back to him. "That's the puzzling thing. The security guard at the gate said nobody came in for the key until Simon showed up for work. And he was the one who put it back the previous morning when the market closed." McDonald gave an expressive shrug: *so?* "How do you think the limb got in there?"

"I was out on me boat last night. We came in with the catch. Drove to the market and Si was already waiting for us. You're the detectives, you figure it out."

Garrick and Fanta had quickly reviewed the security recordings in the gatehouse. It was an old digital system, but at least it was timestamped. They only have three cameras on the gate, which also covered the security booth. It recorded images every second, creating an animated-style video of comings and goings. There seemed to be no unauthorised access to the key, or any unregistered visitor. However, after a quick walk around the poorly maintained fence, it was clear sneaking inside wouldn't be too challenging.

Fanta used both hands to illustrate a line of lockers. "Your units are midway down the row. They're not the furthest from the entrance, which is a logical choice if you're trying to hide from the guard. And with no vehicles entering, the body would have had to have been carried there, which would require maximum effort."

Garrick had found a loose fencing panel on his walk around, ideal for sneaking inside, but he didn't raise that option as Fanta continued:

"At first glance it appears to be a random choice. One in thirty."

McDonald folded his arms and leaned back in his seat. "Unless you find pieces of the fella in others. Or unless he comes back for this leg."

Fanta treated him to a cold smile. "Or unless you were *specifically* targeted."

A heavy silence hung in the room before McDonald slowly shook his head. "In that case, you better find out who has a grudge against me, 'cause I don't have a clue." He glanced at his solicitor. "You better make a note that this bunch are now making me feared for me life."

The solicitor duly made a quick note on his pad. Garrick's brow creased. With McDonald's thinly veiled threat, the conversation had quickly turned sour. He forced a warm smile.

"I assure you investigating this incident is a priority, which is why anything you may remember, no matter how trivial, could shed light on the matter."

"I'll keep me thinking hat on," McDonald said belligerently. It was clear the interview was over.

Garrick returned to his desk as Fanta escorted McDonald and his solicitor out. He sat heavily at his desk, a deep sigh escaping from his lips. Interviewing McDonald had been draining. The man was prickly, but that didn't mean he was guilty. A part of Garrick sympathised that the fisherman was facing fresh damage to his already shrinking business. However, it had also raised the question as to whether he was being targeted.

He glanced at his phone to see he'd missed three messages from Wendy informing him that Amy had slept peacefully before needing a diabolic nappy change. Garrick couldn't shake the feeling that his daughter was saving all her waking moments for when he tried to sleep. He also couldn't help but notice his messages with Wendy had become more perfunctory, lacking kisses or emojis. Not that he'd ever been a fan of them, but their absence was notable. What had changed during his unconscious weeks? Or was he being too judgemental towards a woman who was also the victim of sleeplessness.

Fanta returned to her desk in a huff. "Thank God he's gone. What a pillock."

"The man's livelihood is suffering. Do you blame him?"

She gave him a cynical side-long look. "Seriously? *That's* what you took from that?"

"Well..." Garrick didn't know what to say. "Are you questioning my judgement, now?"

"I'm just saying..." Fanta trailed off in frustration. She cradled her head in her hands and caught Garrick's curious expression. They knew each other well enough to second-guess what was eating her.

"Have you received a date for your exam?" She nodded. Garrick grinned. "I was nervous as hell when I got mine through."

"That was *years* ago..." she muttered, running her hands through her hair.

"Yep. Exams were easier then."

"Exactly." She caught the annoyance on his face and couldn't hold back a laugh. "It's in three weeks."

Garrick nodded. "It's nothing you don't know. What really counts is your track record." He regarded her steadily. "And you've got nothing to prove there." She gave a small nod. Garrick cleared his throat as he tried to frame a friendly warning. "You can only move backwards, really. We're all behind you here. Just make sure you don't push so hard, that they start to officially complain."

Fanta stared into space for a long moment. Garrick couldn't work out if his hint was getting through. Witnesses had been known to press complaints after rigorous interviews, and although McDonald had been nothing more than irritable, the last thing she needed was a petulant complaint against her techniques. Eventually she nodded, and he hoped she understood.

"Besides, I'm going to be the one in a bad mood after that, because I'll be stuck looking for a bloody replacement DC."

That made her smile, and she logged onto her computer. Garrick considered whether he should go home early and take some of the pressure off Wendy. But all he really wanted to do was sleep, and that would cause more tension at home. He considered his options when he heard a note of surprise from Fanta.

"Have you seen the update from forensics?"

"No. Sean is down there to oversee things."

"They found another body part. A hand." She looked meaningfully at Garrick. "It was in McDonald's second storage locker."

Chapter Five

DCI Garrick was feeling sickly when he hung up from Wendy after explaining he would be home even later than anticipated. The reality was he was relieved that the case had suddenly expanded to occupy his time, and the unpleasant feeling was due to drinking an instant coffee Fanta had forced on him before leaving the office. He'd given coffee a wide berth for years as it never agreed with him, and had settled on herbal teas. Now he was in desperate need of focusing, so he had caved in under his team's insistence.

Fanta volunteered to join DC Wilkes at the market to investigate the new limb. Garrick had no objections; they were an item living together, so he hoped that translated to efficient teamwork. DS Chib Okon had finally tracked down the owner of storage depot and had swung by to pick Garrick up as they travelled to Sevenoaks. She was still looking refreshed after her postponed honeymoon in the Maldives. At the best of times, she'd inherited a youthful Nigerian complexion from her mother, but after a fortnight in the sun, she looked younger than ever. Which made her opening gambit sting even more when Garrick got in the car.

"Jeez, Guv, you look knackered!"

"Thanks a bunch, Chib. I'd say the same, but it would be a lie."

"Amy keeping you awake?"

"Do I really look that bad? You're lucky you can't have kids." He immediately flinched at his own carelessness. Chib was in a same sex relationship, and Garrick was just on the rough end of still saying the first thing that came to his mind. He spluttered as he tried to correct himself, which only made Chib chuckle.

"If that's an offer, I'll pass. Thanks." His cheeks flushed red, which just amused her further. "And you we're going to adopt. We decided when we were away."

"Is that good news? I mean, having two senior officers sleep-deprived might not be the best idea."

"That's another advantage I have over you. We're looking at a three or four-year-old. Bypass all the hard work you're going through. We've started filling out the paperwork." She became tactfully silent for a moment. "And I may need a character reference..." She smiled sidelong at him.

Garrick rolled his eyes. "If there is anything I can do to make your life as uncomfortable as mine is, count me in."

It was approaching seven-thirty in the evening when they drove through the small village of Seal and turned off on a private road. Chib buzzed an intercom that controlled the gated community beyond. It was answered by a remote operator at the security company that looked after the estate. Their logo, Pegasus Security, and a flying horse emblem were on the intercom. She flashed her police credentials, then was told she would have to open the gate manually as the motor was broken. Garrick got out of the car to oblige, and closed it after she pulled through.

Sevenoaks was a well-heeled area of Kent, but this private community took a page out of the Beverly Hills handbook. Large mansions with pillared entrances, open tennis courts, and - as they pulled up to their destination - outdoor swimming pools, most concealed by walled gardens and well-manicured hedges. Garrick thought the pools were a luxury that was completely at odds with the turbulent British weather.

They pulled up at the property gate and Chib buzzed the intercom. They took in the large, whitewashed house, ivy artfully creeping up the walls to add a flash of colour. There were no cars in the gravel driveway, but two large, shuttered garages to the side no doubt hid something expensive. The intercom was answered and after Chib had held up her ID to the embedded camera, the gate opened and they drove inside. Garrick gave a low whistle as they climbed out of the Range Rover Chib had appropriated from the police pool.

"This is exactly like the houses I've been looking at buying. Looking at... but not being able to afford. This guy got rich from a fish market?"

"Alexender Kontos," Chib reminded him. "And no, he's into property. That's where the real money is."

Garrick had expected them to be met at the door by a housekeeper, so was surprised when Kontos himself greeted them with a wide smile. Slightly shorter than Garrick, Kontos was handsome, with markedly defined Greek heritage, shoulder-length hair that was still dark with the occasional strand of grey, and a build that indicated he took pride in his appearance. He guided them through a palatial hallway, and into the kitchen where he had already prepared a cafetière of coffee and a jug of freshly squeezed orange juice. Garrick took both. Even the kitchen was the size of Garrick's home. With recessed lighting and speakers, black marble worktops, a top of the range hob, and a massive double doored refrigerator. It looked more like a photoshoot than a real kitchen.

"This is beautiful," Chib commented as she looked around.

"I am something of a cook," Kontos said. "I had ambitions to start my own restaurant, but real-world interests have a habit of overriding your dreams."

"I didn't think we'd manage to have the chance to talk to you today," Garrick said, his tongue tingling from the juice, which was a million miles away from the processed cartons he bought in Asda. "Your office was less than helpful."

Kontos joined them at a marble topped kitchen table that overlooked the swimming pool. A canvas pool over was drawn across it, but steam gently rose from the water, lit from lights below the water.

"My apologies. But I am essentially a one-man show. Details can be lost with staff and offices. It has been a hectic morning. I have twenty-two tenants who rely on my facilities and have now been told their livelihood are on hold for a day or two. Some of them do not have insurance to cover that, so you can imagine what they're going through."

"It may be longer than that," Chib said. "You have heard something else was found in another locker?" Kontos nodded solemnly. "One also rented by Mr McDonald."

"I find the whole thing unbelievable."

Chib pressed him. "We've had plenty of experience dealing with the unbelievable. What can you tell us about Mr McDonald?"

"He was a tenant when I bought the business six years ago."

"Would you say he was a model tenant?"

Kontos laughed. "There is no such thing. When I took ownership, I restructured the charges. Naturally, nobody was happy. Rents went up, yes, but I updated the power grid, because there had been consistent failures. I improved security. I added five extra units, and I invested in an advertising push to draw more trade to our facilities so retail could get the freshest catches before they even went to the market next door, something the previous owner had never done. Tenants only focused on the price hike and not the benefits."

"McDonald voiced his displeasure?"

"I would call it, his cynicism. Even though he did well from it for the first two years. Even rented an extra unit. That was until trade took an inevitable hit because of politics and he tried to get out of his contract early. For that extra unit."

"But you wouldn't let him?"

Kontos gave a helpless gesture. "We had a contract. If I did that with everybody then I wouldn't have a viable business."

"In voicing his opinion, did he upset any of the other tenants?"

Kontos shrugged. "I don't often visit the site. Most of my dealings are done over the telephone, or better yet, email. Interaction with them is not something of interest to me."

"So, you wouldn't know if somebody was trying to send McDonald a message?"

"I should think if anybody was sending a message, it could be aimed at any of them. Surely, unplugging a freezer or swapping a padlock on the door would be disruptive enough. As far as murder goes..." His eyes went wide as he tried to comprehend the facts.

Chib made a quick note in her notepad. As usual, Garrick admired her perfect penwork, it was like a piece of art. She tapped the page thoughtfully.

"You said your tenants wouldn't have insurance to cover this. What about you?"

Kontos gave a humourless chuckle as he poured himself another coffee from the cafetiere.

"You said I had been difficult to get hold of. I spent most of the day trying to get an answer from my insurance company. I'm still waiting. Nobody likes losing money."

Before she had left the office, Fanta had made a disgusting coffee and dredged a piece of news from the internet. It was on a community Facebook group that had been griping about the depot. It somehow loomed as important in Garrick's mind, so he jumped in before Chib could ask her follow-up question. "Except you."

"I don't know what you mean."

"You've invested in the site. More lockers, power, etcetera. But the industry has been dwindling, hasn't it?"

"By providing the best facilities, one hopes, as others fold, I would get their custom."

"And are you?"

"No."

"Is that why you're trying to sell the land?"

Kontos's posture sharpened a little and his tone became a little edgier. "When the land is worth more than the business sitting on it, then there is a problem. I'm a property developer, detective. Not a fishmonger."

"Does that mean you bought the depot to eventually sell it off?"

"Of course. Always have an exit plan. It was a speculative purchase, and showed promise of breaking even. The future of the industry was always questionable; therefore, it was just a matter of time before a seafront warehouse was not worth terribly much."

"But seafront *apartments* are worth a lot more."

"Considerably."

This was news to Chib. She glanced between Garrick and Kontos. "Have you tried to sell it yet?"

Kontos put his cup down as his face hardened. "My first attempt faced short shrift from the community. They sentimentally cling to the idea that the industry has value in Whitstable, rather than accepting the more pragmatic fact that it is being consigned to history."

Garrick nodded. "Meaning that your vision is gentrification of the area?"

Kontos nodded. "The industry is the backbone of a lovely area of Kent. But it's declining. People seldom look beyond their next pay packet. They are not seeing that the town could become a slum unless action is taken."

Garrick smiled. "You see yourself as the saviour of the community."

Kontos laughed, his eyes crunkling good-naturedly. "Not all heroes wear capes, eh, detective?" He raised his cup in a toast. "And it makes me a profit. Which makes me a businessman. Everybody benefits if things are done correctly."

"Planning permission was declined?"

"I am required to have the site's usage reclassified from business to residential use. The council didn't agree with me."

"But you can apply again?"

"Of course."

"So, it is safe to say that there is some community resentment against your plans."

"There is always resentment when it comes to progress."

Garrick's mind raced as a broader spectrum of possible ill-wishers beckoned. Chib seized the moment to ask something that had been nagging her.

"Have you had many health and safety incidents on site? Specifically, rodent infestations."

Kontos flinched in surprise. "None at all. It's a very hygienic environment and we have always maintained higher standards than required by law."

"Although security seems minimal."

"I assure you it's far better than it was. We have cameras at the gate, and a guard who patrols the units on an hourly basis."

Having visited industrial sites over his career, Garrick doubt that was the case even if the intention was there. Shift work ruined the body clock of even the most diligent guard, most of whom were on minimum wage, so they would try to snatch sleep when they could, and if the weather was cold, it was even more reason to stay inside and put the kettle on.

It was dark by the time the detectives wrapped up their questions. Kontos gave them his mobile number and assured them he'd be around for the next few weeks. As they clambered back into Chib's car, Garrick was deep in thought.

"What's eating you, Guv?"

"How did he strike you?"

Chib turned the ignition on, and they rolled out of the plush estate as she considered.

"He seemed straightforward. Self-made man from the little I Googled. You?"

"I don't know. I got a whiff of *eau du desperation*. I'll get

Harry to investigate his portfolio. If he's lumbered with a business he can't sell, I'm sure that's a big issue no matter how wealthy you are."

"It would help if we could identify the victims. So far, nobody from any of the tenants has reported anybody missing. I'm willing to bet they're not connected."

Garrick wasn't sure if that made things clearer or not. Lost in thought he scrolled through the messages on his phone until he stopped at one from Fanta. It was about to add a new dimension to the case.

"Fanta's still with forensics on site," he said, re-reading the words. "Their first assessment is the bite marks on the leg are not from rodents."

He looked levelly at her.

"They're human."

Chapter Six

The silver blade slid through the tender flesh with almost no resistance. Red juice leaked from the incision and dribbled down the sparkling silver before pooling underneath the slice of meat. It was quickly followed by the short jab of a fork before Zoe raised the morsel to her mouth, and scooped it in with a low "*mmm*" of delight.

Garrick watched, his mouth watering, as the CSI officer savoured the T-bone before her wide green eyes widened. She nodded, her bobbed, blue-blonde tinged hair swayed hypnotically. Then she beamed her approval at Garrick.

"Oh mate," she said, sipping the Coke Zero she'd selected to accompany her midday lunch. "You don't know what you're missing."

"I think I do." Garrick's eyes shot to his plate of pasta, which had sounded nice and healthy on the menu, until the minuscule portion arrived and indicated the rest of his day would be spent in a state of hunger. His doctor had been on at him during his recovery to lose weight, and he'd started eating healthily. But the sight of Zoe's steak threw all notions of that out of the window.

He usually spent time with Zoe at crime scenes and, very occasionally, in the lab, which reminded him more of James Bond's Q's cool high-tech gadget shop. She had little to officially add to her forensics report, and it left Garrick burning with more questions. She was fond of him and always open to meet up, but as the team was exceptionally busy, she had the perfect excuse to evade any additional work. So, he'd lured her out with the promise of lunch, anticipating a trip to McDonald's, and ending up in *Bleù Steakhouse* in Staplehurst, one of the best steak restaurants in Kent and definitely not one of the cheapest.

"You said those teeth marks on the leg were human," he said, steering the conversation back to the case.

Zoe gave him a careful look as she sliced into her steak again. "I wrote in the report 'bite marks.' As in deliberately repeated bites, not just one."

Already his hopes were raised. Hard dental evidence was enough to identify a suspect in a court case. She caught his look and pulled a face.

"Multiple bites suggest that it wasn't a defensive wound, say when the attacker is trying to force somebody off them. This looks like deliberate gnawing at the raw flesh, *after* it'd been severed."

Garrick opened his mouth to ask a question, but Zoe beat him to it.

"But we only have fragmented dental recreation." She put her fork down and mimed a biting action, a rapid biting motion with her fingers. "I'd say three or four times, each bite erasing part of the last one, so it's not a clean wound. It all becomes a bit of a blur. It's not enough for court evidence."

Garrick pulled a face, already disappointed. "What does this suggest to you?"

"Well," she considered the question, "the reason you'd bite is in defence or to further weaken an opponent, but this leg was already lobbed off. And done with precision. I doubt they were trying to remove a tattoo or identifying feature just using their teeth – that's far too sloppy. This, in my opinion, is a very deliberate cannibalistic action."

Garrick reluctantly shoved one of the four large pieces of ravioli into his mouth, chewing slowly, his appetite slowly extinguishing at the thought of cannibalism.

"Have you ever come across this before?"

Zoe shook her head. "No, mate. It's been on my bucket list."

Garrick blinked in surprise. "You have a weird bucket list."

"Well, me professional one. With cannibalism, you'd expect the flesh to be cooked, at the very least. This was raw. That suggests it was an opportunistic act. Curiosity, maybe? It's difficult to say."

"What about any genetic evidence?"

"Huh! Therein lies another problem. The number of times the freezer door had opened and shut created a layer of frost over everything. You know, like when you leave the freezer door accidentally open and fine ice covers everything. It's called freezer frost, created by water vapour in the air condensing on any exposed surface. It's thin, powdery stuff that easily melts. And when it melts, it washes away into the room's drainage system. I reckon that happened at least half a dozen times before we got to it. Carrying away DNA, blood, hairs, all the good stuff we need. My boys isolated the drainage filters so we're gonna to check those, but to be honest, I'm don't hold out much hope. My hunch is the dissection took place in that locker. There would have been blood everywhere. If that was on a layer of white frost, it would've been so easy to spot and flush away."

"Any indication of the cause of death?"

Zoe almost spat out one of her chips in response. She flashed him a wide, freckled smile.

"Are you serious? The cause of death is loss of his *entire* body." She shrugged. "Assuming he's dead, that is."

Garrick gave her a curious look. "Now you're joking."

"The limb was very professionally dissected. I'm talking not just some sloppy wild hack job. I'm talking professional abattoir butchery going on here. Maybe better than that. Surgical. I've reached out to a few experts to analyse the cut, but this was very well performed, which opens up the possibility this was done intentionally."

"You mean, torture?"

She took another handful of chips from the metal container they shared and chewed on them thoughtfully.

"Sure, although I imagine if you're torturing someone, it'd be a little bit more of a hatchet job than precision. My first thought was it was the work of a mob doctor."

Garrick looked puzzled. "If you've been shot in the leg and about to die, sure, but again there's no indication of that. And then there's the hand found in the other locker."

She nodded. "Then there is that, although it doesn't discount my mob-doc theory because it's not from the same person."

Garrick's eyes widened slightly. He hadn't had any details about the find, so this was news to him.

Again, Zoe smiled. "You're losing your edge, mate. It's all this married life."

"We're not married," Garrick muttered.

Zoe gave him a coy look. "Ah, there's hope for me yet then."

Garrick felt his cheeks flush. "You're certain they're not connected?"

"Well, the hand is from a black fella, and that white leg is pastier than I am. We're running everything through for DNA profiling, but that's going to take a bit of time. There are clear tats on the hand, which gives us something to ID. And it was also cut with the same precision."

"Meaning that this wasn't a batch order job."

Zoe shook her head. "Too early to tell for sure. And again, if they're dead." She was amused by his disbelieving look. "I think it's weird that here you class murder as one thing. Premeditated, impulsive, it's all the same. In the States there's murder by degrees. First degree if it's planned, second if you just meant to beat the fella up be accidentally caved his skull in. And manslaughter. There are degrees of murder because nothing's back or white."

"I would argue death is black or white." He toyed with another chunk of ravioli. Four bites in and he was already halfway through his meal.

He didn't buy the mob doctor angle, and his gut told him the owners of the limbs were dead. So, he was dealing with two killings from a skilled perpetrator in a highly controlled environment. Already his alarm bells were going off. These were the traits of a serial killer. Someone very different from an individual who'd impulsively killed multiple times. There was an absolute world of difference between the two. It was the gnawing marks that worried him the most.

He mused further, as he pushed a ravioli around his plate, his appetite fading. "Cannibalism is something I associate with old-timey explorers or kids' books, where people are cast away on a desert island."

Zoe polished off the last chunk of steak and her emerald eyes flicked across his face as she tried not to smile too broadly. "Oh, mate, you've tickled my sweet spot right there."

Garrick glanced away. She always had a way of slipping in an innuendo he still found uncomfortable after all this time. She lay her cutlery across the plate and swooped up the Coke glass.

"As a matter of fact, I did a dissertation about it in uni. You've got the Jeffrey Dahmers and their like, who are really dull, yawn-o-ramas. Cannibalism is so much more fascinating than those dolts. Throughout time, cultures have engaged in it. It's built into religious beliefs. Roman Catholics believe in *transubstantiation*. I mean... no offense, but technically believing a piece of bread and wine turns into human flesh the moment you eat it?"

"I'll put my priest on the suspect list."

"Sometimes cannibalism emerges out of necessity, like sheer hunger. Remember those films about the aeroplane that crashed in the Andes? That's a true story. They ate the dead. Most often it's ritualistic, like winning a battle."

"Disgusting."

"Apparently humans taste of pork, and who doesn't like bacon? Islanders around Fiji called us *long pigs*. Everything has been eaten one time or another. The Asmat tribe in Papua New Guinea used to even eat the skull." She was amused by Garrick's repulsion. "Until Christian missionaries stamped all that out." She took a big sip from the glass as her enthusiasm increased. "But the Fore tribe out there take the biscuit. They were involved in *endocannibalism*." She said the word with relish before registering Garrick's confusion.

"It means they ate the dead as part of a funeral ritual. They weren't weird or anything."

"Clearly not."

"It sorta faded because people were contracting *Kuru*. That's a neurogenerative disease. Not a nice one. You catch it by eating the brain. Remember you guys had mad cow disease here? Similar thing."

"So, the idea of Soylent Green isn't such an environmental saver then?"

After a few seconds wearing a puzzled frown, she finally remembered the old sci-fi reference. "Some cultures really believed eating parts of the victim transferred those traits over. Like a heart for strength. Or a big penis." She smirked sidelong at him.

"But this is all a long time ago."

Zoe shrugged. "The Fore tribe only stopped in the sixties. And you heard about Armin Meiwes, of course."

Garrick's appetite had fled. He put his fork down. "Would it surprise you if I had no idea who Mr Meiwes is."

"*Herr* Meiwes. He was German. The *Rotenburg Cannibal!* He was caught when he advertised for victims on the internet back in 2001."

"Advertised?"

She nodded emphatically. "And people replied. They volunteered to be killed and eaten."

Garrick sipped his water, wondering why he wasted his time being a detective when people were calling such tragic blights down on themselves. "Savages."

"Cannibals are mostly educated blokes. Very few women. Maybe we're just better at getting away with it?"

After picking up the bill, which Garrick assumed was the most somebody had paid for two pieces of ravioli, including at Michelin-starred restaurants, he was hugged goodbye outside and Zoe promised to send him some reading materials.

Walking back to the car park, Garrick tried to work out why the conversation had affected him so much. During his career, he had seen many grisly sights and acts of depravity. Was he just being oversensitive due to lack of sleep, or was he being protective now that he was a new father? The answer wasn't obvious, but for the first time in a long time he felt disjointed. Fractured away from his family; away from his team.

He decided it was time to head home and attempt to focus on something else other than work. Only he knew his mind didn't operate that way. There was a puzzle in front of him, one with only a pair of unconnected pieces; and he was never able to leave a puzzle unfinished.

Chapter Seven

DCI David Garrick loved a fast-moving case. It engaged the senses and seized the mind and imagination, providing a distraction from the trials and tribulations of ordinary life.

This case was certainly not one of them.

For two weeks, it felt as if they were making little progress. The labs hadn't matched any DNA that identified either the potential victims or the killer. The tattoos on the hand, although vivid and striking with the black-inked, curving Maori-inspired lines, did nothing to help identification. A complete forensic sweep of the market had revealed no further clues, and there was nothing revealing in the witness statements. The security guard admitted that he hadn't done any rounds that night because he had a cold and was feeling under the weather.

Harry and Sean had poured over weeks' worth of video footage, which showed nothing unusual with the comings and goings of the usual crews who accessed their storage units. Everything was on point and secure. There was no hint that anything could be amiss.

Still, for every employee identified in the video footage, the team had interviewed each and every one of them. A few people had records for being drunk and disorderly, but for minor incidents, and nobody in Trev MacDonald's employment had anything wrong except one man who had an outstanding parking ticket. The only flag Fanta had uncovered was an official cannabis warning Simon Evans had obtained for having been caught carrying pot on him. It wasn't a criminal record as such, and the next infraction would be a fine, which he appeared to have avoided for the time being.

Fanta had made requests further into Trev McDonald's business accounts, as she kept raising the idea that somebody had been trying to sabotage him. But HMRC and Companies House had both been slow to respond with anything so far.

The slow pace had meant that Garrick was now spending more time at home, which had settled into a regular routine of not sleeping as they waited for Amy to wake them both up. When the weather was nice, they had taken to going to the park together, which he had dreaded but turned out to be enjoyable. Except the two times Amy had thrown up on him, ensuring that he now always kept a spare t-shirt and jogging trousers in the boot, just in case.

The change of routine had been a welcome relief that both he and Wendy had been forced to acknowledge. This had led her to declare she had booked them to visit two properties they had circled on their house-hunting list. Garrick had been reluctant to progress beyond window shopping.

Anything beyond the websites brought the future into scary focus.

The first house had been a wonderful example of photographic excellence. On the screen, it looked spacious and ideal, yet the moment they walked in, they barely recognised the place, despite the acne-covered estate agent's enthusiastic sales patter. For once, Garrick was happy that Amy had woken in Wendy's arms and thrown a tantrum as they completed the first lap of the house. It gave them the perfect opportunity to cut the visit short.

However, the second house, which had a driveway extending from a quiet cul-de-sac at the edge of the quiet village of Kingsnorth, backed onto a farmer's field and woods beyond. Wendy was captivated when she spotted the faun flanks of a deer cutting through the farmer's field backing onto the property. It made the home feel enchanted and a million miles away from the bustling town centre, which was only four kilometres away.

This estate agent was a more mature woman who had mastered the art of subtlety, which bordered on indifference, as Garrick and Wendy pushed for further details.

They were the ideal buyers. They had cash because Garrick had sold his previous house, and they were already pre-approved for the small mortgage needed to top up their funds. They were not in a chain, so could move in instantly. And, as if fate was dancing a jig for them, the estate agent casually mentioned that the property once belonged to the owner's mother, who had recently passed, and so the sellers were not caught in the dreaded housing chain, either.

It offered twice the space of their cramped rented terrace and an infinite amount of privacy and luxury compared to what they were used to. On a practical level, Garrick knew a change of environment would do nothing to make their daughter sleep, but perhaps it would do wonders for his and Wendy's relationship.

They were halfway back home when they decided they should put in an offer, just to see what would happen. Garrick suggested going in under the asking price, giving them a little bargaining power, but the idea was vetoed by Wendy, who insisted they just pay what was asked. She sent the email on her mobile phone, and with a whoosh, their potential future lay in a digital message flashing across the internet.

Just as the investigation team was running dry after three weeks, Garrick assembled them all at the office. They stood in front of the evidence wall, staring at pictures of the two severed limbs, and photos of the storage depot. Various pictures of Simon Evans, Trev McDonald, and Alexander Kontos, taken from social media or copies of their driving licences, circled the edge of the board.

The cannibalistic overtones of the case had been kept secret after an initial flurry of press interest. But that had waned after forty-eight hours. In fact, there was no outside pressure at all.

Garrick bit his lip thoughtfully. "You know what's really bothering me?" he said with a nod towards the wall. "Nobody's reported missing people. And if the owners of these limbs were still alive, they haven't reported it."

"Lost property's not what it used to be, eh?" said DC Harry Lord as he sipped his tea.

"Losing a hand is not the same as losing a suitcase, mate," Garrick said, shaking his head. "So, what does that tell us?"

Chib opened her mouth to speak, but Fanta leapt in. For the past few weeks, she'd been revising for her exam and was irritated that the case she was involved in wasn't going to further help her promotional prospects.

"These people were already registered as missing, are loners, or don't live here."

Garrick nodded. "Yes, yes, and yes. Sean, you liaised with missing persons. Anything?"

"A big fat zero, Guv. They ran a check on anyone who could match the tats. Nothing."

"Wonderful," said Garrick. "Well, I suppose there's not much more we can do except wait for something else to pop up."

It wasn't widely recognised, but a lot of criminal cases meandered into cold cases. It wasn't something the police or the government wanted to talk about, but the statistics showed a high percentage of cases remained unsolved. Most detectives felt a cold case was a black mark on their own record, and right now, after a successful run of high-profile convictions, it was the last thing Fanta needed. She was literally writhing with frustration, rubbing her hands together nervously.

"What about the bite marks?" said Sean, clacking his teeth together and then making a Hannibal Lecter slurping imitation that made the others chuckle dryly. Zoe had sent Garrick a lot of reading material on cannibalism. Too much. She was clearly enthralled by the topic, and it made him rather uncomfortable.

"We've drawn a blank there too. We found nothing that mirrors it," Garrick shrugged. "Maybe it was just a bizarre impulse from the killer, um, attacker, whatever." He spun his finger in the air. "Okay, let's wrap this up before we go crazy staring at the wall."

He was about to turn away when Fanta spoke up. "Guv, but there are a couple of things."

He stopped in surprise. At the beginning of the meeting, he'd asked for updates, and none had been forthcoming. Yet now, she was awkwardly pacing back and forth.

"Yes, DC Liu, have we overlooked something blindingly obvious?"

"It's not quite true that there were no other cases that mirror it. See, we'd all been looking for *cannibalism*, for eating flesh, that sort of thing. And nothing flagged up."

Garrick nodded. "Go on."

"But if you broaden that search, there are *thousands* of records, which indicate bite marks sustained in a fight or a struggle. Mostly defensive wounds."

Chib spoke up. "Yeah, far too many. And forensics said no reliable dental records could be made from what we had."

"Uh-huh. But there are some telltale signs. Look." Fanta hammered away at her computer keyboard to call up close-ups of the bite wounds. "Forensics said these are multiple bite marks, so they've left no definitive outline. However, the leading edge—"

"The leading edge?" Chib echoed, puzzled.

"Yeah, the front of the teeth," said Fanta, tapping her own two incisors. "The mark shows a slight unevenness. So, the attacker's left incisor is slightly twisted, like a millimetre or two, just enough not to be even with the one next to it. And that can be seen four times cutting across the flesh."

"Okay, vague," said Chib.

"Vague, yep. So, I ran that through the database," Fanta explained, "using some new AI algorithms."

Chib rolled her eyes and looked at Garrick, shaking her head. Artificial Intelligence systems were increasingly used within law enforcement to make statistical matches and scour computer and data records. They had been used for a while; more so now detectives had easy access to numerous AI systems, they were used to see if there was any probability of matching cases together. It was not yet reliable enough to be applicable in any court of law, but it held the possibility of nudging a detective onto the right track. Chib had been one of the vocal naysayers when it came to using it.

"It made a possible match with an incident in Exeter," Fanta continued. "It was just on the records from two years ago." She called up another photo of a bite mark where a chunk of flesh had been bitten from a victim. "In this case, it was a mouthful that had been taken out. And the victim had been shot."

"And the killer?"

"Unidentified. It was a gang-related killing."

"So not that relevant here." Garrick and Chib exchanged a look and an almost imperceptible, slight shrug, which Fanta noticed. She rolled her eyes.

"Okay, statistically, you might say it's vague, but out of every bite mark on the database, this is the only one that had a 56% chance of matching."

"56%?" Harry scoffed. "Well, it's little better than 50-50: which means it either does match, or it doesn't. That's barely in its favour."

"And still it was the highest match in the *entire* database," Fanta insisted. "That's statistically *something*."

She looked slightly crestfallen with everybody's unenthusiastic reaction. Garrick felt a rare pang of sympathy for her, as he'd always admired her tenacity.

"Fanta, it's always good to chase the extremes and see what's there, but most of the time you have to accept that a dead end is exactly that. I think here, we've just got to be patient."

"Sean found out something." She pointed at Sean. All eyes turned to him, and he looked embarrassed to be at the centre of attention.

"Oh, yeah, well, it's in my notes, but I'm not as sure it's as relevant as she thinks it is," he mumbled apologetically, ignoring the glaring daggers he received from his girlfriend. He gave an embarrassed cough and tapped on Alexander Kontos's picture on the board. "He'd visited the market a few times. We went back through surveillance tapes, and for the last month he'd made three appearances. Okay, he does own the property, so that shouldn't be unusual, except the last time, he is seen arguing with Trev McDonald." He raised a cautionary finger as Garrick's eyebrows raised. "But he was also arguing with practically everybody else."

The others waited for the denouement that didn't come.

"That's it?" said Chib.

Sean shrugged. "I did say I didn't feel it was that important."

"But what is important," said Fanta, springing to her feet, "is it ties in with some paperwork we obtained from the Local Planning Authority. It was the day *after* Alexander Kontos claimed they had caused a deal to fall apart. He needed the land re-designated from business use, to residential. Apparently, the council said it was a done deal, but then they changed their minds."

"He made no secret of his intentions," Chib pointed out.

"No, maybe not. But the day after his deal fell through, he went nuts at everybody there, but the interviews pointed out McDonald was his prime target. And they all universally dislike him."

"He's their landlord. Of course they dislike him."

"Okay, so we have vague motive."

"That we do," said Fanta. "That is more or less what you both heard from the horse's mouth, right?" Chib and Garrick nodded. Fanta smiled. "But what I bet he didn't tell you is the time he had *another* property deal that was about to fall through, and he employed a gang of muscle for hire to apply a little pressure to make sure it didn't. I found the guy Alexender Kontos screwed over."

Chapter Eight

A trip to London was always a welcome diversion in Fanta's opinion. She felt, anything that took a case beyond the pokey borders of the Garden of England was something to be savoured. She'd suggested jumping on the high-speed train, so they'd be there within thirty minutes, and arrive at St Pancras in comfort. But Garrick, muttering about budget cuts and fiscal responsibility, insisted they drove all the way to Sevenoaks and got the much cheaper and crowded train from there. As they pulled into London Bridge, he and Fanta navigated their way to the Underground, flashing their police IDs at the gate guards so they could slip through to the Jubilee line and into the city without paying.

They disembarked at Canary Wharf, and Garrick blinked in surprise as they stepped out into the sunny, but cool day. It had been a long time since he'd been in this neck of the woods, and it had changed into a page from an American postcard, with tall skyscrapers looming around them.

The train journey had been mostly discussing Fanta's

looming exam, which had been a combination of her being overconfident one moment and then terrified the next. Garrick assured her she shouldn't feel *too* cocky, but she was more than capable of acing it. Only when they were out on the open streets, at the risk of their entire conversation being overheard, did they talk about how to approach Fanta's lead.

Once again, Garrick pointed out the connection she'd postulated was wafer-thin. But still, they had a duty to tick every box, and on top of that, they had precious little else to allocate their time to.

"Ian Smith had a warehouse operation out in Essex," Fanta said, recalling case notes from memory. "It was an old out-of-town retail unit that had car maintenance garages, a firework shop, that sort of thing. And Alex Kontos came along once to buy the land, and he had the upper hand. The area is prone to flooding, and over the years Smith had a bunch of tenants complaining about it. It seems like there was nothing he could do. So having somebody buy up the land from under him looked like an advantage." Fanta shrugged. "Let's find out. This was all documented at Companies House and as a legitimate takeover. Kontos bought the land, paid the money, and off Smith went. So far, so normal."

"So, there's nothing to flag up," Garrick said.

"Well, there's only one thing. I ran through the company names, and I came across a legal challenge at the same time when Smith was accusing Kontos of extortion. That case was dropped just before the deal went through."

Garrick nodded as they followed Fanta's Google Maps to Ian Smith's registered office.

"That's how it looks on paper," Fanta said. "But I made some calls with the officer assigned to the case at the time, who said Smith had claimed a couple of his business partners had been assaulted. Although he couldn't prove it because his business partner had also vanished."

"Vanished, how?"

"With one hundred and thirty thousand quid from Smith's business accounts, which happened shortly before all charges were dropped and Kontos got the property."

Garrick nodded silently. Crime took on every possible form, but he had to admit the ones he disliked the most were financial cases. They had the potential for destroying lives almost as much as murder, but the details were often dry and academic, requiring specialist officers to join dots between figures and accounting procedures. He was a man who preferred cold, hard evidence that you could hold in your hands, even though when it came down to it, motivations all boiled down to the basic psychological urges that everybody carried with them.

A few minutes' walk away from the imposing city skyscrapers, they found Smith's office, which was a rented space above a *Costa Coffee*, several hundred metres from the imposing international business skyline, yet a million miles away in business terms. They had decided to cold-call him so as not to give anything away regarding their investigation. Harry had rung through the day before with a bogus query to confirm Ian Smith was in residence.

They buzzed the door intercom, announcing they were police detectives, and they were buzzed in. A narrow, creaking staircase led them up to the first floor, where a young Indian woman greeted them at reception, decorated with a cheap pale blue carpet, a water cooler, and clinically white walls with just one panoramic picture of Manhattan splayed across it.

Garrick grew frustrated pouring himself water from the cooler using the cardboard cones supplied. They took a fraction of the liquid, and couldn't be put down, forcing him to refill it three times before tossing it into the bin. After four minutes feeling irritated, the secretary invited them through the only other door in the office, where Ian Smith was waiting for them.

He was a portly man wearing a smart suit and tie, but was unshaven, with a round pair of tortoise shell glasses perched on his round nose. He stood, one hand straightening his tie, the other reaching to shake Garrick and Fanta's hands.

"Please take a seat," he said, with more than a hint of nerves. He sat back in his creaking swivel chair and waited for his assistant to close the door, before folding his hands on his desk and forcing a smile. "How can I help you, detectives?" he said licking his lips.

"Firstly, I'm thankful you have time to fit us in."

Smith's snicker bordered on sarcasm. "I don't have anything to do other than sit in here all day and act busy."

"We're making some routine investigations," said Garrick. "Your name came up, and we'd like to ask a few questions to clarify things for us. My colleague here is best placed to ask." He gestured towards DC Liu, who looked caught by surprise but quickly recovered.

"It's about Alexander Kontos," she said. Smith gave a terse nod, his knuckles tightening together at the sheer mention of the name. "You had dealings with him, and we'd like to know a little bit more about the details."

"He bought a lot of land from me in Essex. He wasn't the nicest person to do business with, but we managed. He paid. He got the land." Smith shrugged. "Water under the bridge."

Fanta waited for him to give more details, and when he didn't, she pressed on. "You filed a complaint against him for extortion."

Smith gave a nervous chuckle. "That was me being a little *oversensitive*." He chose his words carefully. "Kontos drove a hard bargain and paid under the asking price. I felt it wasn't fair. On top of that, he sold it shortly afterwards, and they built a whopping big Tesco there. He made a huge profit, and he only had the site for four months."

"You felt that you were manipulated?"

Smith licked his lips. "You could say that. Which is why I filed a complaint. It was the police who were more than happy to point out I was overreacting. So, what can a man do?"

"How did Kontos pressured you?"

Smith shook his head. "What does it matter? I got stiffed, but I got some money. He walked away happy. I walked away wiser."

Garrick gestured around the office. "What exactly is the nature of your business now?"

"I advise people buying and selling land."

"Ironic." Garrick brightened up. "Let me know if you know a good conveyancer. I'm buying a house and our offer got accepted."

Smith gave a dry chuckle. "I can tell you who to avoid, that's for sure."

"That's always handy to know, too," said Garrick. "I believe you had business partners?"

"I used to have bigger offices, too. And staff! More than just a secretary doom-scrolling at the desk." His knuckles tightened, and he nodded. "He screwed me over, too. He did a runner. Took a whole bunch of money and vanished."

"Do you think he was linked to what Kontos was doing to you?" said Fanta.

Garrick suppressed a smile, impressed at the leading question Fanta had composed. It heavily hinted that they suspected a connection and knew far more than they were letting on. It was always a tricky task to pull off during interviews, as they had a duty not to be misleading, so any opportunity that made people divulge more than they were willing was always welcome.

It had the desired effect on Smith, who sighed and then slid his fingers under his glasses to rub his tired eyes. "If you're looking to reopen that whole extortion thing with me, I'm not interested. It's settled. I went through hell. My business hung on by a thread and I had to downscale to this dump. It is what it is. So according to your official report," he used both index fingers to point at the detectives, "which I'm sure you've read, the suggestion was my business partner took the money and ran because Kontos was about to screw us over. I felt Kontos had compelled him to do so. The police said there was no evidence and Kontos' bastard of a lawyer threatened to sue for libel and slander. My options had vanished."

He placed both palms down on the table and composed himself. When he removed his hands, Garrick could see the faint sheen of sweat that he'd left on the table. The man was overly nervous.

"I appreciate that's all on record," Garrick said reassuringly. "We've got no interest in dragging you through anything so stressful again, or reopening that case that was dismissed by you. That's your own business, not ours. But we are very interested in knowing more about Alex Kontos's business ethics." Garrick smiled, giving a warm, friendly smile, telegraphing they were both on the same side. It seemed to have the desired effect.

"That question has an easy answer. He has none." Smith wiped his sweaty palms on his trousers and leaned forward onto his desk, closing the gap between them. "Completely off the record, I think the man is a corrupt pile of shit. He steamrolls into business, knocks you until you're on the ground. Then he swoops in with the worst possible deal. The land I had was prone to flooding, and he knew that was an issue. My tenants were complaining, but all that was due to the local council not maintaining the drainage systems, global warming," he waved his hands dismissively, "all the usual suspects. There was nothing I could do about that. So quite frankly, I would have been happy to sell the land, except he came in at such a lowball price that it was insulting. And when I said no, he went *lower*." He nodded emphatically. "Who does that? So of course, that's a major red flag. We were never going to take that. Then my business partner, Calvin, he started to act all jittery. Started trying to persuade me that we should take the poison plot off our books, move on. Now I've known Calvin since uni. We've been in business for six years. That was not him. That's when I started to suspect Konos was leaning on him, putting a bit of pressure. And when he came in with a broken arm, claiming he'd fallen off a ladder when decorating, I knew something was wrong. Calvin couldn't even spell 'decorating'. Somebody got to him. Obviously."

"Kontos?" said Fanta.

"Yeah, not directly, of course. Oh no. He was always level, polite, nice meals, good bars. He likes the finer things in life. Comes across as a polite guy. When you start pushing against him, suddenly he's got these people around him.

Heavies. You know, Eastern European types, big blokes you don't want to bump into at night."

"Did he threaten you?" said Fanta.

"Not directly. Everything was under the radar. But, you know, when he lowballed his own lowball offer, he stuck to that number. And when it was clear Calvin's persuasion was having no effect on me, suddenly the money went, and Calvin vanished. That put me in a huge financial hole."

"A financial hole you could only fill by selling the land."

Smith nodded. "You've got it. Not only was I forced to take his stupid offer, but I was also one hundred and thirty grand down on what had been stolen from me." He snapped his fingers. "Everything I had, had just been shattered. Oh, and then my wife filed for divorce." He shrugged pathetically.

"And Calvin?"

"Never to be heard from again. Told his family he was going travelling. He had mates around the city, a couple of girlfriends - he wasn't the sort to settle down. They never heard from him again. They all thought he took the money and was lying low in Spain or the Caribbean."

Garrick pulled a face. "One hundred and thirty grand sounds a lot, but not enough to run away and start a whole new life."

Smith nodded in agreement. "Yeah, and he was a bloke who burnt through money. I was the fiscally responsible one out of the two of us."

Fanta shifted in her seat as she worked through the profile of Alex Kontos that was being built. "What do you think happened to Calvin?"

Ian Smith leaned back in his chair again and glanced out

the window, lacing his fingers across his chest as he took a deep breath. "I think exactly what the police concluded."

Fanta gave a sceptical chuckle. "Okay, off the record, what do you think happened to him?"

Smith slowly turned his gaze back to her, fixing her with a penetrating stare. The fear in his eyes was evident. "I think Kontos had him killed. I think some of the money that he paid me for the land was some of my own money. I think one day they'll fish Calvin's body from under that supermarket, and that'll prove I was right. Although I reckon when that happens, I'll be long dead and buried along with Kontos. He's not a man who leaves traces."

"What makes you say that?" said Fanta curiously.

"Because as soon as I started to suspect he was screwing with me, I made enquiries around. Nobody had a bad word to say about him." He gave a thin smile. "When nobody has a bad thing to say, that's when you should start to worry. Can either of you honestly say that you don't have a bad thing to say about your spouses, partners, whatever?"

Garrick remained tactfully silent. All his bad opinions regarding Wendy were reflections of his own bad points. Fanta wasn't so cagy.

"My boyfriend can be a selfish prick sometimes. Less supportive about my career and more about his own..." She caught Garrick's curious look and suddenly clammed up.

"There you go," Smith said. "Normal people have bad things to say even about the people they love most in the world. And in business, *everybody* screws everyone else, even if it's with a friendly handshake and a smile, because that's what business is - getting the best deal." He stabbed the table with his index finger to emphasise his point. "Getting the best deal only really happens to one side, not the other."

"And you found nobody saying anything openly bad," Fanta said.

Smith shook his head. "Conversely, nobody has anything good to say either. So that's got to mean something, right? I never came across anybody who did repeat business with Alexander Kontos. And you're aware of the rumours, right?" He looked expectantly at Fanta, but she shook her head.

"Enlighten us."

"That his family have roots in the Greek Mafia – the sort of people you don't want to run into in Athens. That sort of thing. Obviously, he lives over here now, but still, makes you think, doesn't it? How much of that is true?"

They both left Smith's office deep in thought. As a treat, Garrick suggested they have a coffee at the Costa underneath Smith's office.

They were both thoughtful as Fanta eyed his medium soy latte. "I thought caffeine killed you."

He took a welcome sip. "As we speak, caffeine's the only thing keeping me awake. Blame Harry. So, what do you make of that?"

"I think that's one terrified man who's gone through an ordeal that wrecked his life. He thinks his business partner's been whacked and is probably thankful he hasn't been. Whether that's his imagination or not," she added. "And Kontos has apparently got ties to the Greek Mafia."

"Allegedly," Garrick nodded. "We should look into that, but that could all be hearsay."

"It feels like we have a pattern between what happened to Smith and what's happening at the depot."

"Are two incidents a pattern?" Garrick said, sipping his coffee.

"If it's not a pattern, it's a coincidence," she snapped. "I know what you think about coincidences, Guv, because you drilled that into me."

"There's no such thing as a coincidence," said Garrick.

"Exactly," said Fanta. "Don't convince me that's true, and then sit there and tell me it's not true."

"Point taken," said Garrick. "So, we potentially have a bloke who makes a lot of money on property deals, who uses threatening techniques, steamrolls in with terrible offers once you're in a corner. And he's been left with a trashed business, no money, a divorce and a missing business partner. And the connection is Kontos, except the roles are reversed and he thinks he's been screwed on a deal."

"Two missing people minus their extremities," stated Fanta.

"Well, now you mention it that way," said Garrick, "it does feel a bit more than a coincidence."

"Exactly my point."

She gazed into the middle distance thoughtfully, and something occurred to her. She went straight to her phone, rapidly typing an email. Garrick watched her, then noticed he had several messages from Wendy giving Amy's latest updates on their journey to a soft play centre, a park to feed the ducks, and another confirming they finally had a conveyancer to help them buy the house. The conveyancer also had a surveyor with a free slot who could visit the property to make his assessment within the week. Garrick was surprised at how quickly things were suddenly moving.

He looked up again to talk to Fanta, but his gaze caught Ian Smith hurrying out of his office, his telephone cradled to his ear. He nudged Fanta and nodded towards the man who was quickly striding down the street.

"I thought he said he was in the office all day?" she said.

They exchanged a glance, took their disposable cups, and hurried for the door. For his big size, Smith made rapid progress, constantly talking on his phone and paying little heed to the world around him. Garrick kept several yards behind, desperately trying not to look as if they were trailing him.

Smith only stopped at a pelican crossing as the light lingered on red. He hurried across before the signal changed. The detectives hesitated precious seconds as a taxi passed before the crossing light changed to green. They followed towards the tube station. Smith looked around, but failed to notice them. However, they could clearly see the concern etched on his face. Then the big man stopped in his tracks at the side of the road and looked around as though searching for somebody.

Garrick and Fanta stopped too, pivoting towards the window of a Ryman for cover. In the reflection of the window they could see Ian Smith look around, searching for somebody. Then he jerked as if in recognition, raised an arm, and stepped out into the street.

Exactly at that moment, a black Land Rover roared down the road, switching lanes at the last second and slamming into him with a loud, wet thud.

By the time Garrick spun around from the window, he saw Ian Smith's ample body lifting off the bonnet and several feet into the air, almost in slow motion. Broken limbs twisting at impossible angles - before as his hefty body slammed onto the road in a bloody pool.

Parts of the Land Rover's wing mirror and spoiler clattered down around him. The vehicle itself continued to accelerate, jumped the red light, and with a squeal of tires, turned the corner out of sight just as the crowd around them began to scream.

Chapter Nine

There was nothing David Garrick or Fanta Liu could do, which was made clear as they approached Ian Smith's shattered body lying in an ever-expanding pool of blood that stained the pink tarmacked bus lane. They were both moving on autopilot. Despite their experiences, despite their training, it was such a shocking sight to have witnessed first-hand.

A member of the public identifying herself as a nurse, pushed her way through gawkers filming the tragedy on their phones and joined Garrick at Ian Smith's side. She searched for a pulse on his throat and quickly declared that he was dead.

Fanta called 999 whilst Garrick took to crowd control, which essentially meant stopping traffic so that it moved around them. A black cabbie obligingly stopped at an angle to block the lane, providing a substantial roadblock preventing a red London bus from grinding through the crime scene. As they waited, he made a more personal call to the Met. The ambulance arrived within minutes, although it did so in silence with no need to sound the siren, as time had already caught up with Smith.

Two police cars arrived, subtly marked with the City of London Police's red and white cheques. They operated as a distinct police force within the Square Mile financial district. After exchanging details with the coppers, who then moved on to crowd control, they were finally joined by the man Garrick had called - DCI Oliver Kane. The detective who had relentlessly tormented Garrick whilst at the same time enabling him to be free of his past nightmares, and who was instrumental in undoing the twisted relationship with his psychopathic sister. The relationship between the men was brittle, although Garrick was gracious enough to accept Kane was only doing his job. Since then, they had worked together, but still, the word *friend* stuck in Garrick's throat when he tried to utter it, and he always felt *colleague* was taking the piss.

Kane took a tug on his vape, fruity smoke escaping his lips as he spoke. "Why is it every time I see you, something like this happens? Troubles just follow you around."

"It was a hit-and-run, right in front of us."

"I know you well enough to know the pair of you weren't just passing by. Or are you claiming that you were doing some shopping for the missus? Congratulations on the baby, by the way." Garrick glanced at him. He hadn't told Kane about Amy, so he wondered if the Met detective was still keeping tabs on him. "But I reckon fatherhood hasn't made you any less reckless, has it?"

"As it happens, we were interviewing him about one of your department's old cases and all was fine. A few minutes later, he received a very urgent call, ran out of his office, and was struck by a black Land Rover." Garrick indicated the tyre marks and trim scattered on the floor - all useful evidence he'd photographed and would submit as part of his witness statement. He glanced up. "This place is crawling with cameras. We may have got that on video. We can ANPR the plate. If you hurry, you might actually catch them."

Kane raised a hand. "Whoa! First, this isn't my case. It's a hit-and-run, and these officers who turned up will be dealing with that. And second, this is London City Police's turf. I'm MPS. You've seen *Westside Story*, right? This is police gangland territory right here."

"They'll be happier working with you than me. I'm Kent, so I'm an outsider

Kane gave a weary sigh. "Any indication of why he was in such a hurry?"

"I'm guessing our questioning made him nervous."

Kane nodded. "I've experienced your stellar repartee."

Garrick sighed. "I'd be really *thankful* if you could keep an eye on it."

"You're looking into one of the Met's old cases?"

Garrick nodded. "I'll send you the details." He gave a weak smile. "If you've got time to go through them... or maybe task one of your underlings with digging out anything that may have been missed."

Garrick knew he was pushing his luck. With every police force complaining about budget cuts, there was still a rivalry when it came to the Met cops, who were regarded by the other forces as having a little too much of a good thing. But Kane nodded amiably.

"I'll see what I can do."

Fanta joined them. "DC Liu, always a pleasure to see you."

"Wish I could say the same, Guv," she said with forced jolliness. She still looked pale, and it reminded Garrick that no matter how much her experience was, she was still relatively new to the job. And even if this hit-and-run was an accident - which he doubted - witnessing such things could easily dent an officer's confidence.

"There's nothing we could have done about this, Fanta," Garrick reminded her gently. "It's not your fault."

After finishing with DCI Kane, they headed back to London Bridge in silence. Luckily, the train carriage wasn't as full as it had been on the journey in, and they sat at a table facing one another - Garrick scrolling through his phone and Fanta watching the city fade as they rolled through fields and forests.

"How would anybody know we were there?" she said thoughtfully.

Garrick glanced up from his phone. "What d'you mean?"

"You saw how nervous he was. He wasn't expecting to be talking to the police. And he said he was staying in the office all day. But as soon as we leave, he gets a call and does a runner to meet somebody. Then – wham!" She thumped the table. "In broad daylight in the middle of the city. I mean, think about it. If you're trying to whack DCI Kane, for example-"

"Interesting choice," Garrick muttered.

"Yeah, but to do that, you'd have to plan it, right? I mean, the car's got to be stolen. In the middle of London, with cameras everywhere, that takes balls. Then you call him after we've left, which indicates he's being watched. And then direct him to the kill zone."

"Kill zone? You've been watching too many movies."

"It felt too planned to me."

Garrick couldn't argue. A shower of thoughts struck him at the same time. He shook his head. "You know what, DC Liu? Sometimes you still surprise me." She glanced curiously at him. "Maybe it's your annoying personality quirk of always challenging the bleeding obvious. But sometimes it gets us to the right area." He rapidly began composing an email on his phone. "Let's assume then that he was still tied up in some dodgy dealings, and we come in asking about Kontos." He sent an email. "We need the email and phone records of not just who he was on the phone to when he was killed, but of anyone who contacted the office."

Fanta nodded in agreement.

"Next, he was frightened of something the moment we entered the office, so you're right - it doesn't indicate a clear conscience. Was he already in the middle of something?" Garrick ran through the conversation in his head. "He said he's not working with Kontos anymore, and nobody does repeat business with him. What does that tell you?" Fanta shrugged. "Come on, you use that enormous suspicious brain of yours. What's the first thing that comes to mind?"

"That he's not working with Kontos. That maybe he was trying to screw him over."

Garrick smiled and nodded. "One of the most powerful human motivators, right? *Revenge.*"

"So, what do we do now?"

"We can wait for the records to come in and get a clear idea of who he's talking to. But I'm really curious to see if anyone involved with the storage depot knows our Ian Smith. We should see if his name rings any bells."

. . .

By the time they reached Sevenoaks, Garrick was regretting being so cheap, as they then faced an hour drive to Whitstable, where they knew Trev McDonald's boat was moored. It was about three o'clock by the time they arrived, and Garrick was fretting in case the fishermen had already headed out for the evening. But luckily, they'd made it with plenty of time, and the crew were only just arriving to prepare the boat for a night's fishing.

Trev, clad in a thick Aran jumper under yellow bib and braces oilskins, did a double take when he saw the detectives park up and approach his boat, the old Sea Mutt. He glanced at his crew and then approached the detectives.

"Afternoon."

"Afternoon, Trev," Garrick said, casting his eye over the thirty-foot trawler that clearly had seen better days, pocked with dents, the dark blue paintwork peeling along the hull. "I thought you might be out already."

"Soon, so I haven't got long to sit and chat or invite you on board for a cuppa, if that's what you're hoping."

Garrick shook his head. "No, I have a few follow-up questions. After speaking to you, we spoke to Alexander Kontos."

Trev gave a snort of derision. "Arrested him yet?"

Garrick managed a thin smile. "Not yet. Still working through that, I suppose. There was an incident at the depot when Kontos turned up, and you and he had quite a heated argument."

Trev shrugged. "I couldn't possibly tell you about that."

"Why? Because your lawyer's not with us?"

"No, because every time I'm near that arsehole, we're in a heated argument."

"Fair point. But this was just after his deal to sell the site had collapsed."

"Oh, *that* time." Trev smiled broadly. "Yeah, that one warms the cockles of me heart. We all got together, all his tenants, and petitioned the council office so they didn't give him permission to re-designate the land, so they couldn't close it down."

"It was a concerted effort by everyone?"

Trev nodded. "Oh yeah, he laid into us all. Make no mistake - he hated *everybody*. But y'know, just because you've got a big wallet doesn't mean you can tread on the little fry."

Garrick nodded. "Power to the people." He raised his fist skyward.

"When I asked you if you had anybody who'd sabotage you, why didn't you mention this?"

"'Cause of what you found?" Trev shook his head. "I'm not connecting those dots. If we've all had to close down, Kontos doesn't even get our money, right?"

Garrick nodded. That made sense, but there was something just on the edge of his thinking he couldn't quite grasp - something he knew he should be paying attention to.

"I'm guessing it took quite a lot of effort to rally against Mr Kontos. I assume you'd gone out, spoke to people he'd had dealings to try and work out his weak points, who his enemies are, that sort of thing."

Trev glanced back at his boat as one crewman gave a whistle and indicated to his wristwatch. He gave a thumbs up and turned back to Garrick. "We did everything we could."

"And how was Ian Smith involved in this?"

Trev gave a dismissive shrug. "The fella who got his land

stolen for a song?" Garrick nodded. "Yeah, I think it was actually the woman at the council who put us on to him."

"Oh, do you have her name?"

"Yeah, Anna Campbell. She's not in the office here. She's in the Canterbury Office. And she is bloody wonderful."

Garrick gestured to the boat. "They're already hating me for keeping you talking, Trev. Thanks for your time, and be safe out there."

Trev raised an index finger to his forehead in a salute and then returned to his ship. Garrick turned to Fanta, who was already on her phone.

"Think we can make it to Canterbury before the office closes?"

"I'm already getting her details," she said, without taking her eyes from the phone.

Garrick drove as fast as he legally could back towards Canterbury. Fanta called through to double-check Anna Campbell was in her office. When she got put through, she explained she was a police detective who had a couple of quick questions. Campbell was fine with holding on until they arrived.

By the time Garrick had found a parking space and they hurried to the council office, it was almost closing time. But true to her word, Anna Campbell greeted them with a cheery smile. In her fifties, with curling black hair, big blue, thick-rimmed glasses, bright red lipstick, and a matching bright red jacket, she looked more at home in a holiday camp than working in a bland council planning office. Even towards the end of the week, and at the end of the day, she possessed incredible energy as she led them to her small office.

She gestured to a small plastic kettle and cups in the corner next to a jar of instant coffee and offered them a drink, which Garrick was sure ran afoul of some arcane council rules. But he'd already developed an addictive taste for caffeine.

As she boiled the water and prepared two cups, Garrick got straight to the point. "There was an incident at the freezer storage depot in Whitstable a couple of weeks ago."

Anna frowned and gave a low hum. "I know, I know. Horrible thing. Did you find the rest of them?"

Garrick looked through her quizzically. "You're familiar with it."

"I've been helping the workers there with their clash against the owner, and of course I've got friends down in Health and Safety who are none too pleased about mixing foodstuffs. You can only imagine - if you're serving cod and chips and human, well, health and safety would have a hissy fit." She clinked the spoon several times inside the coffee cups as she stirred them and then handed one to Garrick.

"Well, they were hardly serving them."

She sat down with a little laugh. "And I thought the police had a dark sense of humour, love."

Fanta piped up. "I'm surprised you think the police have any sense of humour."

"I used to date one of them," she said dismissively.

Garrick swung the conversation back to the point. "I was interested to learn that you helped them out when it came to blocking Kontos's application to re-designate the land. The way he tells it, approval had already been granted, and was reversed."

She held up a finger. "Approval had already been *smiled upon*, and then it was voted for, and he didn't achieve the votes required. There was no formal declaration other than the final one."

"And you're responsible for the sudden change of mind?"

"Our committee's responsible for that. I am responsible for keeping people informed and shifting bits of paper between people who never really listen. I'm pretty sure you get that, even in your job."

"Depends on your rank," Fanta muttered.

That seemed to amuse Anna.

"It's a historical area, so I was surprised the council members would have even considered re-designating it. And it's busy, and the facility had expanded," Garrick said.

"Well, Mr Kontos had expanded the facilities," she corrected him, "but let's face it, there were too few businesses using it and that just made the rent go up. On the surface, it looked like Mr Kontos had made a good attempt at modernising the place, but there simply wasn't the uptake."

"Then why keep it running? Surely Mr Kontos had a point in switching it."

"As you said, it's a historic place," she said, nursing her coffee with both hands. "Scale it back, maybe, or find another use, but to turn it into luxury apartments – ones that locals couldn't afford – is another matter. And none of the councilors were up for it at first. No one likes a pushy millionaire wading in, getting his own way. It's never a good look when it comes to local elections. But one by one, they started to side with Mr Kontos."

"Can you supply us with their names?"

"Of course I can get that to you."

"If everyone started to lean in favour, what was the decision that overturned it?"

"Well, there were three people in favour. It looked like

the other three were about to agree, until something that stuck in people's throats."

"And what was that?"

"News about Mr Kontos's last business deal in Essex. It had generated a lot of ill will, legal challenges, and illustrated how he might not be such a nice character after all."

"How did you come across this?"

"We might be out here in the far-flung corner of the southeast, but we do know what's going on in the rest of the world. And as luck would have it, I have a friend who moved from this office to the Essex planning office. The name Kontos is not exactly a common one in the counties. She let me know. It sounded like such a sketchy affair."

Fanta frowned. "But still, it's not your prerogative to interfere in these decisions."

Anna raised an eyebrow. "Interfere? That's a loaded word. Whatever you think of the council, we're not automatons punching buttons. We live in the community, too. It's our duty to make sure everything is done ethically. I can't officially sway opinion, but I can point out moral issues if I see them. And I happened to pass this information on to Mr McDonald."

"McDonald, as in Trev at the fish market?"

"The very same."

"He was singing your praises. How did you get to know him?"

"My nephew works for him, and he's been a pain in the bum for my sister. You know, typical teenager. Unfocused, unwashed, not doing anything except wasting the best years of his life away. There was no hope of him moving out, until he got that job, earned a bit of money and got used to it. It looked like it was turning him around. So, when it was mentioned that he might be out of a job, well... arrest me now?" She giggled, miming putting her hands together to be handcuffed. "But I was thinking about my sister's mental health if the depot closed down, and my nephew didn't have a job."

"Your nephew wouldn't happen to be Simon Evans, would it?"

Anna giggled. "His infamy goes far and wide. Small world, isn't it."

"It is indeed," said Garrick with a smile, as he felt the welcome pleasure of elements slotting Tetris-like into place. They were tiny pixels of information that were once completely unconnected; even the people involved were unaware of their relevance. Yet still, they formed a bigger picture that successful cases were built on. In this instance, it had the whiff of corruption hanging heavy in the air. "Ian Smith gave you information about the incident between Mr Kontos and himself, and then you presented it to the councilors?"

"Well, I got them all on a Zoom. I felt right that they all knew who they were dealing with, and Mr Smith was very persuasive, very emotional. The undecided councillors were touched, and it was evident it was going to be a hung vote, then one who was pro suddenly changed his mind and back-tracked."

"That's good to know. And did you have any direct dealings with Mr Kontos?"

"Everything is generally dealt with by letters and emails. But when this came through, I had the voice of God yelling down the phone," she said dramatically. "And he was displeased. I laid out the facts that the application was simply rejected."

"Out of curiosity, if it is a hung vote, then what would have happened?"

"Well, then it could have gone to a tribunal. And let's face it, with the business case showing the local industry was suffering year on year, that could have swung in Kontos's favour. But luckily for the fish boys, it didn't get that far."

"Did you hear anything from Mr Kontos after that?"

"No, nothing." She shook her head. "You know, if he was going to do any more business in the county - then ringing up yelling at people making decisions wouldn't be the smartest idea. It all went quiet until, well, the other week." She frowned. "How is any of this connected to what happened down at the depot?"

"Oh, it probably isn't," Garrick said dismissively. "But we have to chase all the threads so we can eliminate people from our inquiry."

That seemed to satisfy Anna. The truth of it was, nobody was ever totally eliminated from a line of inquiry until the case was closed.

Chapter Ten

"We traced the last number Ian Smith called," DCI Oliver Kane said, his voice bellowing out through the hands-free kit in Garrick's pool car. "It was an unregistered, pay-as-you-go Vodafone that had only been in use for the last two weeks."

"That's a week after the incident at the storage depot," Chib said from the passenger seat next to him. It had taken less than twenty-four hours for DCI Kane to get the information from the telecoms company, and Garrick felt a twinge of jealousy as he knew it would have taken his department a whole lot longer. Even though he and Kane were the same rank, they didn't have access to quite the same resources.

"Any data, emails, text messages sent from that number?"

"No. The City boys recovered Smith's phone from the scene, and that's currently down at the lab being analysed to see if it can yield any further results."

"The update is appreciated, Oliver."

"Yeah, but I'm not sure what resources we can apply to this. It's a hit-and-run case the City of London is dealing with, and only because I have a pal working there are they being so quick. Unless you give me something solid to go on, it's going to be difficult to dedicate any more resources on it."

"What about IDing the hit-and-run?"

"The car was stolen twenty minutes before, and found abandoned two miles away. Which makes it my turf. A figure was seen leaving it, wearing a baseball cap and mask, and we quickly lost them on the cameras."

"You're kidding! The number of lenses around the capital, and this guy just vanishes?"

"It happens," said Kane. "Now, because there's a fatality, I have managed to squeeze some resources to check for any private CCTV footage in the area. You never know - we may get lucky."

Garrick held back his customary sarcastic response. He was appreciative of all the help they could get, especially as Kane was now dealing with, at best, a manslaughter case, which was only loosely associated with Garrick's investigation - which he still didn't even know if it was a murder case or some bizarre missing limb incident.

"This whole thing stinks to high heaven," Garrick said. "A car stolen twenty minutes before he's mowed down, at which point we were still with him in his office."

"He'd already spilled the beans on Kontos, and spoke to the police before, so my hunch is this is unconnected. City spoke to his secretary. She's obviously in shock, but she said when you left, she went in to see him, but he snapped and told her he needed some time alone. Then he got up and left without any explanation. She said business had been slow for the last few months and he'd hinted that her hours would have to be cut. But, then he got excited dishing the dirt for your fishing guys. Optimistic, even."

Garrick and Chib swapped a knowing glance.

"Maybe Kontos realised who was behind messing up his takeover bid?" she suggested in a low voice.

Garrick nodded. It certainly felt like that to him.

"I have to go," said Oliver. "I'll keep you posted when I can."

"Cheers, mate." Garrick reached for his phone, but Kane had already hung up.

"Okay, the coincidences are stacked, at least regarding timing," said Chib. "But there's this one little thing we're lacking." Garrick shot her a look, knowing what was coming next. "Hard evidence."

Garrick silently shook his head and glanced at the sat-nav when it indicated their destination was on the left. As they reached the turn, Garrick pointed to a tall whit, oblong building with a tall black cross on the roof.

"You know what that is?"

"A church?" She looked again and noticed the cross was a compass, with a large metal ball at its base. "Or some terrible modern art."

"The Deal Time Ball. You're looking at ingenuity. That's how they set Greenwich Mean Time to ships out there." He gestured to the seafront opposite, the pier stretching into rolling green/grey water. A light drizzle had moved in air, and for a moment he felt sorry for Trev and the other fishermen who had to go out in any dismal weather.

Chib frowned and looked sidelong at him. "You know, guv, you're a vault of information. And not all of it is useful."

Garrick extended his hands out, palms up, in a defensive gesture. "I think it's a sign the universe is giving us about the case. Timing seems to be at the core of this thing. I thought it was a terrific connection."

Chib shook her head as they parked up and walked back to the seafront as the rain intensified. They approached a small tea shop and hurried inside. Several elderly people sat at tables having afternoon tea, and she immediately recognised the face of a man in his sixties, sat in the corner alone. She led the way over to him.

"Councillor Stafford? Hi, I'm DS Okon, we spoke on the phone. This is DCI Garrick. Thank you for your time."

Stafford was delighted to have been recognised. "I feel like I'm a celebrity. Please sit."

Garrick and Chib did so.

"Well, to be honest, I recognised your face from your website. You've been a councillor for Whitstable for over twenty years."

His grey eyebrows rose, and he nodded. "And I have always lived in Deal, which makes me a traitor! But I must say, I've enjoyed it for the most part. May I get you something?" He gestured to the counter.

"I think tea all-round," said Garrick.

After ordering a large pot of breakfast tea and two jam scones - one for Stafford and one for Garrick - they settled down.

"We are hoping for a little background information regarding the planning application for Mr Kontos's site."

"Ah, yes. I heard there was something of an incident there, afterwards. It was only in the local paper and no real details," he said, obviously pressing for more information.

"There's not much more to say, really. Something was found, and I wonder, with the timing of Mr Kontos's planned sale, if there could just be any possibility that somebody was trying to sabotage his deal."

Councillor Stafford nodded slowly. "I see. So how can I help?"

"We spoke to Anna Campbell at the planning office, and she told us about what happened. Three of you on the planning committee had already agreed to vote, and then when certain information came to light about Mr Kontos's business practices, the other three decided to vote against, and somebody changed their mind. I was just hoping that you could give us a little peek behind the curtain."

"It's all very simple, and very boring. I was against it, as were two of my colleagues, quite simply because of the historic nature of the area. Fishing is the soul of Whitstable, and we need to preserve it as much as possible. We lose the infrastructure, then what next? The market? That's already waning. Then there is no fleet to support. Then there is no Whitstable. And all because some rich fellow wants to build luxury condos with a sea view. That was my opinion. However, three of my colleagues decided that things are declining anyway. Even Mr Kontos' investment didn't change the barometer of the industry at all. They think it will have to close anyway, and then who knows what would replace it. I could see their argument. There is a risk the site would turn derelict and become an eyesore. Better accommodation and gentrification could certainly help. I'm not an old fuddy-duddy."

"So, there was no real animosity between the two parties?"

"Not at all. I mean, it's odd, I suppose, because when we first discussed it, everybody was in favour of keeping the depot. We'd talked endlessly about how marvellous it is to keep the fishermen on our shores happy. And then Mary, David, and Bob suddenly had a change of heart."

"And which one of them flipped their opinion again?"

"David Freeman. He was always mercurial at best."

"During the process, did Mr Kontos approach you directly?"

Councillor Stafford shook his head. He'd already bitten into his scone, so he had to chew before he could answer, crumbs tumbling from his lips. "Liaison was solely with Anna at the office. Understandably, there must be a firewall between the two parties." He looked thoughtful. "Although, I remember Mary saying she had spoken with him directly."

Chib and Garrick swapped a look. "And that's not normal?"

"It just came up in conversation when I'd asked why she'd changed her mind. She told me Mr Kontos had put up a very sound argument and convinced her the area was in dire need of gentrification. I think she got caught up in that argument. It never occurred to me to ask her how they'd met."

Garrick unfolded a sheet of paper that Chib had printed at the station. It had the names of the six councillors who were on the board. Mary Ganning was one of them. Either Fanta or Harry was set to meet up with her. He made a note for them to ask about her communication with Kontos. Garrick ran his finger down the page to David Freeman's picture. "And this is David?"

"Aye, that's him. As I say, a very mercurial character. He was adamant that apartments shouldn't be built, and then he suddenly decided it would be for the best. It was only when Mr Kontos's dirty dealings came to light that he certainly had a change of heart and decided I was right all along. He's an ex-military chap - Army, I think. One of those stiff-upper-lip types who cheer for King and country." He playfully punched the air. "I thought it was pretty typical for him."

"Have you spoken to any of them since the incident at the market?" Chib said, casting a glance around the tearoom to ensure they hadn't been overheard.

He tapped Garrick's list. "Stephen and Rachel at another committee meeting. We were due to meet last week to take a vote on another application, but since we're at odd numbers, that hasn't happened yet, until we find a replacement."

"Odd numbers?"

Stafford nodded. "Yes, David finally had enough - he retired straight after this. He'd always threatened to, complaining the job didn't pay enough. I don't blame him, to be honest. We do it for service, not for the money. He's probably on the golf links somewhere." Stafford raised his cup in a toast. "But at least he went out voting on the right side of ethics."

The rain had intensified as they walked back to the car. Chib kept her head bowed low, updating Garrick about the forthcoming interviews for her adoption process. Garrick only half-listened, his mind replaying the conversation with Stafford. By the time they reached the car, Chib was looking at him expectantly.

"Sorry, Chib, I completely tuned out. What did you ask me?"

"I was asking about the character reference you said you'd do for my adoption process. It would be very useful to have a letter, you know, by tomorrow. Something super flattering saying how wonderful I am and what an awesome parent I'd make."

Despite Chib's dubious insertion onto his team - all down to his old friend DCI Kane – Garrick had always been fond of her. She was reserved, diligent, but undeniably fun and a huge asset.

On more than one occasion, she had been a good moral sounding board when Garrick had found himself lost in the world. And she'd risked her life for him. That alone spoke volumes.

"I promise I'll get that done tonight," he said, putting his hand on his heart. "You'll make a terrific mum." He hesitated, wondering if he'd made a faux pas with roles in a same-sex relationship.

Chib laughed. "You know, you live in a weird generational grey area, DCI David Garrick," she said with mock disapproval. Then she nodded back to the café. "Are you going to enlighten me on why you've not been listening ever since we found out the very boring workings of council meetings?"

"I'm not sure. But I have questions for David Freeman. He was instrumental in flip-flopping the decision."

They contacted DC Sean Wilkes, who was still at the office, and it took him fifteen minutes to come back with Councillor David Freeman's home address, on the outskirts of Faversham. The rain had caused traffic to slow down, and roadworks seemed to have sprouted up everywhere. It took another fifty-five minutes before they reached a pleasant middle-class neighbourhood with stereotypical Georgian semi-detached houses lining a wide, leafy street. They pulled up outside Freeman's address. A Mercedes S-class was parked in the drive.

"Not bad for a man whining about his wages," said Chib. "He should try being on the Force."

They walked up the gravel driveway and rang the bell. After waiting patiently and receiving no answer, Chib buzzed it again several times. Still, nobody came. Garrick frowned as he impatiently paced back and forth.

Chib waved her mobile. "I've got his mobile number from the council office. Shall we give him a call?"

Garrick craned his head up, noticing small windows upstairs were partially open in the front rooms. A second glance at the car in the drive, revealed that leaves had settled across the base of the windscreen, and there were smatterings of bird shit on the glass and the roof. "That hasn't been moved for a week or so." He pointed at the house windows. "If he was on holiday, he's left the windows open."

Chib nodded as the phone rang. Then she caught Garrick's frown. "What?"

He pointed a finger at her, then the upstairs windows. "It's ringing *inside*."

She moved her phone away from her ear and could hear the sound coming from inside the house. "Maybe he's asleep?" Then the ringing inside the house suddenly stopped, and the answerphone cut in on her mobile. She frowned at Garrick. "Did he hang up?"

"Hello? Mr Freeman, are you home?" Garrick shouted.

This time he thumped hard on the door, just in case there was an issue with the doorbell. He stood back near the gate, peering up for any sign of movement. He flinched when a voice behind him said:

"I don't think he's home, love." Garrick turned round to see a middle-aged woman, pushing a large pram, peering from the end of the drive. "I haven't seen him for a couple of weeks." She gestured diagonally across the road. "I live over there. Always handy to know your local councillor lives across the street."

"Is he on holiday?"

She shrugged. "I suppose. Although, he said he wouldn't really go on another one since his wife passed." Garrick looked at her questioningly. "Last year. She was a lovely woman."

"So, he lives alone now?"

She nodded, and then the baby began to cry. "Sorry, I'm going to have to go." She hurried off.

"Chib, try his phone again."

She dialled the mobile number, and this time it went straight to answerphone.

Garrick banged on the door. "I don't like this," he muttered when there was still no answer. He moved around to the side gate and pushed on it. It was locked. He reached over, his hand blindly fumbling for the bolt, which he eventually found and slid back. The gate swung open. He walked along the side of the house, noting a wireless security camera on the corner pointing at him. He made it around into the garden as Chib hammered on the front door, and shouted Freeman's name.

The garden was well-tended, with a metal table and four sturdy chairs on the patio. The back door was locked, but the kitchen's narrow ventilation windows were slightly ajar - not the behaviour for somebody so security conscious. The windows upstairs were fractionally open, too. The property gave a sense that somebody was home.

Chib joined him in the garden.

"We can get a locksmith out," Garrick suggested.

"Not without just cause for going inside. We don't have a search warrant," she warned.

"Maybe he's fallen? Desperate for help. His phone's in there."

"Then he would have desperately called for help," she said.

"Not if he was unconscious."

She sighed. "We can't justify a locksmith."

"We may not have to." Garrick gestured to the small kitchen window. It was about two feet by one foot.

"No offence, guv, but you're way too fat to fit through that."

He shot her a look. "Well, I was going to suggest you do it, but clearly..." She glared at him, anticipating a weight joke. He cleared his throat. "Your ethics wouldn't fit through."

He repositioned one of the metal seats from the garden table, to under the window. Standing on it, his shoulder was the same height as the open window allowing him to slide his arm through. He groped for the latch to open the larger window. Standing on tiptoes gave him the extra inches to snag the handle and open the window. With a triumphant chuckle, he crawled inside, over the kitchen sink - which had a few dishes coated with a thin layer of mould -and dropped down from the countertop.

"I'll meet you around the front," said Chib.

Garrick didn't dare reply. He listened intently for any sound in the house When his ears failed, he relied on his other early warning system and sniffed the air. He'd read recently an article that suggested the human nose was a more sensitive instrument than anyone gave it credit for. In fact, it was able to pick out a wider range of odours than a dog's. Whilst he doubted that, it was a beat cop's more reliable alarm system. It always helped to hear somebody creeping up on you, but the amount of information a simple sniff of the air could tell - from a gun-toting goon lurking around the corner, out of sight but smoking a cigarette, through to somebody who stunk of booze or drugs, and of course, the always unwelcome scent of decaying flesh.

He crept into the hallway and poked his head into the

dining room to the right. It was empty. Across the hall, there was a door into the living room and a staircase upstairs. He saw Chib's shadow behind the front door but didn't want to make any sudden sounds by rushing to open it.

He cautiously entered the living room, which smelled stale - the windows shut, but nothing was out of place. As he reached the door, he noticed an alarm panel flashing on the wall; it hadn't been activated.

He opened the door in silence to Chib and placed his finger to his lips and pointed upstairs. They both crept up, Garrick wincing when the wooden step subtly creaked under him, despite his diet.

Upstairs, everything seemed normal. Nothing out of place. There were no signs of forced entry, no signs of a struggle. On the bedside table lay David Freeman's mobile phone.

Garrick peeled a blue latex glove from his pocket, which he put on his right hand before picking up the phone and tapping it.

"Battery's dead," he said. "It's been here a while. That's why it went to answerphone."

He put the phone back where he found it, and they exchanged puzzled glances.

David Freeman had vanished.

Chapter Eleven

The weekend rolled around with Garrick hoping for sleep and a little rest, but it wasn't to be. Amy's night-time routine had become turbulent and the sudden barrage of emails they had to deal with, as the conveyancer sorted out the small mortgage they needed, and made plans for the surveyor to visit the property. Admin now consumed Garrick's every hour, but he managed to break that up by spending time writing a glowing letter to support Chib's adoption quest. By the time he finished tweaking it, it was so worthy that he wouldn't be surprised if she got nominated for an OBE, too.

On top of that, all the floating pieces of the case were circling around him like metaphorical vultures. All the indicators pointed towards some form of extortion or property scandal, and Harry Lord had recommended an independent financial expert he had been involved with on a previous case, but without hard data to scrutinise, it was just a list of potential assistance on the off chance the case needed it.

David Freeman was registered as a missing person, and

Chib had discovered no immediate family other than an estranged son who was working on a North Sea oil rig. Contact had been made. The son claimed their relationship had worsened since his mother's death and wasn't surprised that his dad would hightail it and get away from facing reality. It was more of a character trait than anything to be concerned about.

It also meant Garrick couldn't justify assigning a forensic team to search the house for signs of wrongdoing. But luckily, Fanta, always eager to score brownie points, roped in Sean, and they volunteered to comb through the property over the weekend.

By late Saturday afternoon, and eager for a change of scenery, Garrick suggested he take his daughter to the park so Wendy could catch up with some sleep. For the first time in a long while, she hugged him tightly, kissed him, and then gently sobbed with gratitude.

Garrick spent the next hour bewildered in the park, fretting whether he and Wendy were becoming ships that pass in the night. He distracted himself by pushing his daughter in her pram and pointing things out to her, from dogs, to kids on the swings or people with funny walks. She was fascinated with the ducks begging for food at the side of the pond. The pure, innocent moment of interacting with nature made him smile, and he could feel himself regressing to his own youth. He found himself distracted by the number of mothers walking past, throwing admiring glances at him, and wondered what new superpower Amy had bestowed upon him.

He was ready to return home when he got a call from Fanta asking him to stop by Freeman's house. They'd found something, but she was ambiguous as to what it was.

Garrick strapped Amy safely in the baby carrier at the back of his car, eager to leave but just as eager to go through his daughter's safety twice over to make sure she was locked tight. He realised this was a routine he was developing, which was bordering upon obsessive-compulsive. Even driving to Freeman's house, he'd become a dreaded *Sunday driver*, driving dangerously *under* the speed limit. Wendy had stuck a big sticker on the back windscreen: 'Baby on Board'. She said it was to ward off other aggressive drivers, but the reality was it usually pissed them off even more. Garrick pointed out the stickers were originally invented so emergency services would be extra vigilant in searching for a child who could be unable to cry for help during a crash. Wendy thought that fact took the charm off the whole venture.

He pulled up at David Freeman's house, spotting Fanta's pimped-up Volkswagen Polo blocking the drive, and then wondered what he should do with his daughter. Ideally, he should have dropped her off back home, but now it was a little too late. Along with a small stroller and a clean t-shirt in the boot, they kept a papoose to hand. He saw Fanta peering out from the upstairs window, beckoning him inside.

He put the papoose on, convincing himself that it was a kiddie's version of some tactical vest. Only after it was buckled tightly did he place Amy in it and enter the house, feeling self-conscious because Fanta had been impatiently staring from the window.

He made his way up to the bedroom, where he heard low, rhythmic techno music pumping from Fanta's phone. Inside, she and Sean had emptied the wardrobe and cupboards, neatly stacking items in piles. Wearing blue nitrile gloves, they had carefully emptied all the wardrobe and all the drawers and carefully photographed them.

Fanta frowned at Amy who was hanging from Garrick's chest and gently gurgling. "Training my replacement already, Guv?"

"We'll have to start somewhere, Detective. I'm hoping this one won't be so smart-mouthed and talk back so much."

"You'll miss me when I'm gone," she said, arching an eyebrow.

Garrick gave a doubtful snort, but inside he knew that would be true.

"What have you dragged me and my daughter over here for?" he said, looking around the room. When he didn't get an immediate reply, he realised Fanta's expression had changed from her normally stoic resting bitch face to a softer, googly-eyed look as she made cooing noises and started *booping* Amy's nose with a forefinger.

"Hello, little Amy Garrick. Hello, hello," she said in a baby voice Garrick couldn't quite believe was coming from her lips. He felt proud when his daughter's eyes widened and she began to bawl. Fanta jerked back her finger as if she was about to be bitten, her face reverting back to her default look of indifference.

"You take after your dad."

Now, with Amy's added sonic blast to go with the techno music, Garrick tried to hush his daughter by gently, rocking her up and down.

"Thank you for that, Fanta. So why am I here?"

She glanced at Sean and then pointed to a briefcase on the bed. "I found some interesting documents." She waited for him to open it, but he just raised his hands as if to indicate he was covered with *baby*. Fanta took the hint and unlocked the case, lifting it and opening it. It was crammed with bundles of twenty- and fifty-pound notes.

Garrick stared. "Whoa! And they complain about not being paid enough."

"It's ten grand," Fanta said. "I counted it twice."

Garrick nodded, his eyes fixed on the money. He didn't doubt there was ten grand there, and he also didn't doubt that was the exact amount his officers had found. Once you'd placed your life in your colleagues' hands, you had a firm measure of who they really were.

"I take it there's no receipt?"

"Non-sequential bills, different quality. It indicates this wasn't just a standard withdrawal from the ATM. We reckon this has been cobbled together by hand."

"It adds fuel to the idea that our good councillor hasn't slipped away on holiday. Leaving the windows open, the alarm off, unwashed dishes in the sink, and ten grand lying around the house."

"To me, it suggests something else," said Sean, and then hesitated.

Garrick nodded for his young DC to continue. Sean was a smart, diligent lad, but since his girlfriend had excelled on the team and put herself forward for promotion, his confidence had suffered. She was definitely the one in the relationship wearing the trousers.

Sean gestured to the cash. "If I was the one who'd given him this cash, then kidnapped him, I'd assume it was still here. So, I'd take it with me. It doesn't give us any connection to Kontos and the depot. This could easily be cash he's accumulated himself." He wasn't convinced by his own theory.

"We've got the loft and the living room left to check,"

Fanta said. "We found a laptop, which will join the phone at Forensics."

"That's going to be in a locker for a couple of months before they get around to them." Amy's wailing increased, and Garrick automatically made soothing sounds and rocked her a little more as he muttered something that was drowned out.

"What was that, guv?"

"Maybe this gives us a reason to escalate Freeman as a priority. He's missing, phone and money left here, and house essentially unlocked. That's grounds enough to think his life may be in danger. I need to get the Super on the blower and have this thing escalated to a full-on manhunt."

Raising Superintendent Malcolm Reynolds at the weekend was something to be done as a last resort, but Garrick was feeling on safer ground considering the idea that David Freeman's life was potentially in danger. On his drive back home, he got through to Reynolds' voicemail and left a message outlining his request for additional resources to search for the missing councillor.

The cash, although appearing damning on the surface, could still have an innocent explanation. After all, it wasn't against the law to use your own wardrobe as an ATM machine. But Garrick's every instinct was jumping up and down and gesticulating wildly towards Alexander Kontos. In his mind, he'd already built up a picture of the soft-spoken man as a corrupt gangster, maiming and killing his opponents and blackmailing whoever he needed to get his own way. Yet he had to remind himself it was all pure conjecture, like most police investigations were. Nothing more than an educated guess, and the hope evidence would fall in line to confirm a hunch. That was the DNA of an investigation, although more often than not wild hunches and theories were destined for the bin.

It was early the next morning before Superintendent Reynolds got back in touch with Garrick and authorised additional resources so they could launch a manhunt for the missing councillor. Chib and Harry were drafted in to help with door-to-door investigations in David Freeman's street, gleaning any morsel of information about his last sighting. It quickly became apparent that nobody could recall exactly the last time they'd seen him.

Nobody at the council had seen or spoken to him since after the decision to quit, so Garrick set the timeline for his disappearance from that point.

Escalating the situation did have the desired effect of bringing a small forensic team to swab the house for anything Fanta, Sean, Chib, and Garrick had overlooked. As it was a Sunday, Garrick couldn't in all conscience duck out of the operation, so he made his excuses to a furious Wendy, who'd planned a visit to her parents with David and Amy. With a tinge of relief, he joined in the door-to-door investigations.

Reconvening at the office on Monday morning, everybody was tired, and Chib had the unfortunate duty of informing the team they hadn't turned up any useful statements. The only thing the forensics team could tell them was that there was no sign of forced entry and Freeman's own security cameras had been turned off around the assumed time he'd vanished. This focused the search specifically around that date, and from the growth of fungus on the dishes in the kitchen, nobody had been home for the same length of time.

The morning was spent organising a press briefing, which was always a good way to go wide when time was against the police in a search. As that was coming together, Garrick noticed a call on his mobile from Zoe. Curious, he answered and was greeted by her bouncing Aussie charm.

"Morning, sweetheart. You've been keepin' our lab busy over the weekend."

"Yeah, it's turned into a missing person's case right now."

"I've got some news for you. I think that search may have come to an end."

"How?"

"The swabs taken from your missing bloke, David Freeman - they lit up our database like a Chrimbo tree. The limb from the storage freezer is one and the same. The rest of your bloke may be missing, but we've got his leg."

Chapter Twelve

The atmosphere in the police station sharply changed. No longer was this a financial or missing persons distraction - this was a murder, with an identified victim. By the time Garrick arrived at the office, Harry had reconfigured the two large standing boards into a more traditional murder wall. At the centre was a photo of David Freeman, radiating out from it were images of the storage depot, his severed limb, and the still-mysterious hand, and photos of Simon Evans and Trev McDonald. Below that were pictures of the money Fanta and Sean had found, which was now held in a secure evidence locker. To the right was a picture of Ian Smith, and above it all, a picture of Alexander Kontos with a useful printout from Google Maps illustrating his grand home.

The missing persons press conference had been cancelled, and the media outlets that had been contacted were told the person had been found, and none of them pursued the matter any further. David Freeman's name had never been mentioned, and Garrick didn't want to run the risk of the murderer finding out they were now on his trail. He paced anxiously to and fro.

"The working hypothesis is that Alexander Kontos wanted to sell the site. He's been involved in at least one shady deal with Ian Smith that we know of, and Smith indicated there were more and that Kontos had links to organised crime in Greece." Garrick glanced at Harry.

"Still nothing back from our Euro pals," said Harry. He'd been tasked with reaching out to Interpol, Europol, and the Hellenic Police.

Garrick continued pacing and speaking. "Then Smith was abruptly killed in a hit-and-run." He paused for thought, his hands held out before him as if holding an invisible box. "We need to be crystal clear about that timeline. The initial idea of re-designating the site to sell it for luxury condos looked dead in the water from the beginning, with the planning team unanimously against it. Then three of them changed their minds. It was only when Ian Smith came onboard, thanks to Anna Campbell, that David Freeman switched his vote again."

Chib interrupted. "Don't forget, Counsellor Stafford thought Mary Ganning had spoken to Kontos directly to persuade her to vote in his favour. Which shouldn't happen."

"The tide turns back against Kontos because Freeman changes his mind, then quits and disappears, leaving ten grand in cash in his house. A few days after his last sighting, his severed lower leg was found at the depot, sporting bite wounds." He paused again so they could let it all sink in. "And that's about all the hard evidence we have indicating his death was a hit orchestrated by Alexander Kontos."

"If we bring him in for questioning, it's going to rattle the cage," Chib cautioned. "With no evidence against him, we can't even justify an arrest on probable cause. It'll just damage our case."

Garrick was feeling frustrated as they were now staring across a potential chasm between suspicion and proof.

"We need more evidence, folks."

Sean spoke up. "Forensics identified the exact time the cameras were turned off, which was the day before his leg was found."

"Go back door-to-door and focus on that precise moment. Somebody must have seen something off. How were the cameras disabled?"

"They're blaming poor Wi-Fi security. Somebody just jumped onto the network and turned them off."

"So that indicates a degree of technical knowledge."

Harry gave a grunt of disagreement. "If I knew the password, I could do it. So, *degree of technical knowledge* is being quite generous there, Guv. Anyway, around that time, we already focused on trawling through the doorbell cams we had, and we already picked up two things with passing traffic around that time."

On his computer, he called up a video from a house situated across the road, four doors down. Freeman's driveway was just visible as the road bent. It was a good enough angle to make out a car pulling up outside the house from the opposite direction, but too far to make out any details or registration. The headlights turned off. Moments later the clip finished. He clicked on another, showing a car driving past the camera, presumably the same one as it was no longer parked outside Freeman's home.

"The headlights are too glaring, so the plate or occupant can't be made out. The thing both bits of footage have in common is the same shape headlights, which indicate it's a Toyota Rav4."

Garrick nodded. "Okay, that's something."

"We have one other bit of footage that sits between these two moments," Harry opened another video file. It was another doorbell cam, this time taken from the opposite end of the street, that showed the vehicle outside Freeman's house had now backed into the driveway.

"The only reason this camera triggered is because of that cat at the bottom of the screen. I'm betting it was the same cat that triggered the other camera initially, because it wasn't the car. I suggest we do a search for this moggy as a material eyewitness."

A dull chuckle rippled across the room - not because they found it funny, but because of the tension release the new evidence provided.

"The timestamp on this clip is eight minutes after the car arrived. Four minutes later we can assume the vehicle leaves. So that's a twelve-minute window our attacker was inside. From twenty-three-oh-four."

"You say *attacker*," Fanta said. "There were no indications of forced entry, no indications of a struggle. So, either Freeman knew who it was and let them in..."

"Or they just did a bit of easy breaking and entering," Chib added. "I mean, the Guv crawled through the window like Spider-Man. It's not beyond imagination that's exactly what our suspect did. All they had to do was close the window behind them and get Freeman while he was asleep."

"We're still waiting on forensics for that," Garrick said. "Okay, so we need to broaden our search beyond any camera in the vicinity with automatic number plate recognition that's picked up a Rav4 in this time period. Check an hour before and after and see what we can find." He nodded at Fanta. "You seem to be up on all this fancy AI stuff. Is there anything there that can assist?"

She nodded thoughtfully. "Possibly, yeah. I'll look into that."

"Also look for the Toyota around Whitstable because the body must have been transported there somehow. And let's not limit it to here. Look for any similar vehicles in the orbit of Kontos's house. If there's any way we can link the two, it's going to give us something. Factor in the travel time between Sevenoaks and Canterbury." He knew he was reaching, but thinking back to the Land Rover that killed Smith, he also added, "And of course, check for any stolen Rav4s that could fit into this time frame."

"I'll get on that, Guv," Harry said. "But it's a popular car. The likelihood of a Rav4 being on a camera is huge and it will suck up resources. Are we cornering ourselves here?"

"Possibly," said Garrick, "but until something else pops out of the woodwork, what can we do?"

Chib glanced through her notepad. "We're attempting to gain access to Kontos's business files and tax receipts to see what we can find there."

Garrick nodded. "Good. I also passed on his details to DCI Kane to see if our boy was in London at the time Smith was killed.

Chib looked doubtful. "If you ask me, I don't think he's the sort of person who gets his hands dirty himself.

"How about surveillance on Kontos's home?" Fanta suggested.

The tension in the atmosphere in the room became prickly. Their last surveillance operation had taken an ugly turn, which had resulted in Garrick's car crash and hospitalisation. Surveillance was a vital tool in their work, but the recent pain was still all too raw.

Garrick broke the mood. "Fanta's right – so long as she doesn't ram me off the road again." A dull chuckle flowed around the room. He moved closer to the map of Kontos's property on the wall. "But that gives us another problem. This is a private road. Any maintenance that goes in and out is scheduled, so we'll raise every resident's attention parking a car right outside his house."

"Nothing's wrong with a challenge," said Fanta, as she thoughtfully leaned back in her seat.

"A wiretap?" Sean said. "Can we authorise one on his phone?"

"A landline's going to be interesting if he has one. That's a massive amount of probable cause we're going to have to give to Reynolds to get authorisation. And if he's using a mobile, well, that involves a lot more kit. And if it's a burner phone and we don't have his number... and already I've had an angry message from Reynolds when I told him we cancelled the press conference."

The newly installed superintendent wasn't incompetent or bad - he'd just been directed by the powers that be, that every penny spent had to be justified.

Garrick's stomach grumbled, and he was starting to feel lightheaded, perhaps from the copious amount of coffee he'd imbibed. He focused back on the wall, his eyes drifting to the severed hand. They were dealing with multiple murders, and the owner of that appendage was almost certainly caught up in Alexander Kontos's web of brutality...

Assuming they were on the right track and not blindly rushing down a dead end.

It was now late afternoon, and everybody was starting to

feel the burn from the weekend duty. He clapped his hands. "Okay, gang. Let's call it a night. Let's get back in here sleep on it, and figure out a way to nail this character."

When he returned home, Wendy was fast asleep in the chair next to Amy's crib. Remarkably, despite fumbling with the front door lock and accidentally slamming it closed, Amy was still sound asleep. He took the opportunity to creep into his bedroom, undress, and smother himself under the duvet.

His body craved sleep, but his mind was suffering the caffeine version of ADHD. If Kontos had killed Freeman as punishment for reversing his decision, did that mean other councillors had been bribed? They still needed to be interviewed, and Garrick didn't want to leave it to a local bobby who could overlook subtle clues. Perhaps that would have to wait until after an arrest before they could delve deeper.

If David Freeman's death was retribution, did that mean the other councillors' lives were not at risk? In that case, who as the *other* victim? How did they factor into a tale of corruption and revenge? What did Ian Smith know that Kontos would be afraid he'd tell the police? Had news of the dismembered limbs been a warning to Ian Smith that he was next? It would certainly explain the man's nervousness when he and Fanta had shown up.

David Garrick's thoughts flittered to his imminent property purchase. Buying a house was supposed to be one of the most stressful moments in a person's life. He could think of many more, but it certainly hadn't been enjoyable. He'd almost smothered the anxiety of waiting for the surveyor to do the report and announce whether the house would collapse the moment they moved in. His neurosis orbited the world of property before hopping back onto the case via the storage depot.

The very location was the weak link in the theory that Kontos was the murderer.

Why would he take the bodies taken there? Zoe indicated it was a good place to dispose of corpses, but why be so sloppy and leave, not one, but two limbs. The odds of it being accidental - given the precision with which they had been dismembered – were wafer thin. It had to be intentional.

And that intention was difficult to explain.

It was the presence of the limbs that had led Garrick towards Alexander Kontos. And now discovering the leg belonged to a prominent local council figure linked it directly to Kontos and the property deal. That was a slap in the face for the logic Garrick had been constructing.

And then there were the bite marks.

That had taken Garrick down a rabbit hole of cannibalism. He recalled Kontos's immaculate kitchen and his love for cuisine. However, he had to admit it was a tenuous stretch to connect the two.

It was only when Garrick gave up on the idea of sleep that he sank into the deepest slumber he'd had since his daughter had been born. With these conflicting thoughts battling away, the worry and stress of the chaotic case cast its spell over him.

Chapter Thirteen

DCI Garrick didn't even make it into the office before the plan occurred to him. Perhaps sleeping on the thorny issues had forced his subconscious to offer solutions. Or maybe all he needed was a good night's sleep.

He put a call in to DC Harry Lord on his mobile, who was also on his way to work, and talked him into his scheme. He was short on resources, and keen to avoid bumping into his Super until he had made some substantial progress. He needed everybody to focus on the leads at hand, which - as the least vital cog in the team - made him expendable enough to stake out Alexander Kontos's house.

After so much-needed sleep, maybe his brain had created the solution. The image he woke with in his mind was the Google Map of Kontos's home pinned to the murder wall. There were only two access roads into the private estate. Whilst they couldn't get close enough to his house, they at least had a good chance to see Kontos moved off the grounds

Garrick parked up next to the small library, adjacent to

the busy A25 that cut through the village of Seal. He cut his engine, and adjusted his car seat. He had just enough of a view to observe comings and goings via the private road further down the High Street. Harry was positioned at the other entrance, down a narrow B-road, parked up half on the pavement and providing just enough annoyance for the passing cars. All they had to do was sit, wait... and hope, because there was no telling if their suspect would leave at all. Garrick informed Chib of their desperate mission. To his surprise, she agreed that it was worth at least spending the day to see if there was any merit in adding further resources to track Kontos.

She informed him that there were three vehicles registered at Kontos's residence: a black Porsche 911, a black Audi Q7, and an old Jaguar XK, also in black. With the plates noted on his phone propped on the dashboard, Garrick settled back for the improvised stakeout.

It became a very dull waiting game, but one that didn't last quite as long as he'd feared. After a variety of delivery trucks, resident vehicles, and a Pegasus security van had moved in and out, Harry reported the Q7 had emerged from the side exit and was on the move towards Sevenoaks.

Garrick hesitated. They hadn't formulated much of a strategy beyond sitting and waiting. Now Harry was following Alexander Kontos. He wondered if he should wait in case there was further activity from any of the other vehicles, or if he should join his DC. He chose the latter and merged with the busy traffic on the A25. Without radios, he was forced to spiral his mobile phone bill by keeping the line open to Harry for regular updates. Only when pulling towards the train station did Harry realise Kontos was indicating to turn off and park there.

Garrick instructed Harry to do the same and follow him onto the train, if need be. At least Kontos wouldn't recognise the detective. By the time Garrick arrived, he parked up on the forecourt of the local Shell petrol station, popped his bonnet, and pretended to fill the windscreen washer tank from the machine on the forecourt. Harry reported Kontos hadn't left his vehicle.

After eight minutes, curiosity gnawed at Garrick. He closed the bonnet of his car and jogged to the road bridge that overlooked the station car park. He guessed the petrol station attendant would have something to say about him parking there.

He made it onto the bridge just as Harry called back to tell him there was movement. From his raised vantage point on the road bridge, Garrick could look down into the car park. Harry had left his vehicle and was loitering at the station entrance, talking on his phone but acting far more animated, as if he was having a full-on discussion rather than providing an intel report.

Alexander Kontos had exited his vehicle and moved around to the boot, opening it up as two burly men exited the train station, both carrying silver metal flight cases. Garrick took photos on his phone, zooming in to detail the men's close-cropped hair, tattoos on their necks, and a build that telegraphed a violent, military bearing. He could see words exchanged with Kontos, but there was no friendly greeting as they placed the cases in the boot. Then all three men climbed into the car.

Garrick darted back to his vehicle and was halfway into it when the petrol station attendant announced over the intercom that he couldn't park there and if he didn't want to get a fine, he'd better come in and buy something. Garrick gave a friendly wave - then completely ignored him as he reversed and positioned himself at the petrol station exit. He waited, allowing the traffic to pass, until the big black Audi Q7 rolled by. He pushed himself into the traffic flow three cars behind Kontos. Harry complained he was now stuck at the traffic lights trying to get out of the station.

Garrick was able to follow Kontos all the way back to Seal without any incident. The traffic was heavy, and his suspect was not in any hurry to break any laws. Garrick watched as Kontos indicated and pulled into the estate, through the gate and beyond Garrick's immediate grasp. He parked back next to the library and instructed Harry to resume his previous surveillance position while they tried to figure out what to do next.

His stomach was rumbling two hours later, and he regretted not taking the petrol station attendant's advice. Right now, he'd kill for a packet of Quavers. Harry texted him a few times with increasing boredom. Whoever the men were, whatever was in the cases, they seemed content to stay put right now.

Garrick had sent the photos through to Chib and, as an afterthought, to DCI Kane, too. As Kontos was a person of interest in the Smith incident, he hoped the Met detective would be able to help with any possible identifications.

It was approaching six o'clock, and the traffic had already built up since the school rush, becoming a morass of sluggish vehicles as people headed home. DCI Kane finally called him, and Garrick answered on the second ring.

"Things just got really interesting," Kane said without preamble. "The two men matched up on a database with a string of false identities. As far as we can tell, they're a pair of hired thugs, part of a gang with connections to Ukraine."

"You mean muscles for hire?"

"Worse than that," said Kane. "Mercenaries. There's no hard evidence on them, but they've been seen with automatic weaponry and potential links to several shootings."

"This gets better and better," said Garrick.

"Then you'll like this. Their usual victims seem to be informers who've been speaking to the cops when they shouldn't."

"The sort of charmers who'd pay a visit to Mr Freeman?"

"Exactly. And those cases - who knows? But my money is on weapons inside."

Garrick's thoughts snapped to the remanning council members. He was sure they were safe from Kontos's wrath. Freeman had been the sacrifice, and he couldn't for the life of him figure out why Kontos would need to apply pressure to the remaining council members, especially if he wanted to re-submit his application. The only other person who'd actively shown to be a threat was Anna Campbell. But she had just been doing her job as a happy-go-lucky, innocent woman. Did it really require the terror of two Eastern European bruisers to teach her a lesson? Or was he so thin-skinned that revenge was the order of the day? Voicing his thoughts to Kane they rapidly concluded that's *exactly* what Alexander Kontos would do.

"Okay, this is muddy now," said Kane. "We have a growing list of suspects and still no evidence. What you've got there is Schrödinger's gun."

"Huh?" said Garrick.

"Either there are weapons in the cases or there aren't. If you move in now, it will spook them and probably destroy your case if things go south. If you wait, they could move in on Campbell. Either way, it's your call, mate," said Kane, firmly transferring the responsibility to his colleague. "I'd suggest you get a firearms unit on standby, just in case. Keep me posted."

Garrick's next call was straight to Chib, asking her to send somebody to quietly watch Anna Campbell. Chib volunteered to do it herself, although she pointed out this was still all speculation, and it was now spreading the team thin.

Next, Garrick updated Harry of the latest developments, and both men resigned themselves to the fact this turning into an impromptu twenty-four-hour surveillance assignment. To that end, Garrick got out of his car to stretch his legs. He darted into the post office as it was about to shut, to buy several cans of Coke, three packets of Quavers, and a pair of Mars bars, hoping it would be enough to keep him awake when night came.

Chapter Fourteen

The only further social interaction Garrick had had was when a policeman had rapped on his window to say he'd received word Garrick had been loitering all day. Garrick flashed his badge and commented that he was at least glad the Neighbourhood Watch network was alive and well.

He'd made a couple of video calls to Wendy, but couldn't shake the feeling she was annoyed with him staying out. Chib had got back in touch to say she was watching Anna Campbell's house in Canterbury, but so far everything was quiet. Garrick debated whether he should tell her to go home, since the potential assassins hadn't left Kontos's home yet. Still, they couldn't gamble if her life was genuinely at risk.

He and Harry exchanged text messages the rest of the evening, and he suspected at some point Harry had nodded off and just hoped he hadn't missed a vital moment, but was loath to accuse his colleague of such incompetence. Chib had liaised with the Armed Response Unit, who were based thirteen miles away in Aylesford.

Garrick stretched in his seat when his buttocks and legs had become numb - when, at nine o'clock, there was another loud rap on the window. Fanta held up a coffee and teased a bag of doughnuts. He unlocked the doors, and she climbed into the passenger seat. He thankfully, and greedily, took both from her, taking a deep gulp of coffee and cramming one of the three jam doughnuts in his mouth, barely getting his words out.

"Oh, you're a lifesaver!"

"Me and Sean decided perhaps you'd need to be relieved. He's gone to see Harry."

Garrick nodded but didn't break his stride, laying into the second doughnut with gusto and enjoying the instant sugar rush. He was silently pleased that at least she and Sean now seemed to be back on speaking terms.

"I also put a request to Sevenoaks to send some uniformed coppers here. They reckon they might have people after midnight, but to say they were reluctant is an understatement."

Garrick knew that too well. The local force wouldn't want to admit they had free officers who could be readily deployed to sit in a car overnight. The chances were they didn't have the manpower, and with no real operation in motion, there was no incentive to simply *help out*.

"Don't you think this is weird?" she said.

"What specifically?" he said through a mouthful of crumbs.

"Kontos picks up two burly blokes, takes them back to his house, and they just quietly sit there. I mean, why? Is he hosting a dinner party for them?" Garrick chewed thoughtfully. "They arrived at midday. Nine hours later, they're doing nothing. Why hurry and get here? Especially if they're intending to go down to Canterbury - why not just go straight there and use the time to stake out Campbell's house?"

Garrick had to admit it was unusual. His mind whirled as he licked his fingers and finished off the coffee. He'd been so focused on the moment at hand - the tantalising prospect that the keys to unlocking the web of clue lay in the gated community, just out of reach – that the actual logistical motivations were questionable.

"I take it that you don't think Campbell is the intended target?" he finally said picking bits of doughnut from his teeth.

"I was wondering how Trev McDonald fits into this, other than being the one who shouted the loudest. Is the connection between Trev, Simon Evans, and his aunty enough to piss off our favourite suspected gangster?"

Garrick fell silent as he thought about it.

"We could wait out here all night as a complete waste of time. Then tomorrow, when we're all knackered and useless."

Garrick looked straight at Fanta. "Why do I suspect your plan was for you and Sean to take over from us and then sneak inside to see what's going on?"

Fanta gave an indifferent shrug. "Because that's the smart thing to do, guv."

Garrick shook his head. "It's also reckless, DC Liu. You remember what happened on our last stakeout?"

She met his gaze almost apologetically. "That was different, and you know it. You were a hostage. That's very different from slipping over the fence and having a snoop around."

He shook his head again. "The last time we barrelled into a suspect's house, I nearly got you blown apart," he said, his voice breaking with guilt as he remembered seeing Fanta in hospital.

Remarkably, she smiled. "I still remember every painful moment of that, Guv. But I'm still doing the job, and we're still doing it together, aren't we? That doesn't make any of those past decisions wrong."

Garrick gritted his teeth and nodded towards the gated community. "We don't even know what security they've got there."

"You don't know," said Fanta, as she pulled out her phone. "I approached the security firm who monitor the estate." She scrolled through to find the email. "There are entrance cameras at both gates, and there's a network of twenty motion-sensor cameras along the road inside. It's all broadcast to a manned hub which monitors the feeds. On top of that, each house has an alarm connected to the company. And every hour from dusk to dawn, a patrol does the rounds."

"Blimey, Fanta, you've really been thinking about this."

"Yeah, and I told them that around this time, two suspicious police officers are going to be running through there to check on a situation, and that the patrol should absolutely ignore them."

"I can't, in all good conscience, allow you and Sean to do this."

Her brow creased in frustration. "Fine. Then you'll have to do it with me. Let's go." She opened the door and stepped out. "I'll just take the last doughnut, and we'll go."

Garrick looked at the empty bag in his hand and then crunched it into a ball, staring at her.

"The last one was mine. I haven't eaten all day. You owe me, Guv."

Garrick threw the rolled-up bag at Fanta, and it bounced off her arm into the car's footwell.

She looked disapprovingly at him. "Assault and battery's going to get you nowhere. Let's go." She slammed the door shut.

Garrick blew a sigh of frustration between his lips before following her. She was already texting Sean about the change of plan.

"You've really got all this figured out," he said as they approached the pelican crossing and crossed when it was still on the red man, because there were no vehicles passing by.

"I've had time to think since we had nothing fun to do."

It was already dark, which would provide them with enough cover.

"What happens if they're looking at the gate camera - which I assume has an intercom to each house - and they see us waltzing in? Or if we push the gate and it triggers the alarm?"

She stopped in her tracks as they crossed the road. "That's a possibility." Then she waved her arm, and an approaching car indicated as it pulled over. It was a small white transit van marked with *Pegasus Security*.

She waved at the driver. "You're Martin, right?"

"Detective Liu? I recognised you."

She met Garrick's astonished gaze and grinned. "The folks at Pegasus are lovely. It's family run. Premium client base. They were more than happy to help." She indicated the driver. "They put me in touch with Carl, and we had a little

FaceTime chat to get to know each other. We can hop in the back of the van to get inside unseen."

Garrick couldn't argue as Carl climbed out and opened the rear door for them. "Have you been watching any Greek tragedies lately?" Fanta looked at him curiously as they clambered into the back of the transit van. "The Trojan Horse," he clarified when she didn't get the reference. "That all turned into tragedy."

Carl slammed the door behind them, and the van rocked as he climbed back into the cab. A moment later they pulled into the private road.

"It was only a tragedy for one of the sides," Fanta said. "You should stop being so pessimistic and pick the winning side."

They'd been in the back of the van for a minute, jostled around as hit speed bumps, before it pulled to a halt. Moments later, Carl opened the back of the van.

"Here you go. Good luck."

"Thanks, Carl," said Fanta, and then winked. "Don't forget - you never saw us."

"Didn't see a thing." He gave a smile, climbed back into the driver's seat and pulling away with an almost silent whine of the electric motor.

It took a moment for Garrick to get his bearings.

"I asked him to drop us off two houses down," Fanta said. "This way."

The streetlights were low impact, casting just enough light to see ahead yet giving the huge houses their own sense of privacy. They walked in silence for another minute before rounding the bend and seeing the closed gates of Alexander Kontos's house. Inside, every light was on. Even from here, they could see every light was on, and parked outside the front door was his black Audi Q7.

"Still home. I guess they didn't pop out for a picnic," said Fanta.

Garrick looked expectantly at her. "Now what?"

As they deliberated, Garrick felt a sudden tremor of concern as headlights appeared on the road ahead, moving in their direction. Skulking around outside would raise suspicion from the wealthy residents. He nudged Fanta, and they quickly started to walk in the direction of the lights, heads bowed low and trying to act as if they were out for an evening stroll. As the vehicle neared, it stopped opposite them, and the driver gave a low whistle. It was Carl in his van.

Fanta hurried over. "Hey, mate, what's up?"

Looking concerned, Carl pointed towards Kontos's house. "Is this the property you wanted to take a look at?"

Fanta hesitated. She hadn't told the company who their target was, but now they were here, she just nodded.

"Three minutes ago, the silent alarm triggered."

Garrick looked at the house. "Do you know the nature of the alarm?"

"It was from the back door. Head office called the owner, but nobody responded." He gave a wry smile as he girded his courage. "Now, muggins here has to go and check it out."

"Are you armed?" said Fanta.

He gave her a double take. "Are you crazy? Of course not. The most I've got is a Taser."

"This isn't America," Garrick pointed out to Fanta. "Out here, we're going to catch bullets with our teeth. We'll come with you."

Carl nodded thankfully and got out of his van. Using his flashlight, he led the way to the front gate and gently pushed it. It was locked. He gestured for Garrick and Fanta to stand out of sight as he approached the intercom and pressed the button. He frowned and pressed it again.

"Okay, that's not good. The power's cut." He glanced up between the intercom and the house. Lights were on inside, but the power was off outside. It stank of sabotage. "What the hell is going on?" he muttered. "Come on."

They followed him around the high wall that penned the property into its plot, reaching a far corner away from the road where the wall ran parallel to the neighbour's open garden. Garrick tried to call Harry on his mobile to update him but was dismayed to find he had no signal.

As they reached the far rear corner, Carl stopped, his flashlight hovering over a plank of wood positioned at a forty-five-degree angle against the wall. A quick sprint up it would provide a handy springboard over the wall and into the garden.

He looked at the two detectives and then shrugged. "Well, I've got to go in."

"I'll come with you," Fanta said.

Carl took a gentle run-up to the wood and in a single bound he easily hopped onto the wall and lowered himself over. Fanta followed next with the agility of a cat. Garrick swore under his breath, fretting that the plank would snap under his weight, but still managed to splay himself flat along the wall before lowering himself to the other side, his arms shaking. He dropped the last two feet and sent shock waves through his knackered knees.

"You made a pig's ear out of that, Guv," Fanta teased.

Garrick responded with a muffled curse.

Carl turned off his flashlight so as not to draw attention. The ground-floor lights at the rear of the property were all on, including the external ones illuminating the patio. Steam rose from the covered pool, lit by submerged lights. As they watched, the back door swung open, caught in a gentle breeze.

Carl took a resigned breath and walked boldly forward. "Pegasus Security, this is a routine visit. Anybody home?" He stepped forward so the lights bathed him and shouted again, "Pegasus Security! Your alarm has been triggered. Householders, please identify yourselves."

His hand gripped the stubby black grip of his Taser, the yellow striped business end shaking with his nerves.

Garrick was sure they had enough justification now to officially enter the property. He was about to identify himself as a police officer when the patio windows exploded in a shower of glass, accompanied by a sudden crack of automatic gunfire.

Carl was between Garrick and the door as he fell to the floor when broken glass showered him. Garrick was able to shield Fanta, fragments bouncing off his jacket, as he tackled her to the floor. Then he pushed himself against the side of the shattered door as one of the thugs from the train station ran out - a small sub-machine gun in his hand.

The big man hesitated when he saw Carl - then spun around with wide, frantic eyes as he spotted Garrick. Their gaze met. Garrick was transfixed. The man had multiple cuts across his face, blood pouring down from one side. He automatically raised the machine gun directly at Garrick–

One squeeze of the trigger and a dozen rounds would tear him apart.

But instead, Muscles hesitated, jerked the gun sideways, and fired into the house until his clip was empty. A second later, there came a whoosh and sharp thump as a knife, thrown with precision from the house, embedded in the guy's chest. The gun clattered to the floor as his hand reached for the blade an inch from his heart. He gurgled in shock and pain, staggered backwards, then fell into the pool.

In seconds, the pool cover wrapped around his frantically thrashing limbs, and he was dragged down into the deep end.

Garrick wasn't thinking. He sprang forward, throwing off his jacket, and in several steps dived in after the gunman. He used one hand and a powerful kick to push down, the other hand pushed away the pool cover as it tried to wrap around him like some tentacled beast. The submerged lighting made his view look like a scene from hell as clouds of blood floated up like volcanic plumes from the sinking man's chest. His every thrash was becoming weaker.

Garrick kicked hard to close the gap between them. He hooked his arm around the man's neck, and quickly repositioned his body so he could kick as powerfully towards the surface. The guy was heavy - no fat to float, just lean, hard muscle. It felt as if he was about to drag Garrick down. But the man still had enough presence of mind and energy for a few feeble kicks that propelled them towards the ladder.

Garrick's free hand probed for the rungs, and when he found them, he gripped on for dear life, groaning with effort as he tried to haul himself higher with one hand whilst lifting the drowning man's head above the waterline with the other. The resulting actions forced Garrick further beneath the water, and the tightness in his chest warned him that he was about to run out of air.

But the manoeuvre just about worked, and the guy's head popped out of the water. Garrick quickly followed, gulping for air.

"Come on, arsehole," said Garrick. "Grab onto the ladder."

The man was conscious enough to obey and looped his elbow through a rung, so he was locked in place. Garrick almost stepped on him as he scrambled up the ladder, before turning round and hauling the man out. It was no easy task; he was waterlogged and built from dense muscle - and almost dragged Garrick back into the pool. Garrick fought on, dragging him out an inch at a time onto the patio and rolling him onto his side. Water trickled from the man's mouth, but he was able to breathe.

Only then did Garrick become aware Fanta was nowhere to be seen. Several metres away, Carl lay on the ground groaning, but alive and not shot. His Taser had been taken.

"Oh, shit," said Garrick, and then flinched as another burst of gunfire came from within the house.

Garrick sprang to his feet and was surprised when the gunman feebly gripped his ankle to stop him. "Don't..." the words came as a feeble gasp, and Garrick wasn't sure if he'd misheard.

Confused, Garrick shook him off and bolted into the kitchen. Broken plates and pans on the floor indicated a struggle. Bullets had pocked the marble worktops. He saw Alexander Kontos slumped against a cupboard, covered in blood. But Fanta's scream from the hallway propelled him onwards.

He sprinted through the doorway and saw Fanta was on her knees - she had shot the second gun-toting thug with the Taser. The guy was still jerking, dropping to his knees as his muscles spasmed, causing him to squeeze the trigger of the machine gun in his hand. A volley of bullets strafed the wall, shattering pictures until his clip emptied.

But that wasn't what snagged Garrick's attention. The front door was open, and a third figure stood in the doorway. He was dressed all in black, a cloth mask covering his face, leaving only a narrow slit to see through. He wielded a thin sword in a deadly arc – and decapitated the gunman.

A column of blood shot into the air, and Fanta screamed again as she was covered in it. Repulsed, Garrick was frozen to the spot – his gaze fixated on the dead man. By the time he looked back to the door, the assailant had disappeared through it.

Garrick made a couple of steps in pursuit, but the blood flowing across the hallway tiles, and his wet shoes, made him slip, and he fell hard onto his back, knocking the wind out of him.

Fanta had stopped screaming and was making loud, retching sounds, trying to wipe the blood from herself with her sleeve.

Garrick pulled himself back to his knees and grabbed hold of her by the shoulders. "Are you okay? Are you hurt?"

"I'm fine, I'm fine," she said in a shaky voice. "Kontos–" She gestured back to the kitchen.

Remembering the state he'd fleetingly seen the Greek in, Garrick found his feet and dashed into the kitchen.

Alexander Kontos was bleeding heavily on the floor. His breaths came in staccato gasps as his gaze met Garrick's. Garrick had seen that look many times; it was one of helplessness people wore when faced with their dwindling mortality. His forearm had been severed before the elbow and was pumping blood everywhere. The dismembered hand lay several feet away, still clutching an automatic pistol.

For one macabre moment, Garrick considered taking the gun and sprinting after the killer, but the overwhelming need to save a life stayed the impulse. He crouched at Kontos's side and slipped off his belt to use as a tourniquet to staunch the flow of blood. By the time he pulled it tight, he was drenched in the man's blood.

"Shit, shit, shit," he muttered, reaching for his phone. He had no signal earlier, but now he had full bars. Confused, Garrick made the call for help.

Chapter Fifteen

Garrick jolted awake, his body convulsing as nightmares clawed at the edges of his blurred dreams. His flailing arm nearly sent the coffee in Chib's hand flying. She jerked backward, eyes sharp with concern.

"Easy, Guv." Her voice sliced through the fog of his terror.

He gulped, disoriented, the sterile scent of disinfectant bringing him back to reality. He was in the waiting room of Tunbridge Wells Hospital, where exhaustion had finally claimed him.

"Thought you might get us thrown out," Chib said, offering him the coffee with a wry smile. "You were snoring loud enough to wake the dead."

As the fragments of the previous night reassembled themselves into a coherent nightmare, Garrick's stomach clenched. "Anything?"

She shook her head. "Fanta's got cuts and bruises - paramedics patched her up and Sean forced her home eventually, but she didn't want to leave. None of us have slept in twenty-four hours. We're running on fumes and adrenaline, and that's a recipe for disaster."

The coffee scalded his throat, but the pain felt grounding. Real.

"When the ambulance arrived, Sean and Harry took control of the scene. Kontos and the gunman Garrick had saved from drowning went straight into surgery. The security bloke needed stitches from flying glass, but physically he's intact. Mentally...?" She shrugged. "He kept breaking down. Wouldn't stop sobbing."

Garrick nodded grimly. He'd given Carl space - emotional storms weren't his forte.

They'd secured Kontos and the gunman in private rooms at the opposite side of the wing, with uniformed officers stationed outside each door. After six gruelling hours of surgery, the doctors had managed to save Kontos's arm. The wound had been inflicted by the same medieval weapon that had separated the other gunman's head from his shoulders.

The beheading replayed behind Garrick's eyelids every time he blinked. Twenty years on the force, and he'd never seen anything so brutally primitive.

He'd texted Wendy once: *Won't be home tonight.* Uncharacteristically, he'd added two x's for kisses. She hadn't replied. Either she was sleeping soundly or furious with him. He presumed it was both.

"You need to go home," Chib was saying when his attention drifted back.

"There's a sword-wielding maniac loose on the streets—"

"And the sleepiest coppers on the force after him. There's an all-ports bulletin out on him. The press office has already issued a public warning across breakfast radio." Her sarcasm was acidic. "Complete with helpful advice: 'do not approach the masked swordsman as he may be dangerous.'"

"What about Anna Campbell?"

"There's a uniformed officer plonked outside her house for round-the-clock protection. But here's the thing, Guv, we assumed our gunmen were hired to kill her. Now it looks like they were hired to *protect* Kontos."

They'd both reached the same conclusion, but neither understood what it meant.

"So, us being there probably saved his life," Garrick mused.

"I'd be careful how you phrase that around Fanta," Chib warned. "She's tearing herself apart, thinks because she Tasered the guy, it made him an easier target for beheading. And she might be right."

Garrick's chest tightened. "She can't blame herself for that."

"Try telling her that. You know how stubborn she is. I've sent everyone else home. Look, we both need sleep. Time we did the same, David."

It was the genuine tenderness when she said his name that made him cave in. He couldn't recall her ever calling him *David*. It made him thankful that she had all their backs. He gave his mobile number to the two officers outside the doors, with instructions to call him the moment there was any news. Then he walked with her outside and blinked as his eyes adjusted to the morning light. He walked Chib to her car, and she thanked him for the adoption letter. He headed for his own car which some wily officer had driven down from Seal, waved goodbye to Chib, then crawled into the back seat to sleep.

. . .

Just over six hours later, his phone's shrill ringtone dragged him awake. It was the officer stationed outside the gunman's room. It was quarter past one and he'd missed a call from Wendy, but she hadn't left a voicemail. Ignoring the parking ticket tucked under his windshield wiper - at least the warden had the courtesy not to wake him - Garrick hurried inside with only a quick stop at the vending machine for an overpriced bottle of water, which he drained before reaching the lift.

In the lift, he scrolled through emails, consisting mostly of operation updates, but nothing directly from his team - hopefully they were all resting. One that made him pause came from DCI Kane. The gunman Garrick had saved in the pool matched images of a hooded figure caught on CCTV from a jewellery shop's door camera, as he hurried away from the abandoned Land Rover that had killed Ian Smith in the hit-and-run. It wasn't the sharpest image, but the man's chin, nose, and build were consistent. Kane also confirmed that the automatic weapons found at the scene were robust Heckler & Koch MP7s.

The doors opened, and Garrick strode quickly to the private room.

"Afternoon, sir." The officer who called him was the same one from the early hours. She was now munching crisps for her lunch.

"Is he awake?"

"Kontos's still in an induced coma. But this one–" She nodded toward the door. "He's been conscious for the last twenty minutes. The doctor just left."

Garrick composed himself before entering, pushing the door open with deliberate force, so that it banged against the doorstop, jolting the patient awake. The muscular thug who'd been the stereotypical image of an unstoppable killing machine, now looked fragile, wearing only a paper gown, and tucked beneath hospital sheets. Sensors tethered him to a bank of monitors, and a drip fed him a clear solution. His steely grey eyes fixed on Garrick, followed by a grunt of dark amusement.

"You," the accent was thick, Eastern European. "You're the one who pulled me from the pool."

"Not bad for my second swimming lesson." Garrick pulled up a chair, and poured water from the bedside jug. "Nice pool. I appreciated that it was heated."

The man accepted the water, and he sipped through cracked and parched lips. "Why did you?"

It was a question Garrick had been asking himself. Why save a killer? Why not let him drown?

"Instinct," he said finally. "It seemed rude to let a man die when I didn't even know his name. I'm DCI Garrick."

The man's head bobbed – was it acknowledgment or contempt? It was impossible to tell.

"And you are?"

"Boris."

Of course. "Okay, Boris. That was quite a situation last night. Help me understand what happened."

Boris stared at the ceiling, marshalling thoughts or constructing lies. Finally: "We were hired to protect Alexander Kontos."

"From who?"

"You know about him. You know his business interests bring attention from unwelcome characters who want him dead."

"And Zorro?" When Boris didn't get the reference, he added: "The masked man."

Boris's eyes went distant. "Crazy man."

It was the understatement of the century. Garrick leaned forward. "That crazy man is still out there. He threw a knife at you. And missed your big old heart by an inch. Your buddy is dead. And if he walks through that door right now, only you can identify him."

Boris looked away.

"I saved your life in that pool," Garrick continued. "Now I'm trying to do it again. Help me stop him."

He decided not to raise the moment Boris had aimed the submachine gun directly at him before changing his mind. Had it been mercy or desperation? The distinction might matter later.

"Right now, the Met wants to arrest you for that hit-and-run in London."

The flicker of surprise in Boris's eyes was confession enough for Garrick to know they had the man responsible for Ian Smith's murder.

Boris met his gaze. "Thank you for diving in after me." Then his eyes closed. His head rolled back. He'd decided that the interview was over.

Garrick stood, beckoned the officer guarding the door inside, and started recording on his phone. "Boris, I'm arresting you on suspicion of murder and possession of an unlicensed automatic weapon. You have the right to remain silent..."

Boris nodded, but never opened his eyes.

Outside the room, Garrick spoke quietly to the officer. "Log everyone who enters - including hospital staff. Someone might come back to finish the job on him. When your shift ends, make sure your replacement has my number. The moment Kontos wakes up, call me immediately."

A Degree of Murder

It was hour's drive through heavy traffic, back to the office in Maidstone. But first, he had to go home to shower off the blood and terror and beg Wendy's forgiveness. Since becoming a father, he had found himself apologising more than he ever had in his life. He wondered if this would continue until Amy was eighteen. That was just another six and a half thousand days away, give or take.

It was always nice to have something to look forward to.

Chapter Sixteen

Sometimes, Garrick wondered why he was buying a house at all, because he always felt he was certainly living in the doghouse when it came to Wendy. He was met with a resigned look when he entered the house - a look that went cold when she saw the bundle of bloody clothes he was carrying.

"It's been a hell of a day," he said with a wry smile.

Her gaze flickered over him, and she gave a dry, repressed sob before pulling herself together. Since they'd started dating, Wendy had been aware of the danger David put himself in. He always insisted it was par for the course, but she pointed out that even the best TV detectives, whose writers were desperate to grab the ratings, still didn't end up half-killing themselves like he did.

Garrick had learned when and when not to bring up any work subject matter. And as she'd been deeply involved with some serious incidents in the past, she now asked fewer questions and stoically accepted the situation. That had changed the moment they knew Amy was on her way. The dynamic had taken a silent but significant shift in a direction that he couldn't ascertain.

He threw the bloody clothes and everything else he was wearing into the washing machine and put it on the highest temperature that wouldn't incinerate the garments. Then he went upstairs and remained in the shower for over thirty minutes, scrubbing every inch of himself clean several times over. In the final moments, he crouched down, leaning against the wall and quietly sobbed as the horrors and tension bled from him.

For all the trials and torments that he'd been through with his insane sister, he'd always managed to keep a tight rein on his feelings. That situation was buried in the past, and his future was tied to the two women downstairs. For some reason, the pressure now felt worse.

He freshened himself up, combed the knots from his hair, and put on some fresh jeans and a T-shirt to give the semblance of being casual. When he went downstairs, he was pleasantly surprised to see Wendy had cooked a jacket potato in the microwave, slathered hot beans over it, and fried three Cumberland sausages.

"I thought you'd be half-starved," she said. "Quavers are not a balanced diet."

He gave her a big kiss on the forehead and a crushing hug, which she latched onto with a satisfying feeling that suggested she wasn't going to let go. Then he dived into the food.

"How have you and Amy been?"

Wendy sat opposite with her laptop and gave a bemused smile. "Oddly, she sleeps like an angel when you're not here."

"Oh," said Garrick in surprise, before considering, "or you sleep so heavily, you don't hear her." He hesitated, aware that may have sounded argumentative, but was happy when Wendy smiled and shrugged.

"That's also a possibility. It's the only time either of us get any peace."

"Oh, how are your parents?" he said, suddenly remembering the situation he'd managed to avoid.

"Exactly as you'd imagined. They were not surprised you were busy. I think mum suspects you kill people just to avoid seeing them."

Garrick didn't take the bait but instead finished his meal with deep satisfaction, if pending indigestion, because he'd guzzled it down far too quickly.

"That was the best thing I've eaten all year," he stated, sincerely.

"And the surveyor's been to the house." Wendy opened the laptop and called up an email. Garrick had clean forgotten the logistics of house-buying.

"Is it still standing?"

"It was when he left yesterday. Because he hasn't got a massive amount on, he reckons he'll get the report by the end of the week."

"Well, that's brilliant news."

"Do you remember Betty, who I used to work with?"

When they met, Wendy had been a classroom assistant in a school. But since quitting the job, intending to study to build a better career, life had got in the way, and she had ultimately fallen pregnant. In the darker moments of self-loathing and doubt, Garrick wondered if she held that against him, and had even voiced his suspicions during his therapy sessions. It was pointed out that Wendy had never raised the situation, never breathed a word about it, therefore it was entirely his own issue. The therapist had wisely told him that, like so many things when we think life is against us, it's often our own demons who are the ones trying to sabotage our plans.

"Anyway," Wendy shook her head dismissively, knowing full well he didn't recall any of her friends. "It took Betty six months from putting an offer in, getting a mortgage, getting the reports, selling her own house, and waiting for the people in the house she was buying to move out. Talk about stressful. But our conveyancer reckons we could get all of this sorted within the next week. The property market is in the doldrums."

Garrick gave a low whistle, impressed. "Okay, so they're really desperate to sell that house. Now I want to know what's wrong with it."

She playfully slapped him. The thought of moving to pastures new was making her overlook his work commitments.

"Don't jinx it," she warned him. "So, when the report comes in, I'm going to need you available to talk to the conveyancer and get things rolling."

Garrick nodded. "Of course."

She closed the laptop lid and looked at him meaningfully. "I mean it, David. I know you've got things you need to do, but *we* have things *we* need to do." She glanced towards the cot in the corner where Amy was slumbering. "You've heard the expression - they grow up so fast."

Garrick opened his mouth to argue but sensibly decided to shut up. He hadn't been conscious for the birth. He'd missed out on the first few weeks of bonding. And when they spent time together, Amy was either vomiting over him, or he was making excuses to leave. In his head, he was the very image of a doting father, but the reality made him think of his daughter's future therapy sessions when she complained about the lack of a father figure in her life, and it felt crushingly depressing to him.

He gripped Wendy's hand and held her gaze earnestly. "I promise I'm going to do my very best."

She smiled, and at least she didn't respond with the line that was buzzing around Garrick's own head: *what if his best wasn't good enough?*

"Well, at least I've got you for the rest of the day," she said, smiled, and squeezed his hands. "We can just slob out in front of the TV. Oh, and then we have to go shopping at Asda."

Garrick nodded. "Yeah, that sounds like a plan," he said, even as the phone in his jeans pocket vibrated for attention.

Chapter Seventeen

Garrick arrived back at the station at six o'clock in the evening. He'd tried to ignore his buzzing phone most of the afternoon, and when Wendy finally fell asleep after their leisurely sojourn around Asda, he left her slumped on the couch as late-afternoon game shows started on TV, vowing to only be a couple of hours. He'd missed several calls from DCI Kane, and when he tried to call back, he'd just got his voicemail.

He was pleasantly surprised to see everybody was in the office. The murder board had been extended and updated, everybody was moving with purpose, and one desk had two boxes of doughnuts and several Tesco meal deal sandwiches laid out, along with multi-pack crisps which had already been half-devastated by the hungry crew.

Fanta stood in the middle of the board, attaching pictures of the two gunmen then extending her arms like an orchestra conductor. She forced a weak smile when she saw Garrick.

"Holiday over, Guv?"

"I saw all the sights. Went for a dip in the pool. I don't think I'm going to give that place a good review on Airbnb."

"I know the feeling."

He smiled warmly at her. "You don't have to be here."

"Of course I do. How're you feeling?"

"Okay, surprisingly. It was the initial shock of what happened that hit me hard."

Garrick still hadn't got the full picture of what occurred when Fanta entered the house. Saving both Kontos and the half-drowned Boris had been all-consuming.

Fanta picked up on his silent cue and slowly busied herself, pinning more pictures of the crime scene at Kontos's house on the wall.

"When you went in the pool, I got Carl's Taser and legged it into the house when I heard the scream. I was just in time to see Kontos's arm go flying. The swordsman was standing over him like a demon - dressed all in black, head covered, and a samurai sword..."

"Samurai sword?" Garrick said in surprise.

She nodded. "I've seen enough films and been to enough Comic-Cons to know one when I see one. I must've made a noise, screamed, yelled, *something* - 'cause he spun around, saw the Taser in my hand - although maybe he didn't register it as a Taser, maybe a gun. I don't know... he didn't finish the job. Instead, he fled into the hallway. I practically wet myself at that point, I've got to say."

She paused and sniffled, her whole body shaking. "Stupidly I ran after him. He reached the front door and opened it, but stopped and spun around, raising the sword." She paled as she relived the events. "And then the other guy stepped out between me and him." She stared reflectively at the paper in her hand before slowly pinning it to the board.

"I fired the Taser straight into his back, and he fell. And then–" She made a *whooshing* sound and mimed the decapitation. She sighed. "Now, I think that guy saved my life. He wasn't attacking me - I don't even know if he was defending me - but he was out to stop our ninja. You know the rest." She stared blankly at the board.

"I visited Boris at the hospital earlier. He was in a talkative mood."

"Uh-huh."

"He said they were both there as bodyguards for Kontos. So maybe we shouldn't feel too bad. I think if you and I had blundered in without our mad samurai sword-wielding assailant being around, then we would've been shot without a second thought. They don't strike me as the sort of fellas who do cops a good turn."

Even as he said the words, Boris's sincere 'thank you' flashed through his mind. That hadn't been sarcastic; there was no hint of the *them-versus-us* bitterness usually experienced between crooks and cops. It was a genuine moment.

He saw Harry enter with a tray of drinks, followed by Sean with more paperwork. "You two look bright and breezy."

"Oh yeah, we had it easy - trolling through stuff. And there's a *lot* of stuff coming in."

Sean handed the papers to Chib who was hidden behind the boards, searching through a mound of printouts.

"Forensics are going through the house," she said. "There's a ton of things. The guns were unregistered and all of them fit into the flight cases you saw them carrying at the train station. Including the pistol Kontos had. There's a safe in Kontos's study we can't open. We've got his computers, laptops, everybody's mobile. Surprise, surprise, they're all password protected. Unless he starts squealing, we're going to have to send it to Digital Forensics, and I wouldn't hold my breath for how long that's going to take. If we're lucky, it might just be before we retire."

"Great, so we need his cooperation," said Garrick. "Well, he didn't say much, but funnily enough, our man Boris gave me quite a lot at the hospital."

He noticed their reaction. "No, that's *not* really his name – but that's all he's giving away. Kane confirmed he's the guy involved in Ian Smith's hit-and-run." He crossed to the boards and indicated between Kontos's picture, Boris, and Ian Smith. "Which means there's definite retaliation going on here. And it is all linked to the storage depot deal. Smith blocks any chance Kontos has for a sale. That results in Councillor Freeman flipping his vote against it, which leads to his death - because he'd been bribed to vote for Kontos."

"I'm certain of that," Sean said, "although we need a paper trail to back that up in court. But it's a good place to start."

"What about the others?"

"Well, before I was called away to babysit Anna Campbell," Chib said, "I interviewed the councillors who Stafford claimed had spoken to Mr Kontos. And let me tell you, Mary Ganning is *not* a good actress. She was nervous, looked as guilty as sin, and was wearing a rather nice, brand-new Apple Watch, and sporting quite a nice tan from the holiday she'd just returned from - Thailand. Now, I'm not saying she took a bribe, but council life is really paying off for some people."

"We can delve into her later." Garrick pointed to the picture of Trev McDonald. "He brought Smith in. This led to Freeman having a change of heart about his vote and he was killed as punishment. Kontos is super-pissed by this, and orders Boris to kill Smith after talking to us." He paused and stared at Smith's picture. "But Smith just feels out of place, don't you think?"

Chib shrugged. "No. He was right at the heart of what went wrong for Kontos."

"True. But weeks had passed. Freeman had already been taken. If he was going after Smith, why not do it earlier? After all, Smith's surely a bigger threat than an indecisive councillor. You saw Smith, Fanta. How would you describe him?"

"Nervous, paranoid, on edge."

Garrick nodded. "A regular day in the office for us. But all the statements we have indicate Smith was taking pleasure in dishing the dirt. He wasn't a man afraid, even though he knew of Kontos' reputation. So, again, why go after Smith?"

"Maybe he had more info to spill," Harry suggested. "Or he was so rattled after Freeman was killed, that it pushed him over the edge. Then when you two rock up to his office asking questions, and old Boris was spying on him, then it could've been quite a quick decision - execute the snitch."

"All of this orbits around Alexander Kontos. What other secrets is he keeping? He's a man with links to the Greek underworld, a man powerful enough to hire professional mercenaries to do his dirty work. What's transformed him into a man frightened enough to need the same protection against our swordsman? Who is *he*?"

"Don't forget," Fanta said, standing up and moving to the far side of the board to indicate a picture of the severed hand. "We still have this John Doe. We never got a match with the tattoos on his hands." She pointed at the two hired guns.

"And we haven't yet got firm IDs on these guys, even though one of them's in custody. What they all have in common is that they operate below the radar."

Garrick didn't get what she was hinting at. He shrugged.

"The murkier people are often those who lurk on the dark web. And perhaps they're working together, and this is a tale of internal rivalries?"

Silence descended on the room.

"We know one victim in the depot was Councillor Freeman. Are you suggesting our handyman could have been another hired gun?"

"It's not implausible," said Chib. "We know Kontos is our big fish, but there's a shark swimming around waiting to get him."

Garrick clapped his hands together. "Okay, people, spitball. What about our mystery Zorro?" He felt some satisfaction that he didn't have to explain his reference this time.

"Yakuza?" said Fanta, which got a snigger from around the room. She looked offended. "What's wrong with you people? They're the Japanese Mafia?"

"Well, we could accuse you of stereotyping," Harry scoffed.

"I beg your pardon? I'm Chinese - totally different place. That would be the Triads. We don't all run around with samurai swords, y'know." She glared defiantly at him, which stopped Harry's retaliation, which Garrick was ninety per cent certain would've been accidentally racist.

"And yes, I did suggest Yakuza, based on the sword," Fanta said, pulling a face. "Admittedly, yes, but it's another organised gang rival to the Greek Mafia. What's their name? You know, like the Italians have Cosa Coffee. That kind of stuff."

"The Costa Nostra," Harry said in despair before realising Fanta was winding him up. "Funny. I'll look it up." He Googled the phrase, then frowned. "Apparently, the Greek Mafia is called the Greek Mafia. Not very imaginative, is it? How about the Keb–"

Fanta talked over him. "It doesn't matter, but what if this is a gang war sort of thing?"

Again, silence descended on the room.

"It as good a theory as any, right now," Garrick acknowledge. "Harry, can you liaise with the NCA, and ERSOU."

Harry nodded. "On it." While the National Crime Agency dealt with all aspects of organised crime across the UK, it was ERSOU – the *East Region Special Operations Unit* – who would have intimate knowledge regarding gangs across the area.

"Forensics expect to be in the house for at least another day or so," said Chib. "And because a lot of materials are flowing in, it'd be great if we could get a couple more hands to deal with the paperwork here."

Garrick nodded. "Okay, let's do that. I'll speak to the Super." His phone buzzed in his pocket. He glanced at it, fearing it was Wendy, but instead it was a message from an unknown number. He quickly read it and smiled.

"It's from the uniform posted outside Kontos's room. The Greek has awoken, and there's someone claiming to be a detective who is insisting on speaking to him."

Everybody glanced around in alarm. Could this be the killer making his final move?

Their concern vanished when Garrick burst out laughing. "Some tosser called DCI Kane, who won't take no for an answer and thinks he can barge his way in. This should be fun."

Chapter Eighteen

DCI Garrick marched out of the elevator with so much gusto and authority that the uniformed policewoman outside Kontos's door started in surprise as he raised his warrant card to identify himself.

"DCI Garrick. You messaged me. I want that man arrested as an imposter immediately," he stabbed a finger at a weary DCI Kane, who sat on a chair nursing a half-empty cup of tea.

The officer hesitated, her eyes darted back and forth, and she braced herself, ready to act, only stopping when Garrick cracked into laughter.

"I'm kidding," he chuckled. "But thank you for calling and stopping undesirable members of *rival* police forces from trying to interview *my* witness."

Kane knocked back the rest of his coffee and stood with a shake of his head. "Get your kicks where you can, David," he said with a resigned smile, then turned his attention to the officer. "And you're exactly the sort of person we need on the force." He glanced at Garrick with a wry expression. "She point-blank refused to let me in. She refused to even acknowledge my ID as real until you arrived."

"Well, you're not a real officer," said Garrick. "You're Met, London's Toy Brigade." He smirked and gestured towards the door. "But seeing that my star witness is awake and you are here, I suppose it's only courtesy to invite you to watch."

Kane scratched the stubble on his jaw. "Point taken, Detective. I have been trying to call you all day."

Garrick waved dismissively. "Yeah, I've been busy. Shall we?"

He gave an appreciative nod towards the PC, and they entered Kontos's room. A doctor already there, talking quietly to Alexander Kontos. In the few days since they'd first met, Kontos he now looked like a totally different man. The confident, classy man was somehow paler, his face more haggard than it had been. His arm was cocooned in a plastic brace, with only his fingers visible through the end. It masked the extent of his surgery.

The doctor frowned when he saw Garrick, who held up his warrant card. "DCI Garrick. This one's mine," he said, pointing at Kontos.

The doctor wasn't impressed. "I think whatever you wish to ask him should wait. He's been through a lot. The surgery was very tricky. If we're lucky, he may retain twenty to thirty per cent functionality of the hand. Unfortunately, only time will tell."

"It's not his hand we need. As long as his mouth works, we're good."

The doctor looked helplessly between his patient and Garrick, made several notes on the clipboard, which he hung at the foot of the bed. On the way out, he looked between the two detectives. "Please keep everything *civil*, gentlemen. If his blood pressure alarm goes off, a fleet of nurses will be in here to kick you out."

He gently closed the door behind him. Garrick beamed at Kontos. "Isn't it nice to have the doctor on your side, although I suspect he doesn't like policemen. Maybe he has an outstanding parking ticket? Cheated at golf? What crimes do doctors commit?" He clicked his fingers. "Mass murder, of course. Harold Shipman, anybody?"

Kane stayed near the door as Garrick took the clipboard and made a pretence of understanding what was written down. "How are you feeling, Mr Kontos?"

"Barely alive, Detective."

Unable to understand any of the medical hieroglyphics that passed for handwriting, Garrick hung the clipboard back on the end of the bed. "Had any visitors? Your wife? Children?"

Alex shook his head. "She's away. Out of the country. Sometimes I think it's best she stays there when I have business to attend to."

"And what business is that exactly?"

"You know," Kontos said.

Garrick and Kane exchanged puzzled looks. "I know what you told me, and I know what you *really* do. So, I'm curious which side of that fence you were referring to."

Alex gave a good-natured chuckle, which he immediately regretted as pain spiked through his body, registering on the machine bleeping behind him.

"The irony that I thought my life would end at the tip of a sword blade, but it's a police detective with terrible comedy timing that might be the death of me."

"I assure you, Mr Kontos, your death is the very last thing

I want. Did you know I even dived into your wonderful swimming pool to save the life of one of your hired mercenaries?"

From his reaction, Alex hadn't been told anything about that.

"Yep, he's alive and talkative. The other one died, sadly. You'll have a hell of a time redecorating your hallway because of what happened to him. What can you tell me about a masked, sword-wielding looney bursting into your house, attempting to kill you?"

"That is pretty much the topic on my lips. I was as surprised as anyone."

"Clearly. You have wonderful instincts if you hired security before knowing that you were being targeted for attack. You even possessed the foresight to pick them up from Sevenoaks and bring them to your property the very day it happened. That's very fortuitous. Have you considered doing the lottery?"

He studied Alex Kontos's face. The man may be a master liar, but he was wary about how much Garrick really knew. Garrick pulled up a visitor's chair and sat on it, leaning forward and resting his elbows on his knees, without breaking eye contact with his suspect.

"And, as I told your muscular friend, your assailant got away. He stole the security van outside and dumped it a few miles out of the village, in the woods. It was a meticulously planned attack. It's the sort of mind that doesn't leave business unfinished. And the problem we have as a police force, is by law, I am forced to keep you safe. But if I don't know who to keep you safe from, the chances of me successfully completing that job are thin. That's going to be a real bummer if the only way I can track this guy down is by hoping he left enough forensic evidence during your murder that something will lead me to him."

He glanced at Kane, whose face was twisted in an amused grimace of respect that Garrick wasn't mincing his words.

"My alarm system didn't trigger until he came through the back door."

"Disabling a large and sophisticated security set-up requires planning. Premeditation. If you premeditate a crime, you normally have a very deep emotional connection with the victim." He left the rest of his thought process hanging for Kontos to fill in the blanks himself.

"Perhaps you'd be good enough to call my lawyer. I think he will be very interested in my current circumstances."

"Sure. What's his number?" Garrick smiled when Kontos hesitated. "It's okay, we have your phone. I can bring it here if you want to use it and call him?"

That provoked a smirk from Kontos. "Of course. I'll open my phone and hand it to you so you can call him."

Garrick nodded in agreement. "It would save everyone a lot of trouble."

"As a sign of good faith," Garrick extracted his own phone from his coat pocket. He unlocked it and handed it to Kontos with the keypad ready. "Be my guest."

Alex glared at Garrick, who waited patiently. Finally, he typed in a number, which was answered after five rings. He spoke rapidly in Greek. He caught the name of the hospital in the fast-flowing dialogue. Kontos hung up and handed the phone back.

"Thank you. He's on his way."

Garrick pocketed his phone and sat back down. "Well,

since we have time to waste, why don't you tell me about the gentlemen with the guns?"

Kontos chose his words carefully. "I employ security of all kinds. I pay for security at home, at the depot site, anywhere I require security. I pay for the best, you understand. I contract them. I expect them to pay their taxes and abide by the law. So, if they were suddenly to pull out Heckler & Koch machine guns and start firing at somebody trying to kill me, well, that's their concern, not mine. I'm just thankful they're trying to protect me."

Garrick chuckled and leaned back in his chair. "Yeah, very fortuitous that they were armed to the gills with military-grade firepower. I'm more impressed that a property mogul like you can identify a Heckler & Koch."

Kontos clearly regretted his mistake. His lips went thin as he pressed them together.

"How's business at the storage depot?"

"Terrible."

"I suppose finding parts of Councillor David Freeman strewn around is very concerning."

Kontos shifted his position in the bed when Freeman's name was mentioned. He was a man in control, but some tells - particularly when stressed and tired - are almost impossible to stop.

"I feel sorry for the poor guy. His wife had passed away. He was thinking about quitting his job. He had an estranged son. He left *nothing*, apart from a nice house and a case full of cash."

Another flicker across Kontos's face.

"I hope he left the money to charity in his will. Perhaps a donation to the police benevolent fund."

"Now there's an irony," said Garrick, wagging a finger

mischievously. "I see you've still got your sense of humour. It hasn't been carved out of you yet."

"Detective, we could do this all evening. I'm tired. Without my lawyer, I'm not going to let you trip me up with false allegations. And leading statements."

Garrick looked at Kane with a subtle gesture, indicating he should chip in if he wanted to. He'd decided not to mention Ian Smith just yet, but wondered if Kane wanted to tackle that question.

"This is DCI Kane from the Met. I don't think you two have been introduced."

The mentioning of the Met made Alex Kontos stiffen in his bed once again.

"Pleasure to meet you, Mr Kontos," Kane said, leaning against the wall with his legs crossed and one hand in his coat pocket, almost like he'd walked off a fashion shoot for middle-aged gentlemen. "I've heard a lot about you. Lots of very interesting things. I just wanted to meet you in the flesh, so to speak."

Kontos nervously scratched his ear and didn't reply.

"Tell you what, we'll wait outside to give you time to think whilst your lawyer turns up. I'm guessing a man of your clout has a lawyer who will be jumping red lights to get here. So, should we say, forty minutes?" Garrick started towards the door and stopped. "One final thing – I almost forgot. I'm pleased to see the surgery was able to restore your arm. I believe the paramedics told me that if I hadn't been there and stemmed the flow, and preserved the hand, there would have been nothing to save. Makes you think, doesn't it."

That got a reaction from Kontos.

"So, I'm pleased the operation was successful." He clapped his hands lightly together before stopping. "I'm sorry. That was tasteless. However, I must arrest you. You understand? It's just procedure."

After his rights had been read, both detectives headed towards the canteen and settled down with cups of weak tea. Garrick walked Kane through the moment Kontos picked up his hired goons, and through to the events at the house. For his part, Kane was mostly silent with occasional '*uh-huh*' and nods to prompt Garrick along.

"I've got a lot of resources trying to identify Boris and his chum. As soon as we find out, obviously I'll let you know, so you can move your people off that."

Garrick appreciated the inter-departmental cooperation and wagged his phone. "While we've been talking, I sent the phone number Kontos rang through to my DS, so she's going to do a deep dive on who he is." They were halfway through their drinks when Garrick received a message from the policewoman on Kontos's door that his lawyer had arrived.

Garrick glanced at his watch. "Forty-two minutes. That's impressively fast."

"That's a man on a big retainer," said Kane, knocking back his tea as he stood.

As they strolled back to Kontos's ward, an email came through from Zoe. Garrick stopped in his tracks as he read it twice, but didn't have time to absorb it because he could already hear the raised voices of Alex Kontos's lawyer shouting at the policewoman blocking access to his client.

"Easy, easy," said Garrick. "I'm DCI Garrick."

The balding man turned angrily towards him. "You damn well know who I am. You have my client in there."

"Okay, you must be the mysterious lawyer. Do you have a name?"

He took a deep breath to calm himself. "Edward Markis. Now may I see my client? In private?"

"Of course. You've got three minutes with him."

"I need more than three minutes."

"I don't think you do. He wasn't very talkative. He just wants to sleep. You've got three minutes. Be my guest."

Garrick gestured to the door and then took a seat opposite. He looked at the officer, who was quite flushed from the encounter. "When's your relief coming?"

"Another three hours, sir."

"Do you want to nip off for a drink and a bite to eat? Give us thirty minutes."

"Are you sure?"

"Positive. Don't worry about it."

The look of relief on her face gave him a warm feeling. He felt people should be rewarded a little for doing their job properly.

Garrick gave Edward Markis exactly three minutes before he knocked on the door and barged his way inside without waiting for an answer. Kane followed him.

"Feeling quite chatty all of a sudden, Mr Kontos?" Garrick said breezily.

"No comment," Kontos said smugly.

"Remarkable," said Garrick. He looked askance at Markis. "I believe it takes a lot of money to train to be a lawyer, but that one sentence is really all you need to give to a client. You must learn that on day one. What's the rest of the time filled with?"

Markis scowled. Garrick didn't care. He didn't have a particularly soft spot for career lawyers, who knew categorically they were defending the bad guys, when a real lawyer's purpose was to make sure a trial was fair, not that the guilty escaped punishment.

"And has having your lawyer here helped you recall any details about who attacked you?"

"No comment."

"So, you have no comment to describe the man who cut off your hand? Who we're actively searching for and want to apprehend before he can get to you again?"

Kontos hesitated and glanced at his lawyer, who gave him a shake of the head.

"No comment."

Edward Markis intervened. "This is not the place for an interview. My client is in no medical condition to answer your questions. He almost died, for God's sake."

"Yes, I was there, which is why I'm trying to help him. And if you prefer, we can take him to a nice cell to talk, if that makes you feel any better."

"That would be ridiculous, detective. My client is in no fit state for a cell."

Markis moved so he blocked Garrick's view of his client. "Detective Garrick, I know who you are. I know all about your reputation as a fearless hotshot." Garrick was about to register his surprise at such a flattering description but thought better of it. "I would really consider that a man of such lofty reputation has got a higher place to fall from."

"You know, Mr Markis, that sounds like some sort of fable. Aesop, maybe? I'm not entirely sure, but it's lucky I think that's some kind of fable and not a threat, because, as you pointed out, I'm not above the law. Your client is not above the law, and you are not above the law."

They stared at each other for a long beat before Markis

gave a sharp sniff and made a pretence of looking for something in his open briefcase.

"Well, I think this interview - and any interview with my client - is well and truly over, detectives. There will be no further conversations until he leaves this facility."

Garrick couldn't be bothered to answer. He just raised his eyebrows dismissively and looked at Kontos. "You should rest up, and when you feel like talking, the officer outside the door - the one who will be keeping a vigilant eye out for your unknown assailant - will contact me, and we can talk any time you feel like it."

It was clear Markis was staying with his client, so Garrick and Kane left without another word.

"What a piece of work," said Kane as they walked towards the lift.

Garrick was furious. It was one thing having a suspect clam up - quite another to have to put up with the arrogant brief. He wondered just who the hell the guy was.

As they waited for the lift, Kane glanced at his watch and registered surprise. "Oh, I've got to get back home. Traffic into London shouldn't be bad at this time of night."

The lift door opened, and he stepped inside before realising Garrick wasn't following. Instead, Garrick was staring thoughtfully at the floor.

"Are you okay?"

"I'm going to stay a little longer. As soon as you hear anything, let me know, and I'll make sure we do the same. Fanta and Chib are all over this."

Kane gave a nod and pointed back towards Kontos's room. "Don't let the lawyer get under your skin. It seems to me he's the sort that will take every nuance and bad word and spin it against you when it comes to trying to pin anything on his client."

"That's exactly my thoughts," Garrick said.

The lift door closed, and Garrick sauntered back towards the wards just as the policewoman reappeared with a cup of coffee and a chocolate bar. She raised the cup in thanks.

Garrick spoke quietly to her. "Do me a favour - I'm going to check in with Boris. Can you just make a note of what time the lawyer leaves and text me?"

"Sure thing, sir. Thank you."

If Edward Markis was going to play hardball, so was Garrick. He headed round the corner, and down the long corridor to Boris's room. He read through the message Zoe had sent, and digested the revelation.

Another young, uniformed copper sat outside the room, quietly doing a Sudoku puzzle with his pen hovering over the numbers. He did a double-take when he saw Garrick, who raised his hand as the man started to rise.

"Relax, relax," said Garrick. "You saw me coming - that's your job."

"Sorry, sir," the copper said apologetically.

"Not at all. Don't be silly, son. Finish it. I'm going to see if our friend's awake."

Without knocking, Garrick entered. Boris's eyes flicked open when he heard the door, and he gave a grunt when Garrick entered. Garrick could see there was a new drip attached to the man - this one had a little button trigger to the side, which indicated it was morphine he could self-administer when the pain got too much. It was an indication his condition wasn't improving.

"Now you're on the hard drugs."

Boris gave a weak smile. "I never do drugs, officer."

"Of course you don't - big strong man like you. How're you feeling?"

"Like there is a hole in my chest." He tried to feebly point towards the knife wound.

"I just thought you should know your boss woke up, so congratulations on a job well done - you kept him alive. I'm not sure for how long, I still don't know who we're looking for."

Boris's eyes slowly scanned the room as he thought of what to say. He opted for saying nothing.

"Oh, and just so you're aware - and I know you don't have a solicitor here with you, but don't worry about that - you need to know one of the charges against you is for the murder of Councillor David Freeman. He's the guy who was hacked apart. Such a violent, barbaric way to go."

"It was not me," Boris whispered. "It was not me," he repeated a little more earnestly.

"Now's not the time for you to admit it or deny it. Save your breath. I just thought you should know." He half-turned to the door and stopped. "But there is one thing that made me think. I got the forensic report, and the wound inflicted on Freeman was done by a very sharp blade - a samurai sword. One of very fine quality, so fine it could be confused with a surgical blade. It turns out the marks on his leg, which are beautifully preserved because it was frozen, match the perfect incision across your mate's throat. Same blade, lopping off a head."

Without looking, he knew he'd got through to Boris, as the rhythmic beeps of the machinery monitoring his vitals increased. Garrick pressed on.

"So, if you remember anything, please, just let me know."

"They call him *the Chef*."

Garrick stopped at the door. "The Chef?"

Boris gave a weak nod. "He's not a good man."

"I'm curious where you position yourself within this list of good men."

Boris gave a morphine-fuelled giggle. "Mr Detective, I am a Boy Scout." Garrick gave a low whistle. "The Chef makes people disappear without a trace."

Garrick stepped closer, his hand sliding out his phone and activating the voice recorder. Boris didn't seem to care.

"Disappear how? Leave the country? Shallow graves?"

"Disappear without a trace. He doesn't kill the victim - he *eats* them. Eats them until they're nothing more than a memory. I told you; this man is bad."

Chapter Nineteen

"He doesn't exist," said Chib firmly.

The rest of the team were busy coordinating with some civilian staff who'd been drafted in to provide admin support for the increasing amount of evidence pouring in from the attack at Kontos's home. Garrick had briefed the core team first thing in the morning about the existence of the Chef, but by early afternoon, nothing had been flagged on any database.

Fanta put in a request to a digital specialist to deep dive the dark web, but so far, even that was drawing a blank.

"There's got to be something out there," Garrick insisted.

"We're getting plenty of hits on TV cookery shows and the character from South Park, but none of them are associated with cannibalistic killers," Chib said.

Garrick ran his hand through his hair in frustration. Ever since he had told Chib about the previous night's conversations, she had regarded the whole thing with scepticism.

"You got this information from a man who still refuses to identify himself, and we still haven't matched his details either. Ordinarily I would be saying that this was the whiff of some sort of internal corruption and records must have been erased, especially after everything you've been through with the Murder Club." She hesitated from bringing up the deep-level access Garrick's previous tormentors had; access that stretched into government circles in ways they were still not privy to.

Chib continued cagily, "But in this instance, it feels like this is a band of professional mercenaries who've been careful over their careers not to leave a footprint behind. No online trace, nothing." She pressed on despite Garrick's scepticism. "It happens. Look, statistically, there are serial killers walking the streets who will *never* be caught because their crimes have never been registered."

There were some grim theories that the murder rate in any country was only the tip of the iceberg. It was disturbing to venture down that rabbit hole, and it made one question the foundations of so-called civilised society. Despite everything he'd been through, Garrick still erred on the side that most people were decent.

Still, despite his reservations, he had to admit Chib's reasoning made sense. If in doubt, choose Occam's razor - the simplest solution is usually the correct one.

"Okay, so you're saying this is just a curveball Boris has thrown at me?"

"No, well, I'm saying the killer obviously exists. I'm just wondering if Boris's motivations would be about bringing justice to the case. You told him we suspected he was the killer. If you were in his shoes, why not try and wrongfoot the investigation?"

"The blade markings are a match. He couldn't be the killer."

"There is that," Chib conceded. "There is also the possibility they were all former colleagues. And Fanta's gang war theory has some merit. Harry asked around about Edward Markis. He's Greek, and according to ERSOU, he is the man organised criminals have on speed dial. Not for the rank and file, but the serious players."

That resonated at some level with Garrick, and he moved back to see what the rest of the team were doing. He saw Fanta and Harry were discussing plans of the house, using Google Maps to try and trace the path the perpetrator's entry and exit path.

"What have we got?" he asked, leaning over their shoulders to look.

"What we have is an anomaly," Harry said, his eyes fixed on the screen. "We asked Pegasus Security to send us footage for the entire day leading up to the attack and the hour after. Our phantom Chef is not on any of them."

Garrick frowned. "The security guy said an alarm had been triggered at the back of the house. The killer must have done that when he opened the patio door."

Harry shook his head. "And when we were there, there was no phone signal. Remember, I tried to call you. It was only after the attack I had full signal when I called for an ambulance."

"That's when Zorro fled," Fanta said thoughtfully. "The doors have hardwired sensors. When I spoke with Pegasus originally, they told me all entry points were hard wired sensors. Everything else was wireless."

"There's nothing of him coming or going." Harry massaged the back of his neck and stretched. "And because everyone is on the Pegasus contract, no one has any alternative security cameras. No Ring doorbells, nothing. They all rely on that one system. And on the high street there are no cameras."

"We need to find out why he's not on camera." Garrick went for his coat.

"Where are you going?" said Fanta.

"To Pegasus. I want to know how they're screwing things up." By the time he reached the door, Fanta was already following him. He stopped her. "I really need you here," he said reluctantly.

"How about you stay here, and I'll go?"

"Why?"

"Because one of us is computer literate, and the other is a dinosaur. And I was the one who went through their security procedures with them."

Garrick sighed, his eyes darting around the busy office. Despite the activity, there was little actual progress, and the thought of staying here depressed him. He gave a resigned sigh. "Okay, Liu. Tag along. I'm driving."

Pegasus Security was based in a retail unit just outside of Ashford, a twenty-minute drive south from the station down the M20. Most of the conversation in the car came from Fanta nervously talking about her upcoming exam. It now wasn't so much that she wouldn't ace the questions - it was her concern that she wouldn't be able to attend the exam due to the demands of the case. Garrick reassured her that he'd do his very best to kick her out of the office when the time came. He pointed out that he couldn't force her to come into work if she was ill, and there was a terrible flu going around...

She smiled thankfully but didn't press the matter.

Pegasus was exactly as Garrick assumed it would be - a

bland warehouse with the logo on the side, next door to a plumbing supply shop.

Inside, the identified themselves and Fanta asked for Carol Blakeman, the CEO she had originally spoken with. They signed in and were quickly met by Carol Blakeman, a statuesque middle-aged woman who carried herself with style and power, wearing a bright red dress and matching jacket. She wasn't the usual down-to-earth security type that worked in the industry - she belonged in a prestigious blue-chip corporation. In her office, they declined drinks and got down to the matter at hand.

"As you can imagine, this is terrible PR for us," she leaned earnestly across the desk.

"A man was killed and two more severely injured," Garrick pointed out. "We're not concerned with the optics."

"I am. Our clientele tends to be very high-end - celebrities, tech millionaires, those sorts of people. And we have contracts with luxury gated communities everywhere."

"Then I imagine it's lucrative."

"It is. These are exactly the sorts of people that are targeted by criminals. But why am I telling you this? You're the police - you should know this."

"I do know that people don't just disappear off video footage," said Fanta. "And on the footage you gave us there's no sign of the attacker entering the community. Considering you're a Premier League security company, that just feels odd."

"I gave you everything, the raw unedited files." Carol leaned back in her chair, gripping the armrests. "If you're suggesting our equipment is at fault..."

"Either faulty or has been tampered with," said Garrick.

"My father set this company up. I took it over when he

died. I'm not just an employee. I do have pride in what we do."

"Good," said Garrick with a warm smile. "Then tell us exactly what went wrong."

Less than five minutes later, Carol had escorted them from her office to another room where a young, employee accessed the surveillance files onto his computer. He sported the patchy beginnings of a moustache he was desperately trying to cultivate. He nervously looked between his boss and the two cops as they sat around him.

"The footage is held in cloud storage," Carol pointed out. "With multiple backups. So, there is no single physical place anybody can break into and sabotage the files. Kevin, I'd like you to walk through the footage with these two detectives."

Kevin nodded and went into a stuttering-salesman mode. "As I'm sure you've been told, our system is very sophisticated. There are high-definition cameras with night vision situated on lamp posts across the road. Each property has a gate camera, and doorbell cameras front and back. Here's the footage in question."

He activated the video to show Carl's transit van passing through the front gate and along the road, each camera cutting from one to another in an almost professionally edited television style.

"I want to see the raw footage," Fanta said impatiently.

"This is it. The cameras are activated by motion sensors and form an interlinked mesh across the estate. Each camera warns the next that somebody is around and the feed is automatically recorded like this. It means we don't have to trawl through hours of footage where nothing happens, and minimises storage space."

"We can react to situations in real time, much more quickly," Carol clarified.

The van stopped and they watched Carl release Garrick and Fanta from the back and drive off. The cameras switched three times as they tracked the detectives approaching Kontos's front gate. They saw themselves peering at the gate camera before reacting as the Carl's van returned. Then the three of them could be seen talking and disappearing around the side of the house.

Garrick was confused. "Fine, that shows us, and there's nothing from the gate camera because that had been disabled. Correct?"

"For some reason, that didn't trigger," Carol reluctantly admitted.

"What about the interior sensors?"

Kevin's fingers clattered across the keyboard as he checked a text log of the timestamped activity of every sensor in the house. He shook his head, slightly bewildered.

"The metadata says the rear patio camera was triggered while you were at the front. It should've activated a camera at the rear of the property, but it didn't."

"We received a notification here and alerted Carl to the situation," Carol added.

"Was the network hacked?" asked Fanta.

Kevin shook his head. "Maybe, but there's no obvious indication of that. It just stopped working."

Garrick nodded thoughtfully. "And then, after the attack, there's nothing until the ambulances arrive?"

At that point, Kevin activated a whole new batch of clips which showed blazing blue lights speeding through the estate - three police cars and three ambulances screaming towards the house.

"Stop it there," said Garrick as the vehicles drove through the gates. "Do you see the problem?" Kevin and Carol craned closer to stare at the paused image and shook their heads. Garrick tapped the screen. "The gate was open when the vehicles arrived. It was closed when we were outside. But you don't have any footage of that. We were there. Our suspect fled from the house on foot and stole Carl's van. The van passed through the gate and sped east A25. None of that is here."

Carol and Kevin exchanged an uneasy look.

Fanta broke the silence. "How long do the cameras stay on for?"

Carol found her voice, but the confidence in it had waned. "Thirty seconds once no motion has been detected. It saves power."

"That doesn't seem too smart to me," said Garrick. "I mean, what level of motion are we talking about? Can somebody slowly walk past?"

Carol laughed. "This is state of the art, detective. The footage is analysed by AI. It can distinguish between a person, an animal or a crisp packet blowing in the wind. It knows when the object its tracking has left the frame or no."

"AI. *Artificial Ignorance,*" scoffed Garrick, tired of her defensive tone. "Yet it failed to catch our suspect and your vehicle hightailing it out. Either the cameras don't work, or somebody has tampered with this footage."

Carol shifted uncomfortably. "It is all held remotely on secure servers, with two back-ups. All digitally encrypted. And the feeds are all wirelessly coordinated between the cameras and relayed across a privately encrypted 5G mobile network that is the most secure on the market. Nobody could have interfered with the footage."

"Mmm," said Kevin, about to speak – but then he suddenly thought better of it.

Carol glared at him. "If you have something to say, Kevin?"

The man turned red with embarrassment. "Well, of course, the signal can be *jammed*."

That perked Garrick up. "How?"

"You can jam phone signals. It's not just the military who can do that. There are music venues, all kinds of places that can dampen a local signal, just so the audience's phone doesn't go off in the middle of a play, that sort of thing."

"Can you carry one around?"

"Sure. It'd be very localised, I maybe a hundred feet or so." He trailed off with further embarrassment. "But that's more than enough to interfere with our motion detectors. Disabling them before you physically crossed into the activation zone."

Garrick blew out a long sigh as he processed that information. "So, you're telling me if I had a localised jammer in my pocket, I could walk right along that road, and it would deactivate the cameras remotely before I activated them?"

Kevin nodded. "Well, not deactivate them, just jam the signal before they start recording, and prevent us from accessing them remotely. It would be just like they've temporarily gone offline."

"Like the front gate camera," Fanta pointed out.

Garrick's eyes went wide as he looked at Carol, whose expression was unreadable. "Well, this is a fantastic state-of-the-art system."

"That's purely hypothetical," she said stonily.

"Absolutely," Kevin nodded frantically, but then couldn't

help but add, "but anyone could buy the kit off the internet. I've seen things on Amazon…"

"Outstanding. Now we're talking about the killer potentially having a full understanding of your network. We'll need details of all your employees."

The task of now interviewing a raft of other people would put considerable strain on the already lean investigation team, but with the glaring problems in Pegasus's system unveiled, it was now a priority.

There was something was bugging Garrick as they left the office.

"Back to the station?" said Fanta.

Garrick shook his head. "No, I want to go back to the scene. Maybe if we walk through it, something will jump out."

Chapter Twenty

They drove back to Seal and parked up next to the library where Garrick had maintained his stakeout position.

"Okay, I was here. Harry was on Seal Drive. Let's give him the benefit of the doubt that he hadn't fallen asleep."

"Sean said he was awake when he arrived. So, our killer had walked right past either of us to get through the gates. Harry didn't see anyone come or go on foot, just vehicles. Do you remember any vehicles?"

Garrick shook his head. "No, but there were a couple of Pegasus patrols..."

"He could have been in one of those like us," Fanta finished his sentence. "A security guard, perhaps. That would give him knowledge."

Garrick considered. "True. It also makes him too much of a prime suspect. Our killer feels far too smart for the bleeding obvious. And the patrols are an hour apart. Why would he arrive an hour earlier but not make his move?"

Fanta was thoughtful. "It was dark when we went in. An

hour earlier, it was still light. He'd want to strike when it was dark."

"Okay, makes sense, but he's still got to get inside." He walked across the road to the gate "It was faulty when Chib and I first came. And Carl had to exit the vehicle, so it was still bust."

"Which would give somebody a small window of opportunity to jump out unseen from the back of the van and hide and wait." They took in the leafy tree-lined boulevard leading into the estate. "And it's very easy to hide here."

"You have a devious mind, Fanta." He lifted the gate and pushed it open enough for them both to walk through, making sure he flashed his police badge at the camera. The police were still on site, so his unannounced visit wasn't greeted by any questions.

They walked along the leafy road which opened out into the broader estate. Paying attention to the lamp posts, they could see each had a solar panel, a camera, and a separate motion detector all topped by a tiny antenna through which they communicated with each other.

"If I'm carrying a signal jammer," Garrick said as they moved within a hundred yards, "boom, that one's out before it activates." They walked the two hundred and fifty yards to the next light. "We're already out of range of the one behind us, and now this one's out of action." He shook his head sadly. "If this is what our boy did, then breaking in here was a piece of cake."

He approached Alexander Kontos's house. The gates were shut, but beyond there were still several police forensic vehicles and a white tent erected over the front door. They approached the gate camera, and Garrick regarded it thoughtfully.

"Kevin said this camera was disabled, it just made me wonder how. It's hardwired." He knelt, his knees clicking, and squinted. "Look at this." He indicated the camera lens.

"Okay, I'm going to bet there's a motion sensor linked to the camera. Look what he's done."

Fanta squinted and leaned closer. "Oh my God."

A circular black piece of plastic had been pushed over the lens, disabling it old-school style, but also blocking the motion detector.

"He waltzed over here, jamming the signal so it doesn't activate. Then he covers the lens with a piece of gaffer tape and sidles around the side. Bunks over the wall using a plank of wood content that nothing was going to be triggered until he opens the patio from the outside, which activates the hardwired circuit that he couldn't jam. By which time, it's too late because he's already inside."

"Should we go in?"

Garrick shook his head. "We're not going to find anything else useful in there." The truth was he didn't want to relive the carnage he had freshly witnessed. "Let's carry on following in his footsteps. Our perp stole Carl's van which was parked there–" He indicated where they last saw it, "and speeds out back the way we came, again none of the cameras activated."

They followed the path back out of the estate, and back to his car. They drove along the A road and were soon surrounded by leafy forest on both sides.

"Where was the van found?"

Fanta checked her notes and GPS on her phone and then pointed. There was a lay-by to the side. They pulled over. The road was a busy thoroughfare that sliced through the National Trust's Oldbury Hill.

Fanta scrolled through the notes on her phone. "Forensics found signs of multiple vehicles. It's popular with people walking their dogs. And doggers." She looked at him sidelong. "Which are two separate things, Guv."

"How old do you think I am?" Garrick muttered.

Fanta smirked and continued. "All Pegasus vehicles have trackers which is how they found this one. They also found dashcam footage of the van passing one of the emergency vehicles attending the scene. It was too dark to make out the driver. But he had the balls to keep the van's ambers on."

UK law prohibited non-emergency vehicles from flashing blue lights, so private security details and construction vehicles warned of their presence through flashing amber beacons. Garrick was taken by the killer's audacity at activating them, which would both draw attention, and alleviate suspicion. It was the vehicular equivalent of wearing a highvis jacket to walk unchallenged into restricted areas. People assumed you had the right to be there because nobody would be crazy enough to draw attention.

Garrick looked around. There was nothing to see, other than it would provide a quiet place to exchange vehicles.

"I'm buying into the jamming theory," he said. "It also makes something else very clear to me. This guy is a professional. Everything's meticulously planned, the very best technology employed and almost nothing left to chance. That's the profile of a very determined person. Somebody who's not going to walk away from a half-finished job. He'll be back."

Fanta looked alarmed. "At the hospital?"

"No. That's probably the safest place for Kontos at the moment. Let's assume our talkative friend, Boris, is just collateral. For whatever reason, Kontos is his target"

"So, we need to get Kontos out of the hospital and into a prison cell."

Garrick looked at her in surprise. "Fanta Liu whatever happened to you? You go after a promotion, you start reading books on *official* police procedure, and you become very, very boring all of a sudden. I used to be the one trying to talk you out of hare-brained schemes."

She looked puzzled for a moment and then brightened up. "Are you suggesting we use Kontos as bait?"

Garrick grinned. "As your superior, I could *never* suggest that, but you just did. That would be unethical." He grinned at her. "It could certainly lure his assassin out. The problem is, he's safe in a hospital, he'd be safe in a prison cell. Right now, there's very little in between. If I was the killer, I'd just be watching and waiting for an opportunity."

"What opportunity?"

Garrick bobbed his head from side to side as he wrestled with an idea. "One that might not look so good on your record, Fanta. We're going to have to screw up the investigation."

Chapter Twenty-One

With his appointed duty solicitor standing to one side, Boris was lacing his heavy combat boots under the watchful eyes of three armed Prisoner Custody Officers, each as big as the felon himself. The hired gun was still quite weak, although compared to Garrick, that still made him a formidable foe - and he was certainly in good enough condition to be taken to HM Swaleside, the high-security prison Isle of Sheppey.

Still, he hadn't divulged any further details of his own identity, the search had been extended to police forces across the EU and Eastern Europe - Albania, Romania, Bulgaria, Estonia, Moldova, and Ukraine - in the hope there was something on file.

Garrick gave a friendly nod to the solicitor and then spoke in low tones to Boris. "I'm not saying free legal counsel isn't very professional. I know this guy - he's very good." The truth was Garrick had never seen the solicitor before in his life, and he'd been assigned on a rota as part of the *duty solicitor scheme* to represent Boris. "But Mr Kontos hired the cream of the crop for himself. I thought he would have extended the privilege to his bodyguard. Between you and me, he's going to be walking out of here." He saw a flicker of anger on the big man's face - whether that was from the news or Garrick's persistent teasing, he couldn't be sure. "Shame to see he's going to let you take the fall on this. By the way, we're no closer to fixing an identity to this Chef character."

Boris finished tying his boots, stood, and nodded towards the officers waiting for him. Then he extended his wrists to be cuffed.

"Let's go, matey," said the Custody Officer. They walked out together with Garrick keeping close to Boris's side.

"The doctor told me you've lost a lung from the knife wound," he said as they waited for the lift. "I'm sure that's going to knacker your exercise regime. At least no more mountain climbing for you."

"I don't think I will climb again. That is true."

They entered the lift, and Garrick pulled out his phone. The idea of Boris and his mysterious dead companion being part of the military had been mooted by Harry. It resonated with Garrick because of their efficiency with high-end combat weaponry, and Boris's blasé attitude to death. The more he thought about it, the severed hand, cut with the same blade that had dispatched Councillor Freeman and Boris's pal, was evidence enough that the Chef was the executioner.

Garrick showed him the picture of the severed hand on his phone. "Seeing as you're no good with faces, why don't you take a look at this? This was found in the same location as the dead councillor - the one you were arrested for murdering. Does it look familiar?"

Boris gave it a cursory glance, then looked away as the lift descended. But then, a moment later, he frowned and looked again, his eyes narrowing.

Garrick second-guessed him. "Yeah, the tats." He zoomed in on the picture and caught a grunt from Boris. It was definite recognition.

Again, Garrick rolled the dice - it was better to bluster under the illusion that he knew more than he did, because he knew nothing. "Yeah, another one of your buddies. And I'm supposing the Chef killed him too."

Boris gave a grunt that could only be interpreted as acknowledgement.

The solicitor glanced between them. "You don't have to answer any questions," he cautioned.

"I'm just asking him if he knew the man. I'm not implying he killed anybody else, because I don't think he did." The solicitor looked undecided, and Garrick leaned conspiratorially towards Boris and pointed at the lawyer. "He's going to tell you to say, 'no comment', which is a real shame, since you're being set up for the Chef's crimes. He's killed two of your buddies, and is still walking free."

The lift doors opened, and the party shuffled down the corridor and through the hospital reception, mindful of the eyes of every patient looking in their direction. Boris stared grimly at the floor, his expression becoming darker with each step as they got outside.

The white prisoner transport van was waiting for them. With the yellow-and-blue Battenberg decals running below three narrow, tinted, windows. This would be the last fresh air Boris would feel for a long time. A Custody Officer jogged ahead and unlocked the back door as Boris approached. Garrick walked in lockstep with him.

"If you can give me a name, it would really be useful."

Boris put one foot on the raised step to enter the vehicle, but then paused. He looked at Garrick for a long moment, but it was an anticlimax as he decided not to speak. He clambered into the back, the suspension of the vehicle creaking under the man's weight.

Garrick hissed with frustration as he watched the van pull away. Boris was the third gun for hire to be taken out by the Chef. Garrick now had a strong connection between all the incidents.

But a connection was one thing, and a motive was quite another.

Chapter Twenty-Two

The whir of air conditioning and the subtle vibrations of the digital recording machine were the only sounds in the room as Edward Markis read through the charges against his client.

It had been several days after Boris left the hospital when Kontos was fit enough to be discharged. He was immediately taken to Maidstone to be processed for arrest.

Kontos was the shell of the man he used to be. Thin and pale, he sat quietly in a grey jogging top and slacks, his hands folded on the table as he studied both Chib and Garrick sitting opposite.

Finally, Markis put the sheet down and shrugged. "You have nothing to hold my client on. None of these charges will stick. According to your own statements, you found him in the house with his hand severed, bleeding to death. He was not in possession of anything illegal."

"He was found in the company of two men armed with sub-machine guns."

"They were the ones wielding the weapons, to my client's surprise."

"Your client had a gun in his hand."

"According to your statement, the gun was clutched in the severed hand on the floor. Whether this constitutes my client holding it or not is legally a grey area."

Despite his years of professionalism, Garrick couldn't hold back an impulsive "Bollocks." He cleared his throat, embarrassed. "Excuse me, I'm developing Lawyer Tourette's. His fingerprints are all over that weapon."

"And may I remind you," Markis steamrollered over Garrick, "that he was protecting his property from a man who seemed determined to kill him - who you have not yet found. How is my client anything other than a victim? And there is nothing you have that connects my client with the three other victims you outlined in your charges, other than the very loosest of associations resulting from the fact that he is their landlord."

Chib gave a low snort of disapproval. She'd argued with Garrick about how they should phrase the charge sheet. Whilst the lawyer was technically right, there were still plenty of reasons to keep Kontos in custody. It was very clear he was going to be walking out.

Garrick tapped the table. "Your client has been less than forthcoming in his responses."

"My client has been in hospital for several weeks after pioneering microsurgery to sew his arm back on." The limb was still in a plastic brace, which allowed him limited movement, but whilst Garrick had been watching, Kontos hadn't so much as twitched a finger. Markis continued, "So I scarcely think he's been in any state of mind to want to engage in riveting conversation with you. And not only that, but he also has nothing of value that he could add to the discussion."

Garrick took a breath to speak, but Chib couldn't hold back her frustrations. "He could start with telling us how he knows the two men he hired.

"You have proof of payment?" Markis said with a raised eyebrow.

"He picked them up from the station!" She scowled at Kontos. "You knew they were coming. They worked for you. I want names."

Markis shook his head and looked sidelong at Kontos, who just smiled quietly and said, "No comment."

Garrick sighed. "I was going to get you a gift - a T-shirt with the words 'no comment' written on it. But I'm sure your lawyer would have accused me of trying to sway your opinion."

"Is my client free to go?"

"Your client is still a suspect in a major case with four victims," said Garrick with a sudden edge in his voice. "So, if he's not in a cell, he is still deemed a material witness and a flight risk."

"Nonsense," scoffed the lawyer.

"As you pointed out, he's been in hospital recovering, and I'm glad to see he made a good recovery. So now we can lock him in a cell for thirty-six hours, and because of the ownership of the illegal weapons found in his house - from the men he picked up from the train station - we could invoke the Terrorism Act and keep him tucked up for fourteen days."

"This is preposterous," Markis snapped. "Terrorism?"

Garrick shrugged. "Similar weapons have been found in the hands of terrorist groups before. As your close-lipped client is not assisting us, what are we to think?"

Markis shifted his weight. He was agitated, and Garrick felt satisfied he'd got him on the ropes.

"Or, because I would really like your client to cooperate and quit using the phrase 'no comment', I feel gracious enough that we can release him under house arrest whilst he helps us put the pieces together."

"I need to speak to my client in private," Markis snapped.

Garrick nodded and terminated the interview, pausing the recording. He and Chib walked out into the corridor of the police station and moved to the water cooler, where he filled a cup and drank greedily from it. His mouth was dry.

"I can't believe you're letting this happen," Chib snapped. "Terrorism? Really?"

"Why not? I thought you wanted to keep him in a cell?"

"You offered him house arrest! I don't understand what we're doing here. We should be locking him in a cell and putting pressure on him to talk. Instead, you suggested he walks from here." Her brow furrowed, and she paced back and forth in frustration. "Everything hangs on finding the killer who's probably in hiding now and whom we may never see again. And the only leads we have are wild stories from his victim!"

Garrick held up his finger to interrupt her. "About that - I received some news on the way in here." He hadn't seen Chib all day as he'd been tactfully avoiding her, knowing that she wouldn't agree with his self-sabotaging arrest plan.

"What?"

"DCI Kane made a match. Boris is ex-Ukrainian Special Forces. The CCO... but don't ask me to pronounce it. In fact, ex-CCO gone AWOL." It went some way to mollifying Chib. "We haven't been given a name yet, but we've had confirmation that he, the other guy, and Mr Tats were all in the same unit. All presumed dead on a mission."

"Wow." Chib rubbed her forehead as she let that sink in. "So, they're real hardcore mercs for hire."

"The genuine article. And Kane's team have now found indicators on the dark web about how to hire these guys."

"Can we make a link to Kontos?"

"Not without access to his phone and laptop. And whatever is in the safe in his study. We still don't know what's in there."

Chib tried to work through the details. "If we put him under house arrest, then he's going to assume he's got away with it."

Garrick shrugged and gave a calculating smile. "It gives us a possibility."

"Possibility of what?"

He was about to answer when the interview room door opened, and Edward Markis poked his head out. "We're done."

Garrick and Chib returned to the room and started the recording machine.

"Have you had time to think, Alexander?"

The scowl on Kontos's face told him he had.

Markis cleared his throat. "My client will consent to house arrest for a limited time. One week."

"No problem. One week gives us ample time to discover your client is innocent."

"Also, although he'd like to return to his home, we reserve the right to move him to another property if he feels unsafe."

Garrick nodded. "I can agree with that. His safety is paramount. Of course, if we're going to do this, then he must be ankle-tagged."

Kontos grunted, but Markis thought about it for a moment and then nodded. "Agreed, just for the duration of the house arrest."

Garrick smiled. "We have progress, then." He looked sidelong at Chib, who was doing her best to hide her look of incredulity.

Kontos's release had clashed with Fanta's exam, which wasn't exactly ideal for Garrick as she was the only other person clued in on his maverick plan. To add to the hiccup, her exam was to take place over two days. One an online test, the other at the recruitment centre down the road. Either way, she wouldn't be showing her face in the office, and there was no way Garrick was going to stand in her way. If he'd expressed any uncertainty, Fanta would simply have rescheduled the exam, which wouldn't be for another six months.

He had intended to escort Kontos back to his house, where a plain-clothed officer would be parked permanently outside. The surveillance was a prerequisite of the deal, but it was also an additional cherry on the cake that Garrick took pleasure in knowing would irritate Kontos and draw unwelcome attention from his neighbours.

But with the latest revelations about Boris's identity, Garrick now had other priorities, so it was left to Chib to escort him back home.

Garrick made his way to Swaleside Prison, where Boris had been incarcerated pending his trial. Crossing the Kingsferry Bridge onto the island, his mind wandered to the last time he'd been on the Isle of Sheppey. It had been to look for fossils on the North Sea coast. A pastime he'd loved, but it had become a more fleeting luxury since Wendy and Amy had appeared in his life.

He'd timed the visit outside of standard visiting hours so he could meet Boris alone in the Visits Hall, away from the other inmates.

He waited patiently for ten minutes for the wardens to bring him in.

"Do you want him shackled?" the Prison Officer escorting him asked.

It took a moment for Garrick to recall the Officer's rank from his insignia. Band Four, a Specialist. The unassuming man was trained in security intelligence. They were clearly treating Boris with the caution he deserved.

"Has he been any trouble?"

"Quiet as a lamb."

"Then I think we're going to be okay."

The Officer nodded and moved back towards the door to give them some privacy. Boris folded his arms on the table and gave a small nod of acknowledgement.

"How do you like your new digs?"

"I've had worse."

"Was that in Ukraine, or when you were away on special ops?"

Boris froze like a deer caught in headlights. He stared intently at Garrick, trying to suck out what information he knew. Eventually, his eyes drifted to the ceiling, and he gave a dry chuckle. The fact that his name still hadn't been released by the authorities was now inconsequential to Garrick; they knew who he was. What Garrick now had was purchase on the man's psyche.

"I was surprised to learn that your other two buddies were also apparently killed in action with you. Can you tell me what happened?"

"No."

"But it was a good reason to turn away from that lifestyle. Vanish from the face of the earth and disappear onto the dark web."

Once again, Boris's eyes crinkled almost with mirth, but certainly with the acceptance that his cover had been blown.

"So, Mr Kontos, as I warned you, is freely walking the streets once again. Why are you rotting in here? I guess that there are two sides to this equation. One: professionally, you do what you do - but I suspect that doesn't include taking the rap for your clients. And if it does, I'd charge more."

Boris said nothing, but he was keenly listening.

"Now, bear in mind, your little operation is three men down." Garrick was careful not to quantify how many men operated with Boris because if he got that wrong, the Ukrainian would know that he was making the rest up as he went along. "You're the lucky sod who survived. Albeit spending life behind bars for... something you didn't do."

Garrick let the silence grow, thinking as he slowly tapped the table in what he hoped was an irritating manner.

"As I said, there are two sides to the equation, and I struggle to think a man like you would accept that's worthwhile. You've effectively been set up by your client. If I was in your shoes, I'd be really pissed off about that. But that's just me. I admit, I don't have the training or discipline you do."

For the first time, he could see indecision on Boris's face. He was finally getting through to him.

"Mr Kontos is back in his house now. There's an awful lot of redecorating that needs to go on there, but still..." He shrugged indifferently.

Twice he'd referenced Kontos's home - it was vital information he'd been telling as many people as he could, and as loudly as possible. He still had no idea how the Chef operated, but he just hoped the more people he told, the more the facts would reach the assassin's ears, and the bait would be taken.

His chair creaked as Garrick sat back. He had very little more to say - he'd pressed enough buttons already.

"You seem like a good detective. You know everything."

Garrick raised his hands hopelessly. "Do I? That's nice to know. I'm not entirely certain that's true. For example, I'm asking you for help in proving your own innocence. That's messed up. You're taking the fall for your client, who's doing you no favours, and the killer who tried to kill you both. I'll be straight with you - I don't understand."

"Mr Kontos, without protection, is a dead man walking. It's as simple as that, whether I am in here or not. And the Chef has a reputation for tying up all loose ends. That is how he stays in the shadows. I have no wish to be a loose end."

The penny dropped for Garrick. This ex-Special Forces behemoth was afraid he'd become too involved and be regarded as a loose end to be dealt with. He was afraid for his life.

"I appreciate that you've got this weird sense of pride and loyalty for a mission accomplished, a job well done, that you've saved your client. But you've just told me it doesn't matter; he's going to die anyway. So does that mean you failed?"

He was thankful to see Boris was torn, especially as he couldn't quite work out where that man's sense of honour and loyalty lay. It was all over the place. He wondered if the hardened soldier was suffering from PTSD. Was his mind so fractured there was no real rhyme or reason to what he was doing other than as a paycheque and a disjointed sense of honour?

Eventually, Boris slowly exhaled, then spoke. "Kars Ikigai."

"I beg your pardon?"

"Kars Ikigai is the name you are looking for."

"Kars Ikigai. Is that Ukrainian?"

"Japanese." Boris raised a finger. "And nothing to do with me. I have some morals, after all."

The sincerity of his words sent a chill through Garrick, and he was reminded that Boris regarded himself as a Boy Scout compared to the killer.

"Okay, so a samurai sword-wielding Japanese maniac who eats his victims?"

Boris nodded. "I told you; he's not a man to cross."

"But Mr Kontos managed to do that."

"That was clumsy of him."

"Very. How did he achieve such a spectacular cock-up?"

"I do not know. It wasn't a topic of conversation. Only that we were hired to protect him from Kars."

"Because you guys were the best?"

Boris bobbed his head from side to side modestly. "Perhaps. Or perhaps we were stupid enough to accept. I mean, nobody else did."

Garrick absorbed this information and tried to see how it fitted into the whole storage depot situation, but he drew a blank.

"And you're absolutely convinced Kars will go after him the first opportunity he gets?"

"As night follows day. His reputation relies on never being crossed. Do you know what the motto is for our Special

Forces?" When Garrick shook his head, Boris gave a half-smile. "I Come For You."

"And you don't happen to know how I can get in touch with him?"

Boris slowly leaned across the table, his voice lowering. "My advice, Mr Garrick - even though this is your job, just as it was mine to protect Mr Kontos - don't pursue this."

"You know I can't really do that."

"You can always close your eyes and turn away, Detective. Sometimes it's for the best."

Chapter Twenty-Three

With Alexander Kontos safely ensconced under house arrest with an ankle tag and an officer outside, the next forty-eight hours were spent trying to obtain more details regarding the MIA Ukrainian Special Forces team, which the Ukrainian military were loath to divulge, whilst at the same time asking for access to interview the prisoner.

DCI Kane, who had been responsible for identifying the men, was more than happy to deal with that, freeing Garrick and his team to dig into the name Kars Ikigai. Criminal records had revealed nothing. However, it was the digital forensics team who found references to the name on 4Chan that led to sites on other dark web bulletin boards. Scouring the bits and bytes of the sewer that was the darknet, it still took over forty-eight hours to build any sort of picture, by which time Fanta had returned and eagerly threw herself into that portion of the investigation.

Queries about how her exam had gone were met with vague indifference, although Garrick had caught her browsing job openings on the intranet, so he assumed she was confident it had gone well. It had also rekindled the frostiness between her and DC Sean Wilkes. He wasn't sure if he was being oversensitive, as nobody else commented on it. But if she were to move on to a different county, then the complications in their relationship were self-evident.

He stowed those thoughts away. That was her personal problem, not his. His personal problems were, on the surface at least, a lot more pleasant. The paperwork for their new home had come through at Olympic, record-breaking speed, and they were able to sign the contracts by the end of the day.

That, in turn, had galvanised Wendy into a packing frenzy. So, when he'd returned home, half the living room was already in cardboard boxes, and he was dismayed to see that his precious fossil collection had been half-heartedly tossed into a box, each piece shockingly wrapped in bubble wrap. This had created chips and scratches on his beloved yet ignored collection. That had led to a pointless argument, which in turn had just woken Amy. Her wailing defused the situation.

It was a relief to return to the office to get an update on the serial killer. Fanta had pilfered a third pinboard from another department, and covered it with various printouts of messaging boards with text highlighted.

"Kars Ikigai is a myth," she stood in front of it like a TED Talk speaker. "Almost. That's according to online forums, which explains why he's never popped up on any police database. The name pops up here and there, as does the Chef. There are plenty of tales of eating his victims to remove evidence, and a hundred per cent success rate on eliminating victims. It has all helped grow him to bogeyman proportions for the bad guys." She let that sink in. "Kars is the man the bad guys call in when their own bad dudes need dealing with."

Harry's eyes went wide. "You mean a hitman's hitman?"

She snapped her fingers and pointed at him as she nodded. "Perfect description there, DC Lord," she said with a cheeky smile, and Garrick wondered if she was deliberately practising how to talk to future lower ranks.

"Imagine: you're a mafia boss or a crime lord, and things are going south. Those trusted heavy hitters who usually deal with situations are all useless, or worse, have switched allegiances. You contact the Chef to deal with things one bite at a time. I reckon that's just a lot of chatter or terrific PR work on Kars's part to drum up business. Leave a few bite marks on a victim and let your fans fill in the blanks."

"Cannibalism is also a sign of trophy hunting," said Garrick knowledgeably, the knowledge from Zoe's macabre research papers still very vivid in his imagination. "Fanta, didn't you have a vague match with the bite mark from a case in the Southwest?"

She nodded. "Exeter."

"What were the details?"

She looked thoughtful and then quickly dashed to the computer to call up the file. "A local crime boss who was involved in people smuggling," she said curiously. "He fits the technical profile, I guess - the boss going down. Nothing more than that."

Garrick nodded. "Which suggests, if any of this is true, that Kontos really pissed off somebody influential - some other big shot who employed Kars to take him out." He suddenly froze as a thought struck him. "Smith!"

All eyes turned to him in the room with silent expressions that indicated he needed to elaborate.

"Get Digital to cross-reference anything on the dark web that could be associated with Smith - any of his businesses, aliases he's used that we found on his machines, anything at all."

"Are you suggesting it was Smith who contracted Kars?"

Garrick hesitated. He wasn't entirely sure what he was thinking. Smith certainly wasn't the head of a large cartel, so didn't fit the profile Fanta had pieced together. But since at this stage it was just guesswork, they had nothing to lose.

"Smith's business partner went missing after he stole the cash. He said he wouldn't be surprised if they found him under some foundations. He also suspected that some of his own stolen cash was used by Kontos to pay him. Perhaps that's some sort of revenge-loop he was caught up in?"

"Okay. Any physical descriptions?" Chib asked.

Fanta shook her head. "No. Asian seems to be the only common theme - Japanese, maybe, because of the name. But that's all we've got. The man I saw was a little taller than me. Maybe five-foot-five, five-foot-six?"

Fanta wrapped up her briefing, giving Garrick the sense that they were no longer pursuing a ghost. There was a definite identity behind the masked figure they'd seen in Kontos's house. Garrick noticed several missed calls from Kontos's lawyer. He listened to a voicemail, his face twisting into a slow smile. He hung up and looked at his team.

"Ladies and gentlemen, it turns out Mr Kontos is displeased with his current residence. He does not feel safe."

"I'm amazed he lasted that long," Fanta said.

"Shame. He wants to be relocated off-grid. An Airbnb preferably. We should oblige." He turned to Chib. "I'm already moving my entire life between houses, so it would drive me insane if I had to deal with him too."

She gave him a thumbs up. "I'm on it, Guv."

Garrick addressed the team. "With Kontos moving, it opens a window of opportunity for our mysterious Kars Ikigai. There are a number of things that can go wrong, and we can't afford to take any chances."

The team nodded solemnly. He briefly met Fanta's knowing gaze, but she stayed silent. They'd been waiting for exactly this opportunity, hoping Kars would reveal himself.

He returned to his desk and saw emails from the moving company setting times and dates for his house move. His doctor was requesting a routine appointment, and DCI Kane informed him that Boris was being transferred from his Kent prison to a military facility at the request of the Ukrainians. He hoped that meant good news and that the Ukrainian military was now playing ball so they could obtain an ID.

The disparate pieces of the case were slowly drawing together. He prayed that it would lure the killer out of the shadows...

Chapter Twenty-Four

Alexander Kontos and his lawyer may have thought they had the upper hand when their demands to relocate were accepted, but Garrick had taken great joy in being one step ahead - which was a rare luxury in any case.

Chib had secured a property through Airbnb, in the quiet village of Challock outside of Ashford, which sat high on a hill in the beautiful Kent Downs. Whilst only ten minutes' drive from Ashford, it retained an air of seclusion, and its approach roads were easily watched over.

Garrick and Fanta sat in Garrick's car as they watched Chib escort Kontos from his house to his new location, followed by his lawyer and two police cars maintaining a discreet distance.

As soon as he'd gone, Garrick and Fanta donned rubber gloves, and entered Kontos's house. The front gates and doors were remotely unlocked by Pegasus Security, who were all too willing to improve their dented reputation. Kontos's laptop, mobile phones, and computers had all been confiscated for evidence, and attempts continued to access the data inside.

Edward Markis, the lawyer, had supplied his client with a pay-as-you-go mobile phone, supplying the number and IMEI details to the police, which effectively meant that Kontos had no other official communication to the outside world.

Due to the nature of the house arrest, Garrick had obtained permission to monitor digital traffic through Kontos's router, so the uptick in sudden internet activity from an IP address within the house that wasn't the new phone was a sure indication that the police had missed something of key importance. And Garrick strongly suspected that would be in Kontos's safe, which they had still been unable to unlock. Luckily, Fanta and Garrick had improvised a plan for that.

They made straight for the upstairs room that Kontos used as a study. Garrick opened the cupboard door with the safe behind it, set at head height. He stared at the keypad. The digital display showed six dashes - which gave a million total combinations. If any three were wrong, then the safe would lock for five minutes. That could take up to three years to guess the code. Garrick didn't have that long.

"Okay, Fanta. Hit me."

Fanta crossed to the opposite side of the room and raised her mobile phone. After activating the Bluetooth, she finally detected the small camera they'd positioned there before Kontos had returned home. It was motion activated, and they had planted it to have a perfect view of the keypad. She wirelessly accessed the memory card. It took a couple of minutes for the thumbnail videos to transfer to her phone, but when they did, she could easily identify one showing Kontos on his first evening at home, typing in the code.

She played the video expectantly, then sighed. "Bollocks. He's blocking the camera with his body. I can't see the numbers."

They'd even taken pains to place the camera at an angle to circumnavigate such a problem, but Kontos was standing too close. Garrick groaned - this was the only plan they'd had.

Fanta watched as the safe unlocked and he opened the door, then she gave a yelp of triumph. "Wait, wait." She paused the video and zoomed in on the image. Whilst she couldn't see the code as Kontos had typed it in, once unlocked, it lingered on the display screen for a few seconds as he opened the door. She quickly read out the sequence, and Garrick tapped it in. With a beep, the safe unlocked. He pulled the door open triumphantly.

"Oh, boy."

Inside were bundles of cash: two solid blocks of fifty-pound notes, and three comprising one-hundred-dollar bills, and three similar ones of crisp fifty Euro denominations. There were two passports, one British and one European Union, along with a Samsung phone and a small MacBook Air.

Garrick gingerly took them out. The phone was off, and he suspected it was secured with a passcode. He opened the laptop on the desk and looked expectantly at Fanta, who scrolled through the other images on her phone until she found one showing Kontos doing the same manoeuvre and typing in his password. This time, zooming in and scrubbing through the images in slow motion, she was able to note down each key pressed. She typed in the password and gave a triumphant whoop as it unlocked. She forwarded the password to the forensics team in the hope that it would unlock his other devices.

"All right, let's see what we've got." Garrick slid the laptop to Fanta. "You're the best at doing this."

She rapidly searched through the various programs, finding the Signal messaging app and a Tor browser that offered layers of anonymity. The browser was a good springboard onto the dark web. Both opened without any further need for passwords, and they watched as a string of encrypted Signal messages appeared on the screen.

Garrick blew out between his lips. It was a goldmine of information regarding Kontos's criminal activities, all of which he had assumed were encrypted. Even a quick scroll through revealed messages which must have come from Boris, informing him that Ian Smith was speaking with the police. That was responded to with damning responses from Kontos about taking him out.

That alone was enough for a conviction.

"Jackpot. There's so much stuff here," said Fanta in awe. "Look, that's his lawyer..."

Garrick nodded. "Yep, let's get back to the office and get the kettle on. This is going to take a whilst to sort through."

The thrill and excitement of such a vital breakthrough were all they needed to make them feel rejuvenated. They closed the safe, retrieved the Bluetooth camera from its hiding place, and took the laptop and phone with them. They had bent some rules, but he had no doubt that the sheer scope of evidence outweighed the dubious means of obtaining it.

Whilst the rest of the station was alive with the evening shift, Garrick's office was quiet with only him and Fanta connecting the laptop to a bigger monitor and trawling through the contents of the Signal messages. Although they'd have to turn the machine over to Digital Forensics anyway, Fanta had plugged in an external hard drive to make a Time Machine backup of the contents, just in case anything went wrong.

Evidence in hand, they began to build a picture of Kontos's movements, motivations, and crimes, all of which were as clear as a direct confession from the man himself. They were only interrupted by a message from Chib informing them that Kontos was safely in his new accommodation.

It was approaching midnight before Fanta and Garrick took their first break from reading through the data. When he looked away from the screen, Garrick felt his eyes sting and could see random words and numbers burnt onto his retina when he closed his eyes. The Signal app had revealed a relatively straightforward case of greed and corruption.

Kontos was in severe financial trouble. He'd overextended himself with several property deals that hadn't gone quite the way he'd expected. It had left him owing money to an investor back in Greece. The identity of the investor was nothing more than a codename - Odysseus - and the tone of the messages was very far from friendly. The implication was that Odysseus was a powerful criminal figure, and the money owed to him, the first tranche of which had come from the land sale - or steal, depending on one's opinion - from Ian Smith, wasn't enough.

Kontos's immediate cash reserves had dwindled to practically nothing. His only hope lay in a lucrative deal to sell the storage depot site for luxury apartments in a deal that would net him almost four million pounds, most of which would pay off his debt, even if it left him penniless.

This was the very deal Ian Smith had sabotaged.

With the vast sums at risk, the bribery amounts were just raindrops in an ocean. When the failed deal was reported to Odysseus, it was followed by a swift demand that all assets be handed directly over to him. But that would only amount to paying a quarter of the debt off, leaving Kontos with almost nothing and still in hock to a more powerful criminal gang.

For a man who prided himself as a skilled businessman, every avenue had taken him towards a terrible deal. He stalled for time, claiming he could get the land deal through.

That was time Odysseus didn't want to give him, and all communication ceased.

Desperate for the deal to be done, Kontos reached out to Boris and company for some serious muscle. It was evident from the brief communication that this wasn't the first time their mercenary services had been employed, but that history would require weeks of digging through the archives.

Despite the temptations, Garrick and Fanta forced themselves to focus on the matter at hand. At this point in the timeline, Kontos had discovered that his plan had gone awry because of Smith's meddling. But there was no indication that anything should be done other than to watch Smith's movements carefully. However, there was a clear order to teach Councillor David Freeman a lesson for his betrayal. The goons were sent to deal with him.

At this point, Fanta and Garrick took a break and circled around the kettle as they had both developed separate views of what that meant. Garrick leaned towards the idea that a mercenary - presumably the one whose hand they found - had been dispatched to beat the living snot out of the councillor, but not kill him.

Whereas Fanta was feeling more ruthless, convinced it was a kill order, although the wording was open to both interpretations. However, she reluctantly agreed that Garrick's interpretation - that the tattooed mercenary and Councillor Freeman had met the same fate at Kars Ikigai's hands - was simply down to unfortunate timing that Freeman and Ikigai's paths had crossed.

But they were not at that point in the history yet. So, after their break and ordering two doner kebabs from Deliveroo, they settled back down to trawl through the data. It was satisfying to peel away the layers that answered some questions but threw up more.

Garrick's assumptions were justified when an exchange of messages revealed shock that Councillor Freeman had been killed along with the mercenary. As ruthless as they'd assumed Kontos was, murder hadn't been on his agenda. After all, he still needed the planning team to be on his side.

It was a message in the mercenary's chat group that revealed the name Kars Ikigai and a very simple statement: there was a contract on Alexander Kontos's head.

There was a blaze of panicky messages to Odysseus pleading for him to call off the hit. It was telling that none of them had been marked as read.

The shocking revelation came five minutes later as they digested each Signal message a line at a time. It was presumably Boris reporting that Garrick and Fanta had turned up at Ian Smith's office. Kontos gave the order to kill him, but that may not have been motivated by a simple desire for him not to talk to the cops. During his stakeout, Boris suspected that the contract with Kars Ikigai had been initiated by Smith himself.

Just what had led an apparently mild-mannered businessman - even one who had been screwed over by a notorious property developer - to hire the services of one of the deadliest gangland assassins was something Garrick and Fanta couldn't fathom. That had led to Kontos's gut reaction to take out his enemy, especially as he'd just spoken to the cops. Maybe it was driven by the fact that he was on the verge of losing everything, and police involvement would turn that possibility into certainty. Garrick could only speculate right now, but it certainly pushed the need to go deeper into Ian Smith's files as a matter of pressing urgency.

Fanta and Garrick physically pushed their seats away from the desk, rolling back on the wheels as if to give them more space between the Signal messages on the screen and the enormity of what they had just discovered.

"You know what this means?" Garrick said, rubbing his tired eyes and still trying to process the information. "Kontos ordered a hit on the one man who could call off the assassin. He's the architect of his own downfall."

Fanta nodded thoughtfully. "Which also brings in some basic business rules." Garrick regarded her questioningly. "Was Kars Ikigai paid upfront or to be paid on completion? I mean, I'm not an expert on how to hire a hitman."

Garrick picked up on where she was going with that. Was the assassin aware that his employer was dead? Had he been paid the entirety of his fee upfront? And what did that mean? Would he simply disappear because there was no point in following through with the contract? Or would he see it to completion? Perhaps as a warning to others not to kill the man paying the bills?

Garrick felt the crushing hand of fatigue embrace him, and he saw, despite the torrent of revelations, that Fanta was struggling too.

"Let's call it a night and share this with the team in the morning."

Fanta reluctantly accepted that it was the best course of action. With the hard drive backup complete, they closed the laptop and placed it in a secure evidence locker, curious about what treasures it would unlock with fresh eyes.

They were crossing the car park when Garrick's phone buzzed. He stopped in his tracks when he saw the caller ID. He quickly answered, putting it on speakerphone so Fanta could hear.

"Chib, what is it?"

Her voice sounded frantic. "Surveillance reported an intruder at Kontos's house. I'm on my way there now. I'm having trouble getting back in touch with the officer."

"We're on our way," Garrick barked and gestured towards Fanta's car. "You're the most reckless driver I know - you drive."

They hurried out of the car park, Fanta extracting a squeal from her tyres in their haste. They were fearful that one of their questions had just been answered. Ikigai evidently still had a score to settle, no matter who employed him.

The bait had been taken.

Chapter Twenty-Five

The crazy dash to meet Chib had Fanta triggering every speed camera down the M20 as they raced with the blue lights perched on the dashboard, Fanta gripping the wheel tight as she dominated the outside lane. Once they'd peeled off at Junction Nine, they tore through suburban Ashford housing estates and then accelerated down the narrower country roads, up the steep hill towards Challock. Garrick lost both mobile phone signal and his GPS connection - which was what they needed to find the house address.

Luckily, the GPS was still making a spirited offline guess at their location. As they turned into the road, the houses were a mixture of a few new builds, low-slung cottages, and larger pre-war homes, which, instead of sensible house numbers, all had names. They were forced to slow to a crawl, using the headlights to illuminate each name in turn.

"That one!" said Fanta, pulling over.

Garrick yanked the blue light's power cable from the cigarette lighter - they'd advertised their presence enough.

Up ahead, on the grass verge, was an empty unmarked car, which he guessed belonged to the officer assigned to watching the house.

The driveway gate was open. The property lay on the corner close to a small primary school and was blocked from view by a surrounding large hedge. There were no streetlights, so they were forced to use the flashlights on their phones to light the way.

The house had well-manicured grounds. The driveway sloped down to a garage at basement level, whilst a wide footpath arced higher up an embankment towards the front door. Chib's car was parked at the bottom, its passenger door still open.

They strained to listen for movement. The still air of the countryside around them was interrupted only by the distant squealing of a fox. There was no background traffic, nor the promise of backup Garrick had requested on the drive over. It was so cold they could see their own breath. There was just enough ambient light from a waning moon for Fanta to see Garrick's gestures. He pointed to her and then to the front door, whilst pointing to himself and then arcing his hand towards a rear gate on the right-hand side of the property that, as he neared, he could see was open.

Their eyes flickered to the windows, searching for any movement within. Once at the back gate, Garrick shielded his phone so the light wouldn't spill outwards and betray his presence, and checked if he had a signal - there was still none. He silently cursed and watched as Fanta pushed against the front door. She shook her head - it was locked.

Garrick steeled himself and slipped through the side gate, Fanta hurrying to catch up. He closed his eyes for a moment to let them become accustomed to the darkness.

When he opened them, he could see a doorway leading to the house on the left, and another gate accessing the back garden straight ahead. To the right, bordering the neighbour's fence, was a wooden stand filled with fire logs, next to an old barbecue mounted on brickwork against the wall.

He crept forward, tense and alert. Fatigue had evaporated, replaced by adrenaline and the sound of his own heart hammering in his chest. There should be some noise - the cops shouting, the sounds of Alexander Kontos complaining. Anything. Silence was an assault on his senses.

As they neared the side door, they could see it was ajar. Garrick hesitated and searched the darkness for anything that could be used as a weapon. His hand found the haft of a small axe embedded in one of the logs. He pulled it out and weighed it in his hand - it was old and heavy, putting him in mind of an American Indian tomahawk. Still, it gave him some courage.

He used his foot to push open the kitchen door. It gave a gentle creak as it opened. He turned to Fanta and whispered lowly, "Go back out and call for backup."

She shook her head. "You've already done that. You want me to go out there because you don't want me in here."

She was right, but this was no place to argue against Fanta's stubbornness. Garrick gripped the axe tighter and stepped inside, finding himself in a small laundry room with a washing machine and an open archway leading into a kitchen that had seen its best days in the eighties.

He crept through towards the far door, which was partially open, revealing nothing but blackness beyond. Halfway across the kitchen, he almost slipped and steadied his balance. It was too dark to make out any details, so he was forced to activate his phone, using only the dim light from the screen.

There was blood on the floor.

As he scanned the phone upwards to find the source, he found a man scrunched up in the corner, barely breathing, but alive. He clutched a gash in his side. He gave the tiniest of gasps as he reacted to the light.

Garrick assumed this was the plainclothes officer. He rapidly gestured Fanta over, putting his fingers over his lips. She almost slipped in the man's blood, as she crouched to tend to his wound, using a towel by the kitchen sink to stem the flow.

With mounting panic, Garrick knew there was no time for him to deal with the injury. He turned his phone off and inched towards the door, and, as slowly as he could, peeled it open.

His eyes adjusted to the hallway beyond, which was lit by the decorative sidelight windows surrounding the front door that let moonlight spill in. A staircase led upwards, and there were two doors ahead - one to the right, the other straight ahead, from which he could hear movement.

He crept forward and became aware that the door was mostly opaque glass as he could see a distorted white light bobbing back and forth behind it. Somebody had a torch. He weighed the axe in his hands, considering his options. The sounds beyond were wet and meaty, and his imagination played a hundred and one tricks as to what could be causing them.

With one cop in the kitchen injured, his concern for Chib's welfare was at an all-time high. He listened beyond the sickening noise from the room ahead, for the sounds of approaching sirens, but there was still nothing. He heard faint swishes of movement from the kitchen behind him, and then the accidental scrape of a kitchen stool across the floor. He'd forgotten that Fanta was clumsy.

The noises from the room ahead stopped, and the light bobbed more intensely through the opaque glass door as it turned in his direction - then the light went out.

Every muscle in Garrick's body tensed, and he squeezed the axe handle so tightly that his fingers became numb. The opaque door slowly pulled back, revealing a black figure beyond.

Garrick cowered in the shadows of the hallway, but even there, there wasn't enough room for the figure to pass by without tripping over him. He had to act now or never.

He bit down hard so as not to give an involuntary gasp and propelled himself forward. But his agility was not what it had once been. The figure caught the movement and immediately slammed the door into his path.

Garrick smashed headlong through the glass door. It shattered, most of the impact taken by the axe in his hand. But however sprightly the figure was, they too had no time to evade Garrick's assault - and he ploughed into them at full force.

In the darkness, they both staggered backwards and crashed through a wooden coffee table. They sprawled to the floor. The figure rolled aside - straight into an empty bookshelf. The cheap wood cracked as it toppled down over him. It bought Garrick just enough time to regain his feet, and increase the distance between him and the assailant.

The flashlight flicked back on - it was a head-mounted torch. The glare blinded Garrick, and he was forced to look aside. He caught sight of Alexander Kontos sitting on the sofa. In the fleeting seconds that he saw him, Kontos's eyes were wide open, his body a bloodied pulp.

Garrick blindly swung the axe at his attacker to ward him off. But the man had closed the gap, and it connected with a thud and a sickening crack and a gasp of pain from his attacker, who was vaguely backlit by the thin curtains blocking moonlight from the window.

Garrick didn't waste any time in letting his opponent get the upper hand. He charged forward like a rugby forward. His head was bowed as he crashed into the attacker, and they staggered backwards once again - trampling over the broken furniture, and slamming into the window. There was no shattering of the thick double glazing. However, the old PVC frame lurched as it was struck.

With a roar of frustration, Garrick slammed his opponent against the glass again, and this time the entire window - frame and all - slipped off its mounting and fell outside.

The living room was positioned just above the sloping garage below. The pane shattered on Chib's car below. The figure gave a yell of surprise as they toppled backwards out of the window.

Garrick almost pitched headfirst through but grabbed the windowsill, saving himself from plummeting out. He pulled himself back, glancing at the motionless figure below, and became aware of the approach of emergency sirens.

Then he turned towards Kontos on the sofa. With a trembling hand, he lifted his phone and put the flashlight on. Alexander Kontos's face was one of frozen shock; blood trickled from the corner of his mouth. A massive wound had cleaved him open from his sternum to his bowels, and a coil of guts had spilled out.

Garrick took a hesitant step - there was nothing that could be done. His foot kicked something on the floor. He looked down to see it was a Taser. At first, he thought that's what had felled Kontos, but as he moved his torch to illuminate it, he saw that the weapon had already been deployed; the electric discharge cables snaked away to the dark corner of the living room.

He slowly followed the path with his torch, revealing another figure slumped in the corner.

It was Chib. She'd been Tasered and put out of action.

Garrick felt a sense of relief. "Chib, wake up, come on."

He darted over to her side and was about to kneel - but stopped in horror. She still had her jacket on but was bleeding heavily from under it. Her eyes were open and glazed.

With a trembling hand, he reached out and moved her jacket apart. Just like Kontos, she too had been eviscerated with a gaping wound down her chest, butchered like a long pig.

Intense rage overcame him, and he bolted towards the window. Lights flashed in Garrick's eyes - not from the assailant's flashlight, but perhaps from nervous impulses triggered by absolute loathing and hatred. He was now a raw mass of impulse. He felt dizzy and was forced to steady himself. He peered down –

There was no sign of the killer.

With no rational thought or judgement, Garrick spun around, fully aware of the axe in his hand - an axe he intended to embed in the skull of Chib's murderer. But his path was blocked by the very same figure - a black shadow appearing as a stain on the darkness.

Something struck Garrick in the face. He teetered backwards - and toppled through the window. The sound of impact and breaking glass were the next things he felt - and the last things he heard.

Chapter Twenty-Six

His eyes flicked open, and for a moment he observed a nebula of swirling lights and colours, as if the Northern Lights had come out to greet him in a funeral procession to the afterlife. But this was no afterlife, as the wave of pain coursing through his body assured him.

He blinked away the lights and looked around. He was crumpled on the bonnet of Chib's car, remnants of the shattered double-glazing window around him, but there was no sign of the attacker. A raw animal instinct forced him to roll off the bonnet, landing in a crouch amid shattered glass. He was braced for an attack, but there was no sign of his assailant.

His blurred thoughts started to coalesce into questions. How long had he been unconscious? Then the image of Chib's vivisected corpse struck him.

It took four attempts to climb to his wobbling legs, and he staggered up the stepped embankment to the raised front door, which was still shut. He blindly sprinted back through the side gate the way he'd come, through the kitchen - noticing that both Fanta and the injured officer were not there - retracing his steps into the living room.

Alexander Kontos's body was still splayed on the couch, but there was no sign of Chib. He ran for the light switch, punching it on with his knuckles. The room was immediately lit up by an ageing light bulb that managed to bring the red gore splattered around the room to vivid life. There was no sign of Chib.

"What the hell?"

He moved to the window to get a better look outside, but the light had destroyed his night vision, and the only thing he could see were hints of blue reflected from trees as the sound of the emergency services drew closer. Then his thoughts switched to Fanta.

"Fanta! Fanta Liu!" He tried to bellow, but his voice came out in hoarse desperation. He hurried back into the kitchen, turning on every single light switch to cleanse away the shadows.

"Fanta?" he called from the kitchen, then he noticed bloody traces leading from where the officer had been injured, back out through the side door.

"Out here, Guv!"

He followed her voice out into the darkness of the side passage. "Fanta! Where are you?"

"In the back!"

The back gate, which had been closed when they'd arrived, was now open. He cautiously stepped through, his movement triggering the floodlight outside to illuminate Fanta hunched over the injured officer, covered in his blood. She'd torn her coat off to improvise bandages.

"Are you hurt?"

She shook her head, and then, in the full illumination provided by the floodlight, looked at him with wide eyes. "What happened?" she said, taking in that he was covered in blood, scratches, and looked quite literally as if he'd fallen out of a window.

"Chib," he said. "He killed Chib."

Fanta just stared. Then she slowly looked back at the copper in her arms, but she still couldn't say anything.

Their world had sharply changed.

It took forty minutes to initiate a mass manhunt in the area. Three ambulances arrived - one took the injured undercover officer away for critical surgery, another made no effort to examine Kontos, and declared him obviously dead. The paramedics from the third attempted to tend to Fanta and Garrick but were angrily shooed away. Any pretence of civility had vanished. All Garrick could feel was pure rage and frustration because there was nothing anybody could do quickly enough for his liking.

Although the situation was critical - an officer down - there was still a limit to how fast units could be activated in the dead of night. A police helicopter was dispatched from Redhill in neighbouring Surrey, and it took twenty-five minutes to arrive and circle the area with its powerful beam cutting through every field in the surrounding area. Onboard thermal cameras could reveal anybody hiding in the shadows, but the simple truth was that the attacker would not have fled on foot, but by vehicle, and an unidentified vehicle at that.

Every single unit was now on the lookout for anything suspicious in the area. It was impossible to pull over every vehicle. Garrick calculated that he must have been unconscious for no more than five minutes - that had been enough time for the attacker to steal Chib's body whilst Fanta had taken the wounded officer into the garden to tend to his wounds. With the intervening time before the search party could even be activated, the killer could easily be in another county by now.

With no point in joining the search, Fanta and Garrick had stayed at the property as forensics moved in at record speed. An officer down incident triggered an unspoken loyalty whereby other, less urgent jobs were shunted aside.

The sudden buzz of police activity hadn't gone unnoticed, even at the late hour, so by the time morning light broke, Garrick started to receive calls from various press contacts, including the inimitable Molly Meyers, the reporter he'd made famous. His impulse was to answer and tell her everything, but the remnants of professionalism cautioned him against it. At this stage, he was unsure whether the details wouldn't just damage the case and allow the killer to sink back into the vile recesses of the dark web from whence he'd emerged.

Somebody shoved a polystyrene cup of black coffee into his hands as he sat half out of the passenger seat of Fanta's car. He looked up to see the grim face of Superintendent Reynolds, dressed in a dark blue puffer jacket, his breath coming in wisps from the cold air.

"You sure she was dead?" were the first words out of his mouth.

Garrick nodded.

Reynolds registered more shock than Fanta had. "And the ID we have on this killer?"

"Kars Ikigai. That's all we have."

Garrick nodded again. "The only people who could possibly identify him are both dead - Kontos and Smith. The

Ukrainian claims he never met him. He was just a bogeyman on the Internet."

"We'll need to organise a press conference."

Garrick sighed and rubbed his eyes. He wasn't in the mood to speak to anyone.

"I don't think it should be you." Garrick looked thankfully at the Super. "The press knows you too well. They know your career, your track record. There's a chance they'll put some sensational spin on it that we simply do not need right now. I'm going to do it and keep it short and simple." Reynolds didn't know what else to say, but then added, "Chib's next of kin need to be told."

The thought of that task felt like a wrecking ball to Garrick's chest, which reminded him that he must have broken a rib or two in the fall. Despite his reluctance, he would have to submit to the paramedics soon.

"I'll do it. She just got married. They were just approved for adoption," he said, the last coming out as a sob.

He put his head in his hands as another sob coursed through his body, and he almost welcomed the stabbing pains from his ribcage as punishment. Reynolds was not the tactile type, so there was no comforting hand on his shoulder. Garrick's rage and fury were crashing down, replaced by fatigue, self-loathing, and utter hatred.

David knew it was of huge importance to tell her about Chib's fate, but in an act that he could only blame on his own miserable personality, he had delayed every possible second in doing so.

He had submitted to the paramedics - over a dozen small cuts across his face, hands, and neck were tended to, three requiring stitches. But remarkably, two broken ribs on his left-hand side were the most serious injuries sustained.

Then he'd gone home and collapsed crying into Wendy's arms for close to an hour. She almost had to carry him into the shower and helped him wash the matted blood and glass from his hair and scrub his body clean.

Then he had driven to Chib's home in a journey that felt as if it would never end. Even as he rang the bell, he had no real recollection of how he'd got there.

Gwen knew something was wrong the moment she answered the door to David Garrick. The smile on her face vanished at his lack of greeting. He'd first met her at their wedding, which was a lively, joyous affair and a real mix of cultures. Chib's Nigerian family had attended in a riot of colour, whilst Gwen's family, middle-class white conservative from Bristol, had been more reserved, but no less happy. Chib's third police-family had all been there, too. And they'd all got extremely drunk.

Now he was sat in an armchair in Chib's living room, head bowed, hands clasped together, wearing a clean T-shirt and jeans. His whole body shook as he sobbed along with Gwen.

He had to be sketchy on the details and stayed away from graphic descriptions. He'd spoken to grieving families and partners countless times in his career, and it never got easier. When his old DS, whom Chib had replaced, had died, it left him feeling hollow and empty, but at least he'd never had to deal directly with his family. Speaking to Gwen was like stepping over the threshold of intimacy. He was no longer talking about a stranger.

Even talking about the bravery of Chib rushing ahead to protect a victim was difficult. It was a noble act of courage, but Garrick couldn't help feeling sick that she had died protecting one scumbag from another. For him, that left a bitter taste that fuelled a growing desire to punish the killer.

A few times in his life, he had come face to face with the most grotesque parody of humanity he could imagine, and that had included his own sister, who had died in front of him. Yet somehow, Chib's death felt infinitely more personal.

Gwen showed him pictures of the young girl they'd planned to adopt, which had the effect of turning Garrick's heart to a slab of vengeful stone. Suddenly, he didn't want to be here. There was nothing he could say to take away Gwen's pain, and with every wasted second, Kars Ikigai was getting away with murder.

He tried to offer the services of a specially trained officer to help Gwen deal with the pain. She declined with a shake of the head and a look of courage he'd never possessed.

With an intense pain crushing his chest - whether it was his ribs or the fury burning in his heart - David Garrick had only one mission. To find Kars Ikigai.

The only justice he could conceive of was to murder the son of a bitch.

Chapter Twenty-Seven

Even in the direst of cases, the mood in the office had retained a level of grim humour that combated the horrors they faced. But now the atmosphere was oppressive. There was no small talk, just the shuffling of papers and feet, soft utterances when they were forced to talk to the civilian staff still helping out with the admin, and quiet phone calls that were now conducted with heads held in one hand as they sat at their desks in an attempt to avoid eye contact with one another.

Garrick's hand wouldn't stop shaking when he pinned Chib's ID photo to the board. The image of her peering down at everybody was heartbreaking. Even though he'd seen her mutilated body with his own eyes, some wild part of him was trying to convince him that she was still alive.

This also marked the first time he'd seen Fanta since leaving the crime scene. He didn't recall whether he or she had left first, but since she had stood in the living room looking at the remains of the carnage inside, he hadn't heard a word from her.

She'd entered the office with a nod of acknowledgement, her head bowed. She was wrapped in an oversized black jumper. One part of Garrick that was still playing detective noted that she arrived thirty-five minutes after DC Sean Wilkes, with whom she lived. He didn't have the energy to try and digest what that indicated.

Of course, everybody knew what had happened, but Garrick still had the duty of laying out the facts as he stood at the board, hands clasped together, his head bowed as he solemnly recounted events, pausing only to inhale long, slow breaths to repress rising panic, as his therapist had long ago instructed him to do.

The thought of his therapist, who was killed, sank its teeth into Garrick's soul. He'd felt a bond with Dr Amy Harman as she delved into his darkest secrets. She'd meant a great deal to him; so much so that he'd even named his daughter in her honour, although he'd never admit that to Wendy.

He began to feel that everybody he cared about - from Dr Harman to his best friend, who turned out to be the head of a killing network - right down to his two detective sergeants, who'd lost their lives in the line of duty, and then his own sister, was dying.

It was a trail of death and despair where he was the only common factor.

Had he brought this upon Chib? He realised he'd fallen silent for far too long, and everybody was staring at him. He had to put aside dark, self-destructive thoughts. He looked around the room, realising that DCI Kane had quietly joined them at the back of the room. He closed the door to block the sounds of the corridor beyond, and Garrick saw the news of Chib etched upon Kane's face too. She had worked closely with him before Garrick, and was highly well-liked and trusted by the Met.

With an increasingly dry mouth, Garrick brought everyone up to speed, right up to talking to Gwen.

It was Fanta's turn to update the team next, and she sat in a chair with her feet raised on the edge of the seat, her arms wrapped protectively around her knees. She slowly picked up from Garrick leaving her in the kitchen. How, fearing that the killer was still inside, she had dragged the plainclothes cop into the garden to deal with his wound, hoping to keep him alive.

She'd heard the loud thump of the window giving way and Garrick crashing onto the car on the other side of the house, but, fearful that she was an open target, she'd remained quiet and still - aware that the slightest move would trigger the garden light and betray her presence to the killer.

In the four or five minutes of Garrick being unconscious, she hadn't seen any movement within the house or heard the killer flee with Chib's body, presumably in a vehicle that would have been parked on the road somewhere outside. There was a possibility that she may have heard the engine turn over in the darkness, but for the life of her, she couldn't recall.

However, there was one sliver of light Garrick had to offer, which was that the plainclothes officer was in a stable condition, and the doctor had suggested that it was down to Fanta administering first aid. Otherwise, he would have bled out on the kitchen floor.

From the statement that they'd managed to extract from the cop, he had remained outside until Chib arrived, and they moved in together, armed only with Tasers. When they found the kitchen door open and heard Kontos's screams from the living room, they stormed into the room with Chib leading the way.

Details became vague. The lights had gone out. The assailant disarmed Chib and used her own Taser against her. He remembered that much. Then he remembered being struck in the side by the blade and staggering back into the hallway towards the kitchen.

Forensics were still all over the site, and the manhunt had yielded nothing of use so far, especially as they had no descriptions of the vehicle or the killer. Superintendent Reynolds had given a subdued press conference, and Molly Meyers had grown frustrated with the lack of information, so had left half a dozen messages across voicemail, email, text, and WhatsApp, on Garrick's phone. All of which he ignored.

The briefing circled around to Harry. Whilst he spoke, his eyes kept drifting towards Chib's empty desk. To his credit, his voice never broke, but his face could have been Botoxed for all the emotion it showed.

Finally, it circled back to Garrick to wind things up, and he looked questioningly at DCI Kane, whom the others hadn't even noticed was there. Kane looked around the group and nodded solemnly. This wasn't the place for well-meaning platitudes that often were for the benefit of the one giving them rather than the ones receiving them. Garrick was very much against the usual sorry-for-your-loss comments, even though they were the glue of social convention that meant he was living in a civilised, empathetic world.

"I'm hoping you're here with an ID on Boris," Garrick said, straight to business. "I know he claims never to have seen Kars Ikigai, but to be honest, I don't believe him."

Kane raised his hands, palms upwards, in defeat. "I come bearing worse news than that. Last night - three hours before this," he gestured towards the room in general, "the transport moving Boris from Swaleside was attacked."

That got the first confused reaction from the room. Kane just allowed it to die down of its own accord.

"It was a violent assault on the transport officers. Remarkably, nobody was killed. Injuries were kept down to a minimum because there was the use of non-lethal weapons."

He looked meaningfully at Garrick. Boris may have been ruthless in executing Ian Smith in an improvised hit-and-run, but there was a bizarre, twisted pride that the mercenaries employed when it came to minimising collateral damage. Garrick knew that even the most horrendous villains had their own bizarre codes of conduct. It was widely touted around the digital forensic community that some of the best customer service on the planet often came from those selling drugs or weaponry on the dark web. The value of repeat business was paramount. Or perhaps it was because they knew that their customer base were the sort of people who complained with a bullet rather than a strongly-worded email.

"He escaped three hours before Kontos was killed?" Garrick said flatly.

Kane nodded. "That's about the size of it. Now, I would immediately jump to the conclusion that Kars Ikigai and this Boris were one and the same, except, of course, you've seen both of them together."

Garrick nodded, but then a thought struck him - a detail he hadn't noticed before, one he couldn't readily ascribe relevance to, but it had to be voiced.

"Although when I saw Boris, he was running out of the back door when Ikigai was running out of the front door."

Fanta looked up. "He was running away from trouble!"

Garrick chewed on that. "At the time, I assumed it's because he thought we were additional attackers."

He was conflicted. Boris had been incarcerated and had been switched on enough to know that Garrick had been using Kontos as bait. That was part of Garrick's plan - to spread the word as much as possible that Kontos was under house arrest in the hope that Kars Ikigai would hear. He just hadn't expected the retribution to be so harsh and swift.

Garrick's brow creased as he recalled. "He was about to shoot me. He raised his gun, right at me... and then he hesitated. And for that, he caught a knife in his chest that punctured his lung."

Kane looked at him levelly. "You saw Ikigai throw it? Are you sure it wasn't Kontos?"

Garrick hesitated, his recollection messy. "Kontos's arm was severed off. No, I don't buy that."

It wasn't uncommon in any investigation for facts to twist, turn, and become confusing. Yet he had a hard time believing that Boris had been anything but truthful. Still, the timing of his escape at least indicated that there was some possible connection between him and Ikigai.

"So now we have a double manhunt underway," Kane said, breaking the tension in the room.

There was nothing more to be said, and everybody turned back to their duties, with Kane offering to help if they needed him. Garrick knew he'd be a great asset, but his natural inclination was to refuse. Having Kane around somehow threw salt on the raw wound.

Before leaving, Kane cornered Garrick in the small room they used for brewing tea and attempted small talk. Garrick couldn't find anything to say. What he wanted to do was shout and scream at the world. He was saved from the fate of small talk when he received a message from the coroner dealing with Alexander Kontos.

Lately, Garrick had started to avoid attending any autopsies. He was a seasoned DCI, so it wasn't so much staring at the dead that bothered him - it was the thought of the humanity that had been stolen from the departed. But when it came to Alexander Kontos, he almost felt delight in verifying that the bastard was dead.

He was surprised when Fanta timidly asked if she could come along. He could think of no reason to confine her to the office. Kane also wanted to tag along, which was annoying, but he was mindful that other people mourned in their own way.

Despite the chill in the mortuary, Garrick had to take his coat off and found himself sweating as the coroner lifted back the sheet from Kontos and folded it just over his groin. The incision from the chest down across the stomach was unmissable; almost half the chest was missing. The skin had blackened a little with the blood gone. The once vivid red flesh was now pale and sickly. Bone and internal organs were visible. It looked like a page from a medical textbook.

The three detectives watched stonily as the coroner used a metal rod to indicate areas. "This wound was made by a very sharp blade. I believe it came in here." He indicated the navel. "With one single violent swipe up. To give you an idea of the sharpness of this blade, it cleaved through bone. That requires immense power or a very, very sharp blade."

"Indicating somebody who is passionate about looking after their weapons," said Kane.

"Absolutely. A sword of great value, not one of those cheap things bought off the Internet. That was conducted when he was standing. He was found seated in a chair, which is where he started to bleed out, but would have probably been unable to move due to shock. He was alive for several minutes as he was essentially butchered."

Garrick frowned. "What do you mean, butchered?"

"His liver was carefully removed. His pancreas too."

Fanta flinched as she recalled, "The plainclothes cop said he heard screams when he and Chib ran inside. He was being vivisected."

The coroner nodded. "That's precisely what happened. Both organs are missing too."

Garrick's thoughts tumbled back to Andrea's cannibal lecture and talk of trophy hunting. He felt sickness in his stomach rise as he thought about the fate of Chib.

The coroner, ignorant of the mood, kept his tone upbeat and looked pensive. "Those organs were cut with smaller knives, not the sword. But very clinical blades. The killer knew exactly what they were doing. It takes a lot of skill to do it this well."

"Medical background?" Fanta postulated. Every piece of information went somewhere to build a profile.

"And the way the muscle had been cut near the heart, suggests that he was going for that next."

"Before he was disturbed," Garrick muttered ominously. He found the information difficult to process, but with each morsel of news came fresh horrors about why Kars Ikigai had taken Chib.

Chapter Twenty-Eight

It was twenty-four hours after DS Chibarameze Okon had been murdered and her body taken. The edge of the manhunt was beginning to blunt. Specialist dog units had been deployed in the area and had picked up a trail that led three hundred yards from the house to where it was assumed Kars Ikigai had parked his vehicle.

There were signs of footprints in the muddy verge surrounding the tarmac road, but they were not useful. Nor was there enough data in tyre marks to identify the car, as the partial indents in the mud had been worn away by the damp weather. It was all very unhelpful when it came to an urgent manhunt.

The mood in the office soured further. Lack of sleep and increased tension created a veneer of irritability across the close-knit team. Garrick was able to hold it together enough that he didn't criticise their behaviour, because that would only lead to deeper animosity at a time they couldn't afford it.

Despite the press conference and a surge in national interest regarding an officer killed in the line of duty, the public had nothing to report. The late hour was indeed a witching time for crime - a period when most things could silently slip under the radar, unobserved. But there was always the promise that a single witness could hold the keys to solving everything. However, that single witness had yet to materialise.

Superintendent Reynolds insisted on constant updates as he had been the face of the news conference and now found himself under their laser focus. Garrick had assiduously avoided any contact with Molly Meyers, so Reynolds was now facing pressure from both her and his superiors for not generating any progress.

David's communication with Wendy was brief, but as ever, she was wonderfully understanding. Garrick felt like a spectator in his own life when he was told that moving day was looming, but currently, he couldn't think of anything less interesting than his own domestic affairs.

He would drive home at night to find his girls sleeping and be forced to kip on the sofa, surrounded by packed boxes, because he didn't want to wake Wendy as he broke out into a fever, as the nightmares of discovering Chib's body played remorselessly. With each iteration, he awoke convinced that Chib's dead gaze was becoming more accusing.

Searching for clues in his dreams was a sign of desperation, yet it was proving to be his only respite from his self-inflicted punishment - a respite that was telling him that there must be something he'd overlooked. Not because the dead were calling from beyond the grave - he'd lost far too many people to believe in an afterlife, even though that was something Fanta was beginning to discuss more. Everybody had their own way of dealing with the inevitable unknown.

Yet the sudden itch that the answer was in front of him drove him into the office whilst it was still dark. He found DC Sean Wilkes asleep across two desks, covered by his coat. The exhausted man had worked through the night, reassessing every fragment of evidence he could in the hope of seeing something new.

Garrick had been monitoring case updates on his phone, so hadn't overlooked anything. Kane's initial stream of updates regarding Boris's escape had dwindled into nothing, and he was now beginning to side with the general belief that Boris and Kars Ikigai had been working together.

If that were true, he knew it would be almost impossible to forgive himself for not spotting it earlier. But as it stood, the suspicions didn't affect the shambolic lack of progress they were making, which was the state that had dogged the case from the very beginning. It also made one thing clear to him: with Fanta about to chase her promotion and Chib no longer with them, this was the end of his department. All the speculation about retiring that he'd shared with Harry suddenly had a taste of reality.

At his computer, he aimlessly scrolled through lists of witness interviews and folders containing countless photographs without pause or focus on any one thing. His hand drifted over the mouse in a sort of free association. Yet perhaps there was still a spark of the detective alive in him, because when he stopped, he was hovering over the folder containing Ian Smith's details.

Smith had been the one who'd contacted Kars Ikigai to set him onto Alexander Kontos. In desperation, Kontos had had Smith killed by Boris's hand - a fact that still bothered him when it came to the Ukrainian and Ikigai being in cahoots.

He played through the CCTV footage cut together to follow Smith's progress from his office. Fanta and Garrick tailed him like a pair of Keystone Cops. Smith stood at the crossing, looking around before waving for attention. Then he stepped into the road and was struck by the vehicle. Four different camera angles covered the moment, including one that showed Boris's stolen Land Rover skidding around a corner and accelerating away.

It was at that exact moment that the glaringly obvious question struck Garrick: who had Ian Smith been waving to?

He played the clips repeatedly. His first assumption was that he'd been hailing a cab, but why hadn't he done it earlier? And the more he watched, the more obvious it was that Smith was searching for somebody before giving a familiar wave. Yet none of the cameras covered who he was waving to. That person lay tantalisingly off-screen, which, right now, to Garrick, was the edge of infinity.

He called DCI Kane immediately, waking him as he outlined the need to get footage from the wider area. Whatever strings Kane pulled, it was to his credit, and ninety minutes later he called back, his voice trembling with urgency.

"I've added a new clip to the database. Check it out now."

By this time, Fanta and Harry had arrived at the office to join him and Sean, and they all stood behind Garrick as he opened the file and double-clicked the video within. The footage came from a different CCTV camera. Smith wasn't visible, but there was a figure at the corner of a building, keeping close to the wall, with a mobile phone pressed against their ear as they looked off-screen and waved. Then they reacted, lowering the phone and staring at something before quickly turning and walking off.

"The bus," said Fanta. "There was a bus that cut across the background. Play this and the one of Smith side by side."

Garrick positioned both videos side by side. By the time he'd started them both playing, they were a second out of sync, but it was immediately obvious what Fanta meant. As Smith was struck, a red bus passed in the background as it turned right. Just over a second later, seen from a different angle, the same bus turned behind the figure. It was enough for them all to get a sense of geography. Smith and the figure were standing across the junction, facing one another.

"Holy shit," said Kane, who was still on the phone and had done exactly what Fanta had instructed. "Have you slowed it down?"

Fanta nudged Garrick aside and seized control of the mouse. She slowed the playback speed and zoomed in. The image was clear enough to make out a face. It was Asian and well-defined even with a jogging hood partially covering the ears, but the profile was clear enough.

They had a video of the mysterious Kars Ikigai, and Garrick hated himself that they'd always had it, unseen and nestled amongst pointless evidence.

Chapter Twenty-Nine

Everybody made mistakes, and David Garrick would be the first to acknowledge that his highly lauded, successful career was built on the foundations of wildly inaccurate guesses, dumb hunches, and costly mistakes. That was the harsh reality of a job where even a two per cent success rate could save a life, and be recognised statistically as a win.

Right now, the mysterious Kars Ikigai, who'd been nothing more than a ghost on the Internet and a phantom footnote in the investigation, had succumbed to the same human foible of making a mistake.

It had been unspoken, but there was a sense that the suspect really was a ghost, an enigma, a will-o'-the-wisp that would never be caught. The annals of crime were filled with such figures, the most infamous arguably being Jack the Ripper, whose legacy was chronicled graphically in newspapers across the country - newspapers that Garrick compared to the same sewer system as today's Internet.

Garrick was using his mobile so heavily that he had to

tether himself to his desk and not move so it could be recharged. His first call had been to Superintendent Reynolds, stating that they had a match, and he was going to use every resource at his disposal to identify the killer. It hadn't been a request for fiscal authorisation - it had been a simple statement of fact.

Meanwhile, both Fanta and Kane put the picture through the Police National Database, looking for a facial match. With over twenty million images stored there, Garrick wasn't going to hold his breath.

Kane had made a virtual introduction to the Detective Inspector in charge of the Ian Smith incident for the City of London Police, and they were now strategically pooling their resources to make an identification.

Garrick then got onto the phone, navigating through the raft of departments and flexing his authority in ways he normally didn't, to get them access to the passport database, which, between passport holders and immigration records, held in excess of one hundred and fifty million stored photographs that the AI algorithms could match.

Within an hour, the image of Kars Ikigai was pumping through the system as the retrospective facial recognition operation built up momentum. Around the country, he imagined warehouse-sized data facilities on the verge of overheating as they churned through the request. That translated to a tiny scroll bar on his monitor, moving a pixel at a time as it processed the results.

Despite the technology, this wasn't the fastest system, especially as it was checking against a photograph that was below optimal quality. It was only their ability to narrow down the ethnic group that was giving them any leeway whatsoever.

Coffee was imbibed, and anxiety levels increased in line with the progress bar. It was two and a half hours before they got their first batch of hits.

"Got some matches coming through, Guv," Fanta said excitedly, her hands shaking as she accessed the computer programme, revealing one thousand and four possible hits. Thumbnail images started to appear on a grid with the image of Kars Ikigai to one side so they could compare. Garrick suddenly felt a cold stab of desperation in his chest. At first, casual glance, he would have considered almost all the matches to be perfect. The computer certainly had.

He was unable to stop swearing as he kicked the foot of Fanta's desk in irritation. But his young Detective Constable was far from beaten. She was already scrolling through her phone to make a call. She sprang to her feet when the line connected, and a few minutes later returned to her desk, beaming, as more images were slowly added to the possible matches.

"Why are you grinning?" said Garrick. Despite the tension, he was unable to prevent Fanta's smile from infecting him.

"She's on her way in," Fanta said simply. "Louise Mather." Garrick shook his head blankly. "She's one of the best super recognisers in the country."

Super recognisers were the closest thing the authorities had to the X-Men. Garrick considered he was being charitable when Harry had compared them to freaks. They were people who quite literally never forgot a face, able to consistently outperform the most advanced facial recognition algorithms. He'd read about their abilities, but he'd never understood the process behind it. And the few super recognisers he'd met didn't either. In fact, they were often amused that the rest of the population were unable to see the glaring differences between identical twins, even though these beloved freaks made up less than two per cent of the population.

And typically, Fanta had one on speed dial.

Louise Mather was a bookish, slim woman in her thirties who ran her own hairdressing business and assisted the police on the side. By the time she arrived, the search was already sixty-eight per cent through. She accepted a tea from Harry, although her face pinched after the first sip, and it remained untouched as she slowly scrolled through the three thousand, eight hundred and two images that the AI system thought were a perfect match.

Garrick and Fanta quietly left the room and anxiously waited, whilst Sean and Harry, who were monitoring the more prosaic side of the search, had reverted to their morose attitudes to report that there was nothing new on the investigation. They'd hit another wall. Sean had spent hours widening the CCTV search to backtrack Kars Ikigai's movements, but the killer seemed to know exactly which streets were covered by cameras and had simply vanished.

It was also very notable that Sean and Fanta were not speaking. That pissed Garrick off, and when he glanced at Fanta, she'd read his mind and sharply shook her head, encouraging him to shut the hell up. Garrick may have been feeling low, but not low enough to provoke Fanta's wrath.

Thirty-six minutes later, Louise stepped from the office and politely waved for attention. "Excuse me?" she called.

Garrick leapt to his feet. "I'm sorry, do you need the bathroom? Another drink?"

"No, I've finished."

He blinked in surprise. "Finished?"

She nodded and stepped back into the room as Fanta and Garrick joined her.

"We're casting the net wider for better CCTV images," he said, instantly apologetic, noticing that the search was now a whopping seventy-one per cent complete. "I think in the next hour and a half, we might have everything the system has to throw at us."

Louise sat back in her seat and smiled politely as she nodded. "No need. I've found a match already."

Garrick suddenly felt light-headed. Two hundred people had been added to the list since she'd started, and the computer was still churning, yet here was this mild-mannered woman calmly scrolling through a database of passport photos and CCTV images, some of which were awful quality, until she had settled on one single photograph. She double-clicked it, and a full passport image appeared.

The name on it was not Kars Ikigai, but the similarity to the person on the CCTV image was unmistakable. Then again, Garrick had thought the other thousand-plus images could all be identical too.

His mouth went dry, and he found it difficult to swallow as he found his words. "How certain are you?" he said, his eyes staring at the image.

"I feel very confident. Of course, I could be mistaken, but this is a match," she said with a confident smile.

Garrick's gut instinct could scarcely believe her, but his professional one knew he shouldn't doubt her. Even with another quarter of the search still to be completed, they had identified the killer.

Chapter Thirty

The immediate impulse was to act with immediate urgency, and there was nothing David Garrick wanted more than to kick down the suspect's door and charge in to mete out justice with a baseball bat. He had to remind himself that he was the one who was supposed to uphold the law and behave flawlessly at this critical juncture, with an arrest lying tantalisingly within reach. There was no place for emotions.

They had barely ushered Louise Mather out of the door before the operations room was reconfigured to plan a raid on the suspect's home, all gleaned from the passport ID. Printers were busy spewing out maps of the area, and every available resource was tapping into what was known about the subject. For once, having Kent, the Met, and the City of London forces all working cohesively together was proving to be frictionless. The fact that the suspect's address was in Surrey meant roping in a fourth constabulary.

Meanwhile, Garrick blustered into his super's office,

dragging Reynolds out of a meeting which seemed to consist of more laughter than a typical meeting should, and stressed the need for a search warrant from the magistrate's court, issued under PACE - the Police and Criminal Evidence Act - that would give him full authority to charge in with an armed team. And they needed it by the end of the day.

The firearms unit was put on standby, and were now working directly under the auspices of DCI Kane, who Garrick had to admit was better qualified than he was when it came to gun-toting crowd control. A large TV had been wheeled in from another department, and Fanta and the station's IT technician had cobbled together a large Zoom meeting to discuss the raid.

Surprise was essential. Kars Ikigai - which was the name they were still using until the passport identity that had been selected could be verified - had proved to be a slippery customer, always one step ahead. With such attention to detail, Garrick found it unlikely that a police raid hadn't factored into the villain's thinking at some point. They had to expect extreme resistance.

Dawn raids were conducted to throw suspects off balance, confuse them, and ensure they didn't have a chance to destroy vital evidence. The operation had been conjured out of nothing, yet the armed team leading it had been training their entire careers for exactly these circumstances. Once the property had been analysed using maps, architectural plans, Google Street View, and every other available resource, they formed a watertight plan to lock the location down.

It was towards the end of the business day when the PACE warrant came through, which meant it was now all a matter of waiting until it was time to strike. However, the one curveball still in play was the fact that they didn't know whether Kars Ikigai would be home.

Surrey Constabulary sent a pair of plainclothes officers to casually drive by. Although it was critical that they didn't raise any suspicion, they reported lights on but didn't see anybody.

By nightfall, there was nothing more that could be done. The civilian support workers went home, but the team were too wired, and decided to try and catch some sleep in the office until it was time to roll out.

Garrick was convinced sleep wouldn't come - but that was the very last thought he had as he fell into a dreamless slumber. He awoke with Harry nudging him and offering a steaming black coffee.

"Time to get wheels on the ground," he said.

Everybody else was awake and eating stale pastries that Harry had picked up from a twenty-four-hour petrol station. It was almost a sixty-mile drive to Egham in Surrey - a delightful English town in Runnymede, according to the map, steeped in history and smothered with middle-class decadence. And home to a killer.

They drove in an unmarked police van, with Harry volunteering to drive it because Fanta was regarded as a menace behind the wheel. The journey was conducted in silence, and the team rendezvoused on a quiet retail estate three miles from the suspect's house. The place was already alive with activity - a dozen vehicles comprising the firearms unit, an ambulance, four tactical vans, and a police dog handler with the hound excitedly sniffing around the other officers. There were several more unmarked police cars and five sporting Surrey Constabulary decals.

It looked as if the entire team had descended upon the

Costa and the local petrol station, because they were all carrying cups.

DCI Kane introduced the Surrey representative. "This is DI Fellows from Surrey Constabulary."

Garrick recognised her from the earlier Zoom call. "Thanks for helping to put all this together," he said earnestly.

They went over the plan one more time. The armed response team would move in first, battering the door down, as the suspect was likely to be armed and dangerous. Then Fellows would lead the team in, as it was Surrey's turf. Garrick wasn't concerned about taking any credit or who did what - he just wanted to be one of the first in the room, and Fellows was happy enough to have Garrick by her side.

The only thing left, as dawn approached and the unstoppable fingers of first light turned the sky from inky black to dark blue, was for Garrick and his team to don bulletproof vests with the word 'POLICE' clearly marked. Then everybody psyched up in their vehicles.

It sounded like the starting grid at Silverstone as all the engines rattled to life. Only the armed response unit's new electric vehicles made no noise as they took the lead. The convoy powered towards the unsuspecting sleepy village - no sirens, no bluster, just an ominous convoy cutting through the English country roads like a shark through dark waters.

Garrick's heart was pounding as everybody took up positions yards from the target.

It was an old house, set back from what passed as the main road, overlooked by nobody and with minimal traffic ever passing by. It lay just beyond the range of the streetlights, with trees laced together to form an arched entrance.

It was the sort of place that sent out unwelcome vibes and warned trick-or-treaters away.

Dominating the driveway was a large Mercedes Sprinter that had been converted into a mobile burger van, with simple livery declaring 'Great Roadside Food'. It was the sort of truck commonly seen at festivals, fairgrounds, or lay-bys across the country, bringing homemade fast food to hungry punters.

Garrick watched the assault team close in. He heard three loud thumps as the front door was rammed open, and the team pushed inside, weapons raised, with shouts of "Armed police!"

The shouting continued but with no signs of scuffling. DI Fellows indicated that Garrick, and the rest of the team, should follow her in. They paused at the end of the driveway, where they waited until they heard the distinctive yell of "Clear!"

Then Garrick and Fellows sprinted forward to see what they had found, only to be greeted by an armed response team officer walking out, shaking his head.

"Nobody's home."

Garrick felt a crushing sense of defeat clutch his stomach. "You sure?"

"Unless they're playing hide and seek. We'll pull the place apart just in case," he assured Garrick.

Garrick stood aside as the dog was led inside, the handler pulled forward by the canine enthusiastically sniffing the ground hungrily for a scent.

Garrick approached the food truck, wondering if they'd made some terrible mistake. The sounds around him blended into a hubbub of activity as the officers moved in to search the house. He was drawn towards the wide garden, which was unkempt with dying bushes and knee-high grass. Trees at the back blocked access to the park. But it offered no outbuildings or places to hide.

He was about to turn back when something caught his attention. There was a pile of bricks in the grass - nothing unusual, but there was something about the positioning that bothered him. It took him a moment to work out what it was. There was a patch of gravel behind the Mercedes that felt as if a garage had once stood there. A garage that had since been demolished.

He moved closer to the bricks, and as he did, he became aware of a warm breeze against his hand, countering the chilly morning air. It was like feeling a warm current in the ocean. He swayed his hand back and forth, zeroing in towards the bricks - closer and closer, until in the dim light he saw a letterbox-like opening protected by a mesh grill. It wasn't a random stack of masonry - it was a cover for a ventilation unit that was gently blowing out air.

His head snapped back to the driveway as he slowly imagined the footprint of where a large garage would have stood and circled around to the back of the van, spotting a soft, contoured edge in the gravel. A set of unnaturally straight lines that were barely perceptible if you weren't looking for them.

He moved to the back of the Mercedes, and knelt. He prodded the gravel; his fingers instantly touched metal. He wiped the gravel away, revealing a tarnished black metal handle poking from the floor. Already wearing gloves to prevent contaminating the scene, he gripped the handle and heaved.

It was heavy, but there was some give along the lines in

the gravel. It was a trapdoor. He changed tactic and used both hands to grip it, and remembered to keep his back straight and bend from his knees. He heaved again.

A hatch suddenly opened, aided by a pneumatic hinge, so it locked in place at head height, revealing a steep set of steps sharply angling down. The trapdoor itself was thickly insulated, and, now open, he could feel a rush of cold air escaping from below.

Without thinking, he was drawn slowly down the steps, his hand reaching for his phone to activate the flashlight. The steps ended in a short corridor with plastic hanging strips, forming an insulating barrier. He could hear the dull thump of cooling fans and a blast of frigid air that caught his breath.

Drawn on by morbid curiosity, he pushed the plastic drapes aside with both hands and stepped into a garage-sized freezing room that had been built where once a large double garage had stood above it.

On one wall, a set of metal shelves were stacked with boxes of frozen burgers, bacon, meats, and pre-cut chips. But he was drawn to slabs of meat hanging from large butcher's hooks attached to the ceiling on chains. He took a step, his light shining over one which looked like a section of beef straight out of an abattoir.

As he readjusted his light, he froze in horror, his own heart turning to ice as he saw two figures suspended on hooks.

One was just the torso and head of a powerful black man. His arms and legs had been removed; his flesh perfectly frozen. Garrick might not have had a name, but the distinctive Maori tattoos across his shoulders and up his neck matched the artwork on the severed hand. This was Boris's missing companion.

The next figure stopped his heart. It was Chib. She was completely naked. A hook thrust through her spine to hang her. Her chest torn open.

Garrick dropped to his knees and howled with an uncontrollable bellow of rage and sorrow.

Chapter Thirty-One

Not all cases could be solved.

That was the harsh truth David Garrick was forced to accept. Kars Ikigai had slipped through his fingers three times. It was almost enough for him to start believing that the killer was nothing more than a ghost. Except now they had built a profile of the killer. It was far from comprehensive and had so many holes in it that it threatened to collapse under the weight of the investigation, yet there was the outline of a flesh and blood person there.

A search of Kars's house revealed a wide network of cameras covering every possible approach to the property. There were over a dozen spread out down the streets, covering a three-hundred-yard diameter, which was evidently enough to give the felon a chance to flee the moment the police had arrived. For the second time, a huge manhunt rolled into action, this time across Surrey.

But that had been a fruitless endeavour. Garrick resigned himself to bringing reporter Molly Meyers into the fold, which brought with it BBC News's prestigious resources. A nationwide manhunt had turned up nothing. Forensics had insisted that the bodies remain for almost the whole day as they swept the freezer unit hidden under the driveway. None of the team could bear to watch when Chib's body was removed, along with the unknown Ukrainian Special Ops soldier, and taken to the morgue.

DI Fellows established a new incident room in Guildford, falling under the auspices of the Surrey force, where evidence from the house started to amass. Sean and Harry had returned to Maidstone, whilst Garrick and Fanta remained to coordinate the investigation with Fellows. Garrick was privately relieved to have his team fragmented, as they had barely exchanged a word with one another since the raid.

No computer or phone had been found at the scene. Presumably, Ikigai had fled with them, along with passports or any further identifying documents. It painted a picture of somebody used to relocating their life at a moment's notice. Walking around the house, Garrick had the feeling that it was nothing more than a shell - a place the killer lived behind the facade of a fake personality.

Forensics had revealed multiple fragments of DNA in the freezer locker. Up to six other victims had been brought here, and what turned Garrick's stomach was the evidence that human DNA had been found on the shelves along with burgers, bacon, and other meats that were sold out of the truck. The truck had been a popular stop on the A-road around the area for truckers looking to get a cheaper meal than the extortionate prices the service stations charged. The food quality was celebrated on social media, and it gained a cult-like mystical reputation, offering delicious food before vanishing, sometimes for weeks at a time, and turning up elsewhere. It was a business run on passion, not profit.

And fragments of the same human DNA from the locker were also found in the truck.

The evidence painted a vague contemporary Sweeney Todd-like figure disposing of their victims in the lay-bys of Surrey. The refrigeration unit had been built two years prior, and neighbours vaguely recalled that Ikigai had done most of the work with a small mechanical digger and a lot of effort.

The huge quantity of leads was slowly reaching their own conclusions - some were dead ends, some lingering with the promise of a bigger mystery, and a few others resulted in hard facts. Kane's search for Boris had likewise resulted in no success, but he was building a case that he and Ikigai had been working together, but how and for what purpose remained obscure.

Garrick was dubious about that, but Kane and Fanta both pointed to the fact that Ian Smith had been in communication with Kars, and essentially been lured to a busy corner where Boris was able to kill him in a hit-and-run. Fanta used Garrick's own prejudice against coincidences to get the point across. He begrudgingly accepted the point, but a part of him still struggled to accept it.

The passwords they'd obtained by spying on Alexander Kontos's house had worked a charm across all his devices, opening his world of fraud and heavy-handed business techniques, although the only ones that seemed to have led to murder were Councillor Freeman and Ian Smith's business partner. They knew that Freeman had been killed by Kars, and the assumption was that Smith's business partner had probably been roughed up a little too successfully by Boris and his crew.

Details of the mysterious Greek mobster, Odysseus, to whom Kontos owed money, were shared with the Greek police, but Garrick didn't hear whether there was any further identification. It was out of his jurisdiction.

However, it was when they finally managed to access Ian Smith's computer files that they discovered how the frustrated businessman had been used by practically everyone around him. Smith had initiated contact with the assassin, guided by a mysterious message from none other than Odysseus. It seemed that the Greek, like all good mob bosses, extracted revenge at arm's length.

Knowing that it was Smith who had destroyed Alexander Kontos's plans, Odysseus had approached him under the guise of a fellow comrade who'd been burnt by Kontos and urged him to hire the hitman to 'teach him a lesson.' He had even paid the fees to Smith in untraceable crypto. It had been enough to put a clear firewall between the Greek mobster and Kontos. Smith had desperately thirsted for revenge, so he went along with the sham. To his credit, it appeared he was trying to call the assassin off from fulfilling the hit, perhaps after a crisis of conscience following his meeting with Garrick and Fanta.

All those details lay in a large pile of potential evidence. Every vault of evidence for a criminal case had such things, which were either too vague to justify in court, or far too complicated that they threatened to confuse jurors when there were more digestible motives to hand. A conviction relied on the most solid, unshakeable foundations of easily digestible facts. It was the simple reason why criminals were convicted on only a few aspects of their broader crimes, the rest of which would officially have to go unpunished.

With numerous leads painting a picture of guilt, it felt to the team that it was all for nothing, if the only person they could arrest had most likely fled the country.

Yet inevitably, life went on, and it started with the funeral.

Chapter Thirty-Two

Chibarameze Okon's funeral had turned into a grand affair, even though Gwen had wanted something small and solemn. Chib's family had flown in from Nigeria en masse; representatives from every police department the case had touched wanted to show their solidarity with a big turnout from the Met. And of course, the Kent Constabulary were there to honour one of their finest. On top of that, driven by Molly Meyers, there was nationwide interest in the story, in which she had painted Chib as a heroic cop, a role model people should aspire to.

That was the only sentiment Garrick could agree with. The rest of it, in his view, was pointless noise. He'd rather spend his own private moments alone, grieving over her. He hated that Gwen had asked him to speak in the church. He'd spent days preparing the speech and presumed he'd read it out, but for the life of him, he couldn't remember a single word, nor whether he'd been able to deliver it without his voice cracking.

He stood graveside, several layers back from Chib's

grieving family, as the coffin was lowered into the grave. As the ceremony was completed and people lined up to toss in handfuls of earth, he noticed that Fanta had been standing at his side the whole time, dressed sombrely in a black suit as she had been for the last two weeks.

"I heard the exam results came back," he said. She nodded. "And?"

"I passed."

"Congratulations."

Fanta forced a smile, which didn't reach her eyes. "I've been offered a position in Birmingham."

"Congratulations. I'm sure it's well deserved. When do you start?"

A long moment passed before she answered, her eyes fixed on the grave in front of her. "I haven't got back to them yet."

He caught a fleeting glance between her and Sean, who was standing several yards away. In the last few weeks, he had lost track of their relationship, so he couldn't fathom what that meant at all.

And then the funeral was over, and the wake began. Traditionally, it was an event that was supposed to unite grieving friends and family to share heartfelt moments and tales of the deceased. Whilst people picked over food and drinks, Garrick managed a sausage roll and a glass of luke-warm cola before he left without saying a single word to anybody else.

On the trip home, he cried the entire way. Previously, he'd experienced sharp pangs of remorse and brief moments when the tears flowed so hard that he could barely stand. But now this felt like a tsunami of emotions bursting from every pore in his body. And it didn't stop until he arrived home.

Wiping tears from his bloodshot eyes, he stepped into the house.

He navigated around packing boxes, except this was not the cramped terraced house they'd vacated - this was his family's new forever home, as Wendy had enthusiastically christened it. In the two weeks since they'd moved in, he'd barely spent any time here, and there was much still to unpack. The moments he'd been here, and not sleeping, had been taken up obsessively overseeing the installation of a security system that had cameras at every corner and alarms on every window. At the back of his mind, he wondered if he was building a fortress of solitude he would one day never leave. He'd grown increasingly isolated from both his team and his family, but he hoped that by laying Chib to rest, it would bury such feelings alongside her.

But another part of him suspected that the unresolved case would continue to haunt him.

One thing Superintendent Reynolds had insisted on was that the entire team take a two-week holiday to decompress and come to terms with the situation. For once, Garrick had been uncharacteristically greedy and had taken the first opportunity, leaving Harry and Sean to squabble over who should be next.

The first thing Garrick did was take Amy and Wendy fossil hunting on the Isle of Sheppey. The cold breeze blowing across the beach, and the invigorating scent of crashing waves, did wonders to rejuvenate his mind. Walking with his two girls, crouching against the eroding cliff front, pulling out a chunk of rock where he could just see the possible delineation of a prehistoric shell, turned into a moment of elation. His heart sang when Amy's podgy finger traced across the shape with a look of fascination on her face.

For the first time in a long whilst, he felt that he was turning a corner on a new chapter of his life.

It was one a.m., and Garrick wasn't sure why he was awake. A quick check of his phone showed him that the security systems were operational. Straining to listen, he couldn't hear a peep from Amy. Wendy was next to him, sound asleep. She had been the nervous one waking up in the new house, alerted by the slightest noise. He hadn't been sleeping well for months, and tonight was apparently no exception.

He considered closing his eyes, but knew that sleep was out of the question for the next hour. The old urge to clean and restore his fossils was probably the catharsis he needed, except he still hadn't found which box his equipment was in, as Wendy hadn't labelled any of them. In the kitchen, he poured himself a glass of almond milk, drinking half of it to quench his thirst before ambling into the dining room where the remaining boxes had been stacked. He was determined to find his kit.

Instead, he found what had woken him.

"David Garrick... and you were worried we'd never meet again."

Kars Ikigai was seated at the end of the dining table.

Garrick had stared endlessly at the passport photograph Louise Mather had selected. Although he had assumed the name was false, it had led them to the house in Egham. Only because the super recogniser had been certain it was a match, his initial shock that Kars Ikigai was a woman had been overruled. The suspect's Asian features had erred on the feminine side, but it was only by talking to neighbours and people who'd used the burger van that it had cast his doubts away. And yet here she was - a petite, beautiful, Japanese woman, dressed in black. Her hair was tied into a ponytail as she sat cross-legged with a smug look on her face.

Garrick didn't dare move. On her knee, she was cradling Amy. His daughter was blasé to the danger and softly gurgled in pleasure as she was gently bounced.

Garrick couldn't see any weapons, but didn't doubt for a millisecond what the woman's intentions were. On the table in front of her was a plate taken from his kitchen, on which the killer had arranged a small circular portion of meat. She smiled as she tracked his eyes darting between his daughter and the food.

"You and your team caused me a lot of upset, Detective. I had no intention of harming any of you, because there was no sport in it. But you insisted on getting in the way. Please sit down before you fall down." When Garrick didn't move, her voice became icy. "I insist." She rocked Amy a little bit harder to emphasise her point.

Garrick wordlessly sat at the opposite end of the table, a good six feet away from the person he wanted to kill. He clasped his hands in front of him to stop them from shaking and met Kars's gaze. She smiled, studying him like some sort of lab specimen.

"I feel like I know you well, David. I looked into your history - what a fascinating career. One long trail of corpses, and so much regret. Who would have thought the urban battlefield could be so thrilling?"

"Pass my daughter to me," he said in a low voice.

Kars smiled and bounced Amy until the child gave another little giggle. "I can't believe somebody like you was instrumental in making something so adorable. I can't have children," she said almost with a flash of regret.

"Give me my daughter," Garrick said again firmly.

Kars treated him to an arrogant look. "I have a reputation that I trade on. I always fulfil contracts. I always instil fear. And I never leave loose ends, which is why people thought I was a ghost." She used a free hand to make a gesture of disappearing into smoke. "And that suited everybody just fine. And then you came along with little Fanta Liu, Sean Wilkes, Harry Lord, and dear old Chib, and you exposed me to the world. You destroyed everything I spent so long building. So, I come for you."

"I'm sure you made a lot of money doing it," Garrick said flatly. "So, pass back my child, take your cash, and disappear."

She raised a perfectly manicured eyebrow. "And you would just let me do that?"

"I believe you underestimate just how little I care about you."

That provoked a smile from Kars. She slid the plate several inches towards him.

"I cooked you a meal, Garrick. In honour of your achievements. I hope you're not going to offend me by refusing it."

"I'm not hungry."

"I don't care. It took a lot of effort. I want you to eat it."

"And then what?"

"And then you'll make me happy, and your daughter can go to bed, and, as you promised, I will walk out of here."

She gave the plate a hard shunt, and it drifted across the table, stopping in front of him. Watching with amusement, Kars gently ran a finger down Amy's face, making the baby smile.

"A lot of blood and effort went into preparing that for you. Made from the finest ingredients. Chib's liver. Delicious. There's plenty to go around."

Garrick's fingers clenched into a fist. "You are one sick bitch."

That just elicited a giggle, and she moved her head sharply, causing Garrick to jump. Her tongue lashed out, and she licked Amy across the forehead, which made his daughter laugh mischievously, and a broader grin spread across Kars's face.

"I just have a taste for the finer things in life, and I like to see honour completed. Eat, and all is well. Don't..." she let the sentence trail off.

Garrick's mind raced through every possibility. How quickly could he reach them, covering the six feet across the table before Kars could harm his daughter? How was she armed? He was certain that she would never allow him to leave this room.

He couldn't stop his hands from shaking as he reached for the food. He picked up a small chunk between his thumb and index finger. It was cold to the touch, and he felt bile rising in his throat.

"We'll be here all day if you eat like a baby," she teased him.

He inhaled sharply and raised the lump of meat, staring defiantly at Kars.

"Eat," she said sharply, her eyes wide with intrigue, "and all your sins will be forgiven."

Garrick knew that there was no reasoning with a maniac. Survival lay in capitulation until the opportunity to resist presented itself. Fighting every revulsion, he put the flesh into his mouth and fought every fibre of his being not to spit it out as he closed his mouth.

There came a sudden sharp thud, and Kars jerked in her seat.

The world slowed down around Garrick as his senses were flooded with information. He noticed a small puncture hole in the dining room window at the same time as a red circle blossomed in the centre of Kars's forehead.

Garrick spat out the meat and leapt from his seat, sliding across the table, arms outstretched as he grabbed Amy from the woman's limp grip. He twisted himself off the table onto the floor, pushing hard against the wall, sheltering his child as much as he could with his body.

The motion jerked Kars, and her head lolled to the side, exposing a missing fist-sized chunk of the back of her head. The skull was splattered across the wall behind her - the sign of a bullet exit wound.

He froze in panic as a figure loomed beyond the patio door. The light from the room illuminated the impassive features of Boris. He held a silenced pistol in one hand. With his other black-gloved hand, he pulled the patio door open - the door having been unlocked previously by Kars and the alarm system disabled with her bag of technological tricks.

Boris was dressed all in black as if he'd stepped away from Chib's funeral. With regret, he stared at Kars's body, the gun poised to fire again. Only when he was satisfied that she was dead did his gaze switch to Garrick, who was quietly making shushing noises for Amy. Not for her benefit - she was dealing with the situation in a calm manner, enjoying the chance to finally play with Dad. The soothing was for his own sanity. Boris met his gaze, and the mercenary unscrewed the silencer, and nonchalantly slid the components inside his jacket.

"You gave me the idea to use Mr Kontos as bait."

Garrick finally found his voice. "I don't understand…"

"I could only think of what bait Kars would go for. And it was you."

Garrick pushed himself back to his feet, sliding up along the wall, holding Amy tightly and making sure she couldn't see the corpse.

"You planned for this to happen?"

Boris looked sad. "Not planned. I engineered it."

Garrick's eyes flicked between Kars and the Ukrainian. "You did know her, didn't you?"

Boris gave a sad smile. "We worked together back in the day. She was the reason our unit went MIA."

"She's Special Forces?" Garrick could barely get the words out.

"Started as a medic, then evolved into something far worse."

Garrick's eyes narrowed. "Breaking you out of the prisoner transport. That wasn't you and your merry band of mercs, was it? That was a military operation."

Boris shrugged indifferently. "Some things are best not to be commented on. When we met, I told you to turn away." He looked meaningfully between Amy and Garrick, the sadness intensifying. "We used to have a daughter once."

Garrick looked between Kars and Boris, trying to work out whether he'd read the mercenary correctly.

Boris gave one last look at Kars and sighed. "I think now you and I, we are equal."

He looked meaningfully at Garrick. The only words that sprung to mind parroted those he'd heard from Boris, when they'd first met:

"Thank you."

The Ukrainian nodded and then turned and walked back out of the room, disappearing into the darkness.

Also by M.G. COLE

Twitter: @abriggswriter

Bluesky: @andybriggs42@bsky.social

SLAUGHTER OF INNOCENTS
DCI Garrick 1

MURDER IS SKIN DEEP
DCI Garrick 2

THE DEAD WILL TALK

DCI Garrick 3

DEAD MAN'S GAME

DCI Garrick 4

CLEANSING FIRES

DCI Garrick 5

THE DEAD DON'T PAY

DCI Garrick 6

A MURDER OF LIES

DCI Garrick 7

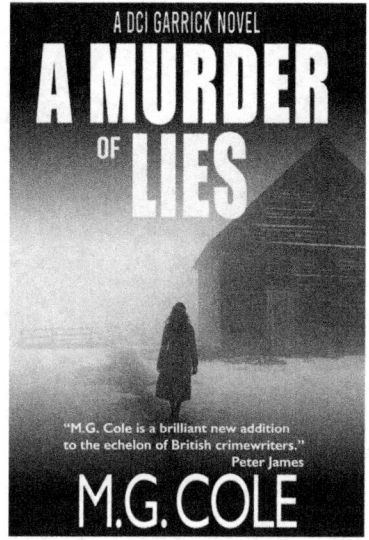

SIREN'S CALL

DCI Garrick 8

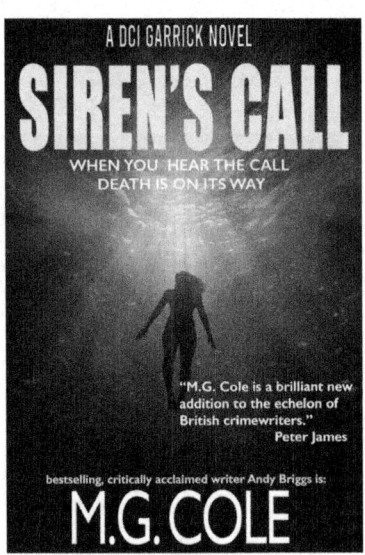

THE WHITE HORSE

DCI Garrick 10 - COMING SOON!

Printed in Dunstable, United Kingdom